STAR TREK®

THE ORIGINAL SERIES

ALLEGIANCE IN EXILE

David R. George III

Based upon *Star Trek*
created by Gene Roddenberry

POCKET BOOKS
New York • London • Toronto • Sydney
New Delhi • Alpha Centauri

Pocket Books
A Division of Simon & Schuster, Inc.
1230 Avenue of the Americas
New York, NY 10020

This book is a work of fiction. Names, characters, places, and incidents either are products of the author's imagination or are used fictitiously. Any resemblance to actual events or locales or persons, living or dead, is entirely coincidental.

First Pocket Books paperback edition February 2013

POCKET and colophon are registered trademarks of Simon & Schuster, Inc.

For information about special discounts for bulk purchases, please contact Simon & Schuster Special Sales at 1-866-506-1949 or business@simonandschuster.com.

The Simon & Schuster Speakers Bureau can bring authors to your live event. For more information or to book an event, contact the Simon & Schuster Speakers Bureau at 1-866-248-3049 or visit our website at www.simonspeakers.com.

Manufactured in the United States of America

10 9 8 7 6 5 4 3 2 1

ISBN 978-1-4767-0022-9
ISBN 978-1-4767-0023-6 (ebook)

FIRE CONTINUED TO CONSUME
THE REMNANTS OF THE SHUTTLECRAFT.

Sulu reached to the back of his hip for his communicator, but his fingers closed on empty air. He found the tricorder, which he'd been carrying on a strap slung across his shoulder, missing as well. Only his hand phaser remained with him, the palm-sized weapon still secured at his waist.

Careful not to make any sudden movements, Sulu glanced at the ground about him. The yellowish grass of the clearing grew in wild tufts, dotting the rich brown expanse of the soil. He quickly spotted his tricorder and retrieved it, but it took longer for him to locate his communicator. It lay in pieces on the ground, obviously smashed beneath his body when he'd been thrown down.

Cut off both from any remaining members of the landing parties as well as from the crew aboard *Enterprise*, Sulu lifted his tricorder before him and activated it with a touch. Its strap, he saw, had been severed halfway along its length. The lieutenant's head pounded, but his vertigo and his queasiness had eased enough for him to concentrate on the device's small screen. He scanned for life signs, beginning in and around the obliterated *da Gama*. He detected no indication of survivors.

The fault, dear Brutus, is not in our stars,
But in ourselves, that we are underlings.

—William Shakespeare,
  The Tragedy of Julius Caesar,
  Act I, Scene 2

. . . . For your great graces
Heap'd upon me, poor undeserver, I
Can nothing render by allegiant thanks;
My pray'rs to heaven for you; my loyalty,
Which ever has and ever shall be growing,
Till death, that winter, kill it.

—William Shakespeare,
  *The Famous History of the Life of
  King Henry the Eighth,*
  Act III, Scene 2

Entry
The Fault in Our Stars

The ground rumbled a moment before the missile lanced through the air toward the clearing at the edge of the vacant city. As the earth quivered beneath his uniform boots, Lieutenant Hikaru Sulu stopped walking, freezing in place after bending his knees and throwing his arms wide to steady himself. At first, the *Enterprise* helmsman thought that seismic activity shook the land, but then he heard the roar overhead. He peered up to the cloud-studded, blue-green sky to see a slender ebon rocket streak past. His mouth fell open in surprise as he followed its flight. He feared where on the supposedly uninhabited planet the menacing projectile would intersect the surface.

Sulu dropped his gaze across the patchy spread of sallow scrub grass to the far side of the clearing, to one of the ship's shuttlecraft and his intended destination, *da Gama*. In the auxiliary vessel, he had led one of several *Enterprise* landing parties down to the surface. The boxy craft, about seven meters from bow to stern, rested motionless atop its paired engine nacelles, its access hatch closed. The shuttle sat broadside across Sulu's path, so he could not see through its forward ports and into the main compartment. He had just enough time to form the desperate hope that the cabin stood empty, but he knew better: at least one of the crew remained aboard.

An instant later, the missile arced downward and plunged into *da Gama*. The vessel exploded in a fiery blast, a ball of flame erupting as the bulkheads flew apart. Sulu instinctively raised his arms up before his face, but his limbs provided scant protection. A concussive wave of blistering air struck him hard, driving him from his feet. He landed meters away, supine, the impact forcing the rear of his head to whip backward into the ground.

Sulu's view of the sky above him wavered, the feel of the heat from the blazing shuttlecraft wreckage faded, the sounds of debris crashing onto the landscape all around him dimmed. He anticipated pain, but none came. Whatever injuries he must have suffered, the resulting sensations didn't seem to make their way to his brain.

He lay there motionless, benumbed, waiting for the normal reactions of his body to return. When that didn't happen, he attempted to rise anyway. He couldn't. Just lifting his head off the ground cost him too much effort.

Weak and overwhelmed, the lieutenant closed his eyes. The simple deed brought him an immediate reprieve, as though the mere act of seeing had proven too intense a task for his battered mind and body. He sought to focus on his breathing, but even that seemed like too great a strain.

A concussion, Sulu realized. *I've got a concussion.*

Despite his compromised condition, he understood that his deduction made sense. He'd endured a trauma to his head, and his responses had dulled. More than that, a fog of fatigue began to enfold him, and he knew that he had to fight to push it away. The planet that the *Enterprise* crew had found—a planet they'd believed a more or less benign environment devoid of intelligent life—all at once seemed something quite different. Sulu therefore needed to see not only to his own well-being, but to that of the crew members forming his landing party.

With his eyes still shut, he struggled to roll over. It required three attempts, but he finally managed to do so, at the same time sliding his hands beneath the side of his head to cushion it against the firm ground. He wanted to push himself up, but the effort of turning his body had drained whatever fleeting strength he'd found. He took a moment in that position to rest.

Sulu couldn't tell whether or not he lost consciousness, but he suddenly became aware of his body trembling. He worried about the possibility of a seizure, a potential consequence of the blow to his head, but then he recognized another roar somewhere in the air above him. Sulu opened his eyes and glanced sidelong at the sky, where he saw a second missile racing beneath the clouds.

The other shuttles, he thought.

Captain Kirk had ordered landing parties to the planet on a trio of *Enterprise*'s auxiliary craft—*Mitrios* and *Christopher* had accompanied *da Gama* to the surface. They'd set down at different points along the outskirts of the world's lone and enigmatic city, allowing the ship's scientists to spread out and conduct their investigations in a variety of locales. The crews had hauled a considerable amount of delicate equipment with them to facilitate their research and analysis.

The sound of distant thunder reached Sulu, but he understood that the din boasted no meteorological origins. He had no doubt that another *Enterprise* shuttlecraft had been attacked and destroyed. Anger and a sense of urgency filled him as he wondered how many of his shipmates had perished.

I've got to find the others, he thought. *We have to protect ourselves.*

It struck him that the surest means of safeguarding the remaining landing party personnel would be escape. Crew members on the planet all carried hand phasers with them, but such weaponry seemed an unlikely deterrent against the rockets Sulu had seen. If he could contact *Enterprise,* though, he could request immediate evacuation of everybody on the surface.

Except why hasn't that happened already? Sulu asked himself. The ship's sensors would have detected explosions like the one that had destroyed *da Gama*. In such a circumstance, Captain Kirk undoubtedly would have ordered the landing parties beamed up at once.

Unless the Enterprise *is also under attack*. With the ship's defensive shields in place, the transporters wouldn't function.

Feeling the weight of his responsibilities as the leader of one of the landing parties, Sulu worked to focus his mind and gather his energy. Slipping his hands beneath his chest, he pushed himself up onto his knees. A surge of nausea rose within him. He waited a few seconds, hoping that it would pass. It diminished somewhat, and so he struggled to his feet. He staggered once, light-headed, but succeeded in staying upright.

Ahead of him, fire continued to consume the remnants of the shuttlecraft.

Sulu reached to the back of his hip for his communicator, but his fingers closed on empty air. He found his tricorder, which he'd been carrying on a strap slung across his shoulder, missing as well. Only his hand phaser remained with him, the palm-sized weapon still secured at his waist.

Careful not to make any sudden movements, Sulu glanced at the ground about him. The yellowish grass of the clearing grew in wild tufts, dotting the rich brown expanse of the soil. He quickly spotted his tricorder and retrieved it, but it took longer for him to locate his communicator. It lay in pieces on the ground, obviously smashed beneath his body when he'd been thrown down.

Cut off both from any remaining members of the landing parties as well as from the crew aboard *Enterprise*, Sulu lifted his tricorder before him and activated it with a touch. Its strap, he saw, had been severed halfway along its length. The lieutenant's head pounded, but his vertigo and his queasiness had eased enough for him to concentrate on the device's small screen. He scanned for life signs, beginning in and around the obliterated *da Gama*. He detected no indication of survivors.

Deeply saddened, Sulu widened his search. As far as the *Enterprise* crew knew, they had arrived at a world unpopulated by sentient beings. The ruins of its single city posed a mystery, one that both Captain Kirk and First Officer Spock wanted to explore. With at least two missiles fired, though, the possibility rose that the landing parties might not be alone on the planet after all. Because of that, Sulu did not limit his scans to the species represented aboard *Enterprise*.

The western border of the ostensibly deserted city sat near the edge of a deep, wide chasm. The trio of *Enterprise* shuttlecraft had alighted just outside the urban borders, at each of the three other compass points. A coniferous wood bordered the city to the south, and it had been in a clearing there that *da Gama* had landed.

As Sulu swept his tricorder about him in slow arcs, five sets of local readings appeared in its display: four human and one Andorian. It pleased the lieutenant to see robust vital signs, but he read no other indications of life in the vicinity, meaning that he could not account for two members of the *da Gama* landing party, both of them human. He gazed up at the burning husk of shuttlecraft that the missile had left behind. A knot tightened in his gut.

Looking back down at the tricorder, Sulu studied its screen. Though divided into a group of three and another of two, the five individuals all moved steadily west, converging on a point outside the city, near the edge of the chasm. The lieutenant knew that a series of caverns descended from the surface there—he'd just come back to *da Gama* from such a cave—and he suspected that his crew pursued refuge in one of them. Given the unexpected appearance of an air-based threat, it seemed a sound strategy for survival. It also pleased him to read a sixth life sign—undoubtedly Lieutenant Hadley, with whom Sulu had been working—already inside the caverns.

Despite the pain throbbing at his temples, Sulu worked the tricorder to measure the distances involved. The first group of landing party members sped toward the nearest caves from a quarter kilometer away, and the second from a half kilometer, while he stood an additional kilometer beyond that. With few choices, he started in that direction.

Previously, Sulu had made his way to and from the caverns via the southwest corner of the city, but under the current circumstances, he chose a more direct, though untraveled, route. At first, he moved with care, trying not to exacerbate the symptoms of his concussion. He crossed the clearing, skirting the destroyed *da Gama,* and entered the unexplored wood. The temperature dropped by several degrees beneath the old-growth evergreens, many of which rose to impressive heights. Sunlight penetrated to the ground only sporadically, considerably limiting the undergrowth. With most of the trees half a dozen or more meters away from their neighbors, Sulu advanced with relative ease. A browning carpet of fallen needles provided him with soft but sturdy footing.

Sulu occasionally consulted his tricorder, but mostly he stared ahead and down as he walked, wanting to keep his field of vision narrow and steady. After a couple of minutes, though, the cooler temperatures and softer light seemed to benefit his condition; he no longer felt sick to his stomach, and his dizziness likewise gave way. Though his head still ached, he began to trot. Shortly after that, he broke into a run.

As he moved, Sulu's head threatened to split in two, but he refused to slow. Trees slipped past him on either side, benchmarks of his progress darting along his peripheral vision. His movements suddenly seemed untamed, as though his arms and legs pumped beyond his control. He thought he might lose his balance, and envisioned hurtling head-first into the unforgiving trunk of an evergreen.

But then Sulu emerged from the wood and skidded to a halt. Not far ahead, he saw the rim of the massive canyon that provided the lost city with a striking backdrop. He'd spied the natural formation from a height as he'd piloted *da Gama* down to the planet, but its considerable extent looked far more imposing from his new vantage. He estimated its depth at a kilometer or more, and it clearly extended far wider than that. Across from his location, a pair of high, narrow waterfalls cascaded in brilliant sprays down to the river coursing along the floor of the great chasm. Amazingly, the beauty of the vista seemed to dull the pulsing pain in his head.

Checking the tricorder once more, Sulu saw that the members of his landing party had already made it into one of the nearby caverns. He peered about, studying the terrain, until he pinpointed the mouth of the cave. He started in that direction and had nearly reached it when another low-pitched sound became audible in the distance. He stopped and listened, hoping that it would resolve into something else as it grew louder, but soon enough he recognized the roar of another missile.

It's headed for us, Sulu thought. *For our landing party.*

He didn't know if all three *Enterprise* shuttlecraft had been destroyed, but as the missile neared, he understood that the ship's planet-bound personnel had become the next target. If the members of his landing party descended far enough belowground, they would likely survive such an attack, but Sulu knew that they had only reached the caves a few moments earlier. His tricorder confirmed that they'd had insufficient opportunity to achieve a safe depth.

Desperate, Sulu attempted to formulate a solution. As he reached to work the controls of his tricorder, his headache returned to its previous, excruciating level. His head hurt so badly that he imagined somebody firing a phaser on heavy stun at him from point-blank range.

Not just on heavy stun, he thought. *It feels like a phaser on overload detonating inside my skull.*

Once more, the land began to rumble. Disregarding his pain as much as he could, Sulu operated his tricorder, setting it to emit the false life signs of a hundred humans and as many Andorians. He didn't know if the missile tracked its prey via sensor scans, but he had no time to devise another plan.

As the roar in the sky and the quaking of the ground both increased, Sulu dashed toward the edge of the canyon. He would have to approach the precipice in order to have any hope of success. Estimating his range from the cliff at about ten meters, he figured to cover at least half that distance.

Sulu stumbled more than once as the earth shook beneath him, but he somehow remained on his feet.

As he topped a slight rise, though, the land suddenly fell away where a sizable fissure had been notched into the rock face. Sulu slammed his feet down as quickly as he could. His knees locked as he skidded forward.

He teetered on the inner point of the fissure, which allowed him an unimpeded view down a thousand or more meters to the canyon floor. His heart seemed to seize up in his chest as he wildly pinwheeled his arms backward. Rocks and clumps of soil kicked forward from beneath his feet and plummeted into the chasm. Sulu barely prevented himself from following them over the edge.

Aware of his rapid heartbeat, as well as of beads of sweat streaming down his face, Sulu knew that he had to ignore the fate he'd nearly suffered. Above him, the boom of the missile had grown almost deafening. Without looking up to measure its progress, Sulu grasped his tricorder as tightly as he could with one hand, reached back, and then heaved it forward with all of his might.

The device sailed out over the fissure, and for a moment, it seemed as though gravity had abdicated its responsibilities. But then the tricorder dropped, and Sulu had to hope that he'd thrown it far enough that it would fall, unhindered and functioning, all the way to the chasm floor. He also had to hope that would be enough.

Sulu retreated a few steps, back to the top of the incline. He started to turn so that he could run for the cave entrance, but then the cacophony of the rocket reached a crescendo. He glanced up to see the deadly projectile already pointed toward the ground, looking as though it might dive directly onto his location. Before he could react, though, the missile shot past him and down into the fissure, clearly chasing the counterfeit life signs fabricated by his tricorder.

The explosion came only seconds later. The clamor of the blast sent fresh slivers of pain deep into Sulu's head. The earth pitched violently beneath him, tossing him from his feet once more. He struck the ground at the top of the incline, and then lurched past it, toward the fissure. His hands clawed at the soil, frantically trying to find purchase.

Then Sulu tumbled over the edge of the canyon.

Ağdam

I

One

The red turbolift doors glided open with their characteristic squeak, revealing beyond them the circular enclosure of the *Enterprise* bridge. Captain James T. Kirk stepped out of the cab onto the raised, outer deck of the compartment. An olio of familiar noises rose to greet him: the background twitter that accompanied the operation of the main viewscreen; the feedback chirps emitted by control stations; the quiet, sporadic dialogue of the personnel present; and the slightly reedy sound of voices transmitted over the intercom. Beneath it all, binding it together, the low-level thrum of the impulse drive suffused the space.

Kirk stopped for a moment to take in the scene and observe his frontline command crew, all of them already at their positions. The captain normally arrived on the bridge before any of them, comfortably ahead of the start of alpha shift. Upon waking in his quarters that day, though, he'd tarried through his dawn routine, slowed by a heavy wistfulness.

But I didn't feel that way just this morning, Kirk thought. Really, his pensive state of mind had arisen the night before. As he recorded the final log entry for the day, he realized that the stardate marked the end of his fourth year aboard *Enterprise*. That time as a starship captain had proven not only the most satisfying of his professional life, but also the most fulfilling from a personal standpoint. It unnerved him to consider that he'd already put eighty percent of *Enterprise*'s five-year mission behind him.

Moving to his right, toward an opening in the railing that rimmed the lower, central portion of the bridge, Kirk passed Uhura where she crewed the communications console. The lieutenant had served as a member of the ship's senior staff for virtually the entire voyage, and although there had been some flux in personnel assignments and the command structure near the beginning of the mission, a similar constancy had held true since that time for most of his officers: Spock doing double duty as exec and the head of *Enterprise*'s science division, Scotty as chief engineer, Sulu at the helm, McCoy down in sickbay as chief medical officer. Even young Chekov had to that point manned navigation for three years.

As Kirk padded down from the outer ring of the bridge to its inner section, he shifted from reflecting on the reliability and longevity of his command crew to the interpersonal relationships that had grown among them. He felt closer to the members of his senior staff than he had to any other group of people he'd ever known; in important ways, they had become like a family to him. It gave him pause to wonder where they all would be a year and a day from that moment.

In the center of the bridge, the captain circled around to the front of the vacant command chair. He knew that another of his officers, Bill Hadley, had drawn the watch as gamma-shift duty officer that month, but even though Spock presently worked at the primary science station, the first officer had clearly relieved the lieutenant. Kirk settled into the empty seat.

Seeking to free himself from his melancholy, the captain turned his attention to the main viewscreen. Over the course of the previous several days, an empty starscape had prevailed as *Enterprise* carried her crew to their next assignment. As Kirk expected, though, the limitless depths of space through which the ship traveled had been replaced by the shallow arc of a planet cutting across the bottom half of the display.

Kirk studied the image on the screen. He saw a topography painted in the hues he normally associated with life-sustaining worlds. Browns and ochers mixed with swatches of deep green to describe a set of continents and outlying archipelagos, vast stretches of aquamarine defined oceans, and great sweeps of white clouds hovered above it all.

The captain glanced to the right, up to where his first officer operated the main science console on the starboard periphery of the bridge. The commander stood bent over the hooded viewer that provided concentrated visual access to sensor readings and other information. "Mister Spock, report."

Spock straightened and turned his lanky frame toward Kirk. "As scheduled, Captain, the *Enterprise* arrived at zero-one-twenty hours at the planetary system designated R-Seven-Seven-Five. The crew has performed basic scans of its three jovian worlds and has dispatched probes into their atmospheres, as well as to seven of their moons; we are continuing to receive telemetry from each of them. We are presently in orbit of the lone terrestrial planet and conducting a detailed survey of it."

Kirk peered back at the viewscreen. "Just one rocky planet?" he asked. "Isn't that unusual?"

"It is true that fewer than three percent of all known systems possess only a single terrestrial world," Spock explained, "but such an occurrence is otherwise of little note." The first officer walked along the railing until he reached the opening beside Uhura, then descended to the center of the bridge to stand beside the command chair. "The number of terrestrial planets that develop about a star is a function of the amount of dust in the nascent solar nebula, as well as of the random collision and accrual of those particles into larger and larger bodies. The cloud of gas and granular matter surrounding R-Seven-Seven-Five after its formation likely contained fewer solid grains than in systems with multiple rocky worlds. It is worth observing, however, that an asteroid belt orbits next to the star, and that another, larger belt does so between the first and second planets, placing the aggregate mass of the system on the low end of, but well within, the normal range."

Kirk looked back at Spock. "What else do we know about R-Seven-Seven-Five?" The captain had read Starfleet's exceedingly brief précis about the system several days earlier, but he liked to hear his first officer's description of such details.

"Prior to our arrival here, we knew very little," Spock said. "It was charted one hundred twenty-three years ago by the crew of a Vulcan starship, the *R'Tor*. They did not explore the system."

During the course of Kirk's career in Starfleet, he had frequently heard and read the phrase *Charted but not explored* employed in reference to astronomical objects identified by agents of the erstwhile Vulcan High Command; it never ceased to confound him. Although the former governmental body had been tasked with the military defense of the Vulcan people, it had also overseen civilian operations, including scientific research and the deployment of their interstellar fleet. Kirk's own interactions with Spock and others of his people revealed among them a uniformly robust curiosity about the universe. Even though Spock's father had disapproved of his son enlisting in Starfleet, he'd wanted him to join the Vulcan Science Academy. Given all of that, the notion that the crew of *R'Tor*, or those of its sister ships, would map an unfamiliar star

system without then exploring that system felt coun-
terintuitive to everything Jim Kirk thought he knew
about Vulcans. He did recall from his history studies
that their society had undergone considerable turmoil
a century or so earlier, at which time they had dis-
banded the High Command, but such a fundamental
shift—not just in their priorities, but in their commu-
nal mind-set—still seemed improbable to Kirk.

And yet here we are, the captain told himself. *In
another solar system that the Vulcans looked at in passing, made note of, and then ignored.*

"Are there any signs of life?" Kirk asked, hope-
ful. Of all his crew's many accomplishments, he most
valued their discoveries of intelligent species previously unknown to the Federation. He in particular
appreciated the opportunity to make first contact with
spacefaring civilizations, though he understood that
no such prospect would arise at R-775; had the crew
detected any ships in or about the system, they would
have notified the captain at once, even during his off-
duty hours.

"The planet is Class-M," Spock said, indicating its
suitability for humanoid life. "It supports a myriad of
complex flora and fauna across its surface and within
its seas, but detailed scans have uncovered no evidence of hominids or other advanced species."

Kirk's lips drew into a thin line as he peered back
at the viewscreen, at the image of the fertile planet displayed there. He looked at the segment of the visible

surface that fell outside the reach of the planet's star, and noted that darkness reigned there unbroken by artificial lighting. He felt more deeply disappointed than usual, doubtless because of his realization that the final year of *Enterprise*'s mission lay immediately before him.

Maybe Starfleet Command will keep me aboard the ship, he thought, searching for any optimism he could find. He might have to replace some members of his senior crew as they progressed in their own careers, but at least he would still have *Enterprise. Or the admirals might transfer me to another ship,* Kirk supposed. Even in that case, though, at least he would retain his captaincy.

Both possibilities seemed reasonable, he tried to tell himself, and perhaps they even seemed likely. But Kirk knew that while he had champions at Starfleet Headquarters in San Francisco, he also had detractors. His tenure aboard *Enterprise* had been marked by a number of significant triumphs—including numerous successful first contacts—but had also been marred by some notable disappointments.

Unable to escape the morass of introspection, he remembered well his inability to keep alive the intelligent creature the crew had encountered on planet M-113—the last being of its kind, and whose death marked the extinction of its species. He had likewise failed to prevent the demise of Kodos, the former governor of the Tarsus IV colony, who had ruthlessly murdered half its population and whom Kirk had wanted to bring to justice. He also recalled with terrible shame arguing with the Organians that the Federation and the Klingon Empire should be permitted to engage in a shooting war—a war that surely would have killed millions, if not billions, of people, destroying life on a planetary scale.

So many mistakes, Kirk thought.

One of those that retained a primacy among his recollections had occurred two and a half years earlier. He had introduced primitive firearms to the hill people of the planet Neural, in what he had come to recognize as a misguided attempt to restore the balance of power between them and the villagers, who'd been supplied weapons by the Klingons. Although Starfleet Command continued to support that arms race, the issue had caused a tremendous amount of heated debate among the admirals. For his part, Kirk regretted implementing his solution, which he had come to regard as a miscalculation not only horrible in its consequences, but immoral in its very conception. He still often reflected on the situation, even going so far as to submit alternate proposals to Command, including the relocation of the hill people to another world.

I wonder if Tyree's still alive.

How many times had he speculated about that? Years before returning to Neural as the captain of *Enterprise,* Kirk had visited the planet as a young officer fresh out of Starfleet Academy. He masqueraded as a native and embedded himself in their culture. The beauty of the place captivated him, as did the tranquil, peaceful life enjoyed by its inhabitants. Tyree, a member of the hill people back then, and later their leader, had befriended him.

And I betrayed his fellowship by providing his tribe—by providing him—*with the concept of vengeance, along with the weapons to carry it out.*

Kirk suddenly realized that an uncomfortable silence surrounded him, that he had become mired in his dour thoughts and dark memories. Willing himself back into the moment, he turned to his first officer. "Very well, Mister Spock," he said, not even recalling the last words the commander had spoken to him—if he'd even heard them at all. "How long do you estimate a full analysis of the planet will take?"

"We have thus far mapped all land masses in detail," Spock said. "We are presently engaging in detailed sensor sweeps of the geology, the hydrosphere, and the climate, as well as cataloguing the abundance of plant and animal life. Given the size of the planet and the diversity of its ecosystem, a complete survey will require—"

"Mister Spock," interrupted a male voice. Kirk looked past the Vulcan toward one of the bridge's secondary stations, the one adjoining Spock's own console. There, a young officer clad in the azure uniform shirt of Starfleet's science division turned from his panel and peered toward the captain and

first officer. Kirk recognized the ensign as Daniel
Davis, a human assigned to *Enterprise* less than
a year earlier. "I'm reading refined metal on the
planet's surface."

Kirk glanced up at Spock. Though the Vulcan's expression remained neutral, the captain could read the
interest in his eyes. During their time together aboard
Enterprise, the two had become the best of friends,
and despite the stoicism with which his first officer
conducted himself, Kirk had come to know him quite
well.

"Specify," Spock said, addressing the ensign. "What
types of refined metal, and in what quantities?" Kirk
understood that Spock would resist venturing an
opinion about what the presence of such materials on
the planet might indicate, but with the lack of intelligent life, the captain suspected they had run across a
spacecraft that had set down there.

"I'm reading steel . . . aluminum . . . even some
smaller amounts of tritanium and rodinium," Davis
said, looking back at his console and reading from
a display. The list seemed to bolster Kirk's theory
that they had discovered a space vessel of some
kind; Starfleet commonly utilized tritanium and
rodinium in the construction of its own starship
hulls. When the ensign peered back up from his
station, he said, "There's enough down there to suggest a city."

Both of Kirk's eyebrows rose in surprise, while

one of Spock's did the same. The first officer strode to a break in the railing on the starboard side of the bridge and mounted the outer deck. Kirk waited in the command chair as Ensign Davis turned back to his console and Spock leaned in over him. The two spoke quietly for a moment as Davis worked his controls. Finally, the first officer stood up and turned toward Kirk.

"Sensors detect not just refined metals, Captain," Spock said, "but also concrete and processed woods."

"Those do sound like urban building materials," Kirk noted.

"Indeed," Spock agreed. "And they appear to be laid out in a grid-like pattern, supporting Ensign Davis's contention that they define a city. But the materials also appear to be in at least partial disarray, and scans show no habitation in the area, other than by local wildlife."

"How do you account for all that?" Kirk asked.

"If it actually is a city, it seems that its builders have departed," Spock said. "It is unclear whether the deterioration was the cause or the result of that abandonment."

Kirk's mind raced with possibilities. He rose from the command chair and paced over to the railing, where he peered up at Spock. "What about radiation levels?"

Spock looked back at Ensign Davis, who once

more operated his panel. "I'm reading nothing out of the ordinary," Davis reported.

"So we're probably not talking about an attack," Kirk concluded.

"At least not one conducted recently," Spock agreed, "or carried out with energy weapons."

Kirk nodded. Though *Enterprise* traveled in unexplored space far from the Klingon and Romulan empires, and away from other known belligerents, the captain knew that the Federation did not reach out beyond its borders alone. While he puzzled over the existence of a single, apparently abandoned city down on the planet, knowing that he and his crew would not be entering a battleground would make his next decision easier.

After first contact, after observing intelligent but pre-warp cultures, Kirk counted the discovery of information about lost peoples among his crew's more satisfying endeavors. Such an opportunity had clearly just arisen. "Mister Spock, outfit a landing party. You'll join me, along with Doctor McCoy and our new A-and-A officer." The captain looked toward Ensign Davis. "I want you to scan the city in detail and be prepared to collate your findings with those of the landing party."

"Yes, Captain," Davis said.

That quickly, the captain's morning had improved. The despondence with which he had awoken gave way to anticipation about visiting the surface of an unexplored world and seeing firsthand the mysterious environs of a deserted alien city. In just moments, he knew, he would enter the transporter room, preparing to face something that he dreaded in his private life, but that exhilarated him in his role as *Enterprise* captain: the unknown.

Two

Ensign Mai Duyen Trinh reached the transporter room almost at a gallop, her stomach aflutter. In one hand, she carried her field jacket, and in the other, a tricorder expressly configured for her specialties, the device's memory packed with a cornucopia of comparative and historical data. She felt foolish rushing through the corridors, but she had no desire to arrive late for her first assignment to a landing party.

Fifteen minutes earlier, Trinh had stood in one of *Enterprise*'s large recreation rooms, collaborating with three of her colleagues. Jacqueline Trieste and Jeurys Mejia served the ship as anthropologists, while Veldaclien ch'Gorin worked as an archaeologist. They'd reserved the space in advance, arriving early in the morning to use it when it would least inconvenience their crewmates. The quartet utilized the rec room's holographic equipment to re-create as best they could a site that the crew had visited three months prior, before Trinh's posting to *Enterprise*.

Although Trinh hadn't taken part in that earlier mission to the previously unexplored world of Drissana II, she had subsequently joined the ship as its so-called A-and-A officer—archaeology and anthropology—and so headed up both departments. Direct observations and sensor scans performed on the planet provided a great deal of information about the most advanced species found there, a type of humanoid roughly equivalent to Neanderthal man on Earth. The ongoing analysis of the data, though, raised some puzzling questions. After several frustrating weeks fruitlessly searching for answers, Trinh suggested employing the rec room's holographic capabilities to examine those issues more closely and to test any hypotheses the team might develop. With recent progress in imaging technology, such methods had grown in their effectiveness as scientific tools.

With the help of Nora Hardy, one of the ship's computer specialists, Trinh and the others had loaded into the control matrix of the recreation room a plethora of sensor readings taken on Drissana II. The resulting projection reproduced one of the hunting grounds of the native people. Tall grass swayed across a stretch of gently rolling hills, the slender stalks pushed in waves by a delicate breeze. Trinh took up a position beside her colleagues on the edge of the veld, anxious for the programmed scene to unfold.

As she waited, Trinh raised her right hand and studied the artifact clasped in her fingers. A reproduction of a stone object found in large numbers among the inhabitants of Drissana II, the rough-hewn tool resembled, more than anything else, a rudimentary blade. It measured nearly as long as Trinh's forearm, with most of its extent tapering to a point at one end. The scientists' confusion arose from the other end of the object, which narrowed at a shallower angle to a second tip. It looked like one short and one tall triangle, both coarsely fashioned out of rock, and fixed together at their bases.

Clearly a tool or a weapon of some sort, the object defied explanation. Sharpened not only at its pointed ends but along its edges, it would slice through the flesh of any hand attempting to wield it with any force whatsoever. None of the many examples of the object that the *Enterprise* crew had seen had been affixed to a handle or shaft, nor did a single one of them possess the balance necessary to make it effective as something hurled.

In the ground beneath Trinh's feet—or what passed for the ground in the holographically reconfigured recreation room—she felt a vibration. Though she had been aboard for only a month, Trinh could already distinguish the different sensations imparted through the deck when *Enterprise* traveled at warp and impulse speeds. As the shaking increased, she could tell that neither of the ship's drive systems caused it. To the others, she said, "Here they come."

Jackie, Jeurys, and Clien all glanced at her before peering back across the savanna. Trinh looked in that direction as well, toward the few small trees that dotted the rise at the far border of the landscape. A low resonance became audible, plainly joined to the trembling ground. It all seemed credible, if not entirely real.

I don't smell anything, Trinh realized. The scene, while visually and aurally accurate, lacked any sort of a scent beyond that of the ship's scrubbed, recirculated air. She detected no musky aroma of soil, no sweet hint of vegetation, no olfactory suggestion at all that she actually stood on the surface of a living world.

Across from Trinh and her team, atop the rise, a cluster of gray beasts burst into view. Bulky and built low to the ground, with a thick, pebbled hide, they reminded Trinh of the Sunda rhinoceros, a creature from her own homeland, though the Drissana II version ran on three pairs of powerful legs rather than two. Half a dozen of the great, single-horned animals ran together, their movements graceful and harmonious, the individuals flowing as one, like the currents of a swift river. Their feet thundered against the ground, the group surging left and right across the countryside, as though with no particular destination, but simply running wild.

Off to the right, near where the creatures would pass, one of the humanoid inhabitants of Drissana II appeared. Dark-skinned and thin, he wore a band of long fronds that reached from his waist to just above his knees. He did not walk into the scene or emerge from hiding in the grass, but simply materialized in place. Though the man's entrance wanted for verisimilitude, Trinh knew it would suffice for their purposes.

Even as the creatures sighted the humanoid and cut in another direction, the man raised his hand and heaved toward the herd a duplicate of the object Trinh herself held. Though such an act in real life would have cut into his palm and fingers, the team wanted to test the efficacy of using the object as a thrown weapon; they even theorized that he could have protected his hand with leaves or a piece of animal hide. It wobbled through the air, flopping lazily end over end in flight, until it struck the closest creature squarely in the middle of its hulking body. The would-be weapon dropped to the ground, ineffective, while the targeted but clearly uninjured animal continued running with the herd.

Trinh watched the beasts cross the final expanse of the grassland. Just a few seconds later, they all vanished, the cacophony of their passage abruptly dropping to an unnatural silence. Trinh turned and saw that the Drissana II humanoid had also disappeared. Coding the simulation for greater realism would have required more time and effort, and so they'd chosen to focus only on what they required to conduct their experiments.

"Well, that's one hypothesis refuted," said Jackie Trieste. She had long, brunette hair, arranged into a beehive atop her head, and deep, brown eyes. A human in her late twenties and younger than Trinh by almost a decade, she nevertheless had quite a bit of experience in space. Unlike Trinh, Jackie had entered Starfleet Academy immediately after completing her secondary education, taking her scientific instruction coincident with her starship training. She'd so far spent seven years as an active member of Starfleet, aboard several different vessels, a fact that made Trinh uncomfortable serving as her superior.

Jeurys and Clien had traced comparable paths through the Academy and into space, as had the majority of personnel in both the archaeology and anthropology departments. Trinh, on the other hand, had greater depths of education and fieldwork in her chosen subjects, and as a science specialist, had taken an abbreviated Starfleet curriculum. She had earned her baccalaureate and master's degrees at Hanoi National University, and both of her doctorates at the University of Alpha Centauri. She also boasted membership in several professional organizations, including the Federation Register of Xenoanthropology and the prestigious Nova Ares Fellowship of Archaeologists. Of greater significance, she'd participated in a wide range of scientific expeditions, mostly in the Sol and Alpha Centauri systems, but also on Tellar and Ophiucus III.

Ophiucus, Trinh thought, the name instantly dredging up unwanted images in her memory. She could have—perhaps *should* have—recalled the beauty of New Dakar, the many exhibitions of art throughout

the bohemian colony, even the dig in which she'd participated on the periphery of the settlement. Instead,
her mind conjured up only the cold, stark interior of
the hospital there.

Trinh felt herself shudder, chilled by the inalter-
able past. She hoped that none of her colleagues had
seen her tremble, and felt grateful when she turned
to see that Clien had started across the veld, drawing
the attention of Jackie and Jeurys. The archaeologist
parted the brownish green stalks with his hands, the
blue of his Andorian flesh standing out against the sea
of color, until he reached the area where the grass lay
flat, trampled by the rhinoceros-like beasts. He peered
about, then trotted to a spot where he reached down
and retrieved the simulacrum of the object thrown by
the native of Drissana II.

Clien turned back and regarded Trinh and the others across the prairie. "Perhaps it's the simulation," he
said. "Just because it didn't work here doesn't mean it
wouldn't in real life."

"We'll check our parameters again," Trinh said,
"but I don't think that's it. We were very diligent in
spelling out all the details for Specialist Hardy. The
simulation might not be perfect in terms of what it
looks like or sounds like—" *Or what it smells like,*
Trinh thought. "—but the size, shape, and keenness of
the weapon are accurate, the force with which a native
could throw it, the texture and density of the creature's
hide. I believe we got enough of the details correct

to demonstrate that the inhabitants of Drissana Two can't possibly hunt these animals in this way."

Clien held up the still unidentified object. "But then what *is* this?" he asked, the slight accent with which he pronounced the words in Federation Standard insufficient to mask his vexation. He walked back through the tall grass to rejoin his colleagues.

"I share your frustration," Trinh said. She looked down at the object in her own hand. She wondered how something so simple in form could prove so inexplicable.

"Maybe if we used vines to attach it to the end of a wooden husk," Jeurys suggested. The Dominican had a swarthy complexion and dark coloring. "We could fashion a spear out of it."

"Or we could attempt to balance it by applying mud from the riverbank to smooth out its shape," Jackie offered.

Trinh shook her head. "Even if we could craft this into the head of a spear, you observed no evidence on Drissana Two that the natives did so. And evening out its aerodynamics with mud would necessarily blunt its sharp edges, which would be counterproductive if this thing really is a weapon."

"It just about has to be," Clien said. "We know the meat of those animals constituted a considerable portion of the natives' diet." The *Enterprise* crew's investigation of Drissana II had lasted several days, but while more than one tribe had been recorded cooking and eating the flesh of the creatures, none of the natives had been seen killing or capturing those or any other animals.

"At this point," Trinh said, holding the object up before her face, "I'd be willing to speculate that the inhabitants of Drissana Two used this to *hypnotize* the creatures into being their dinner." She smiled along with her joke.

For a moment, nobody said anything, obviously lost in their own thoughts. Finally, Jackie said, "It can't be that complicated. The natives just aren't that advanced."

"No," Trinh agreed. Then, tilting her head upward, she said, "Computer."

"Ready," came the immediate response. The ship's computer spoke with a stilted female voice.

"Can you display a static, three-dimensional, life-sized image of the six-legged creature we've been watching?" Trinh asked.

"Affirmative."

"Do so," Trinh ordered.

The air a few meters in front of the scientists shimmered for a moment, almost like the effect of a transporter, then solidified into one of the Drissana II beasts. Trinh walked up to it, and her colleagues followed along with her. She moved to the midsection of the animal, then reached toward it, tentative, unsure what she would feel. As she understood it, the capacity to reproduce or mimic environments and physical objects in the rec room relied on a mix of progressive holography, basic transporter technology, and software engineering. For all of that, though, Trinh expected that her hand might simply pass through the replica of the beast, the animal betraying its existence as merely a cohesive packet of photons. Instead, her fingertips tapped against an uneven surface, no warmer or cooler than the ambient temperature. It felt hard and unyielding, and she said so.

"That's how the computer created it," Clien said. "That doesn't necessarily reflect reality."

"Let's see," Trinh said. "Computer."

"*Ready.*"

"Is this how the creature actually feels?" Trinh asked.

"*The question is nonspecific,*" replied the computer. "*Please rephrase.*"

"When I touch the hide of the simulation of the creature," she said, "are my resulting tactile sensations the same as if I touched a living example of it?"

"*Negative,*" the computer said.

Trinh felt herself deflate. She'd understood that holographic technology worked well enough to employ as a diagnostic tool. "Explain."

"*The outer surface of the creature is not composed of organic matter, but is an approximation,*" the computer said. "*The re-created hide has the same surface geometry and the same hardness as specified in sensor readings of the creature.*"

Trinh nodded, then looked to Clien and the others. "So this may not feel like a living animal," she said, "but it still demonstrates that the inhabitants of Drissana Two certainly can't use this object against them." She closed her empty hand into a fist and rapped her knuckles against the gray hide. It sounded as though she knocked on a thick, wooden door.

Jeurys stepped forward and also rapped his hand against the side of the faux creature. "No," he said. "There's no way that this object, even if they threw it with a great deal of force, could penetrate the creature's hide."

Trinh allowed her gaze to trace the contours of the animal. She stopped at the spot where the middle leg on that side attached to the body. She leaned in and touched all around the area, which felt as hard to her as the rest of the hide. But then Trinh lowered herself to her knees and reached up along the creature's underbelly. "It's soft," she declared, then looked up at her colleagues. "The animal would be vulnerable here."

"But that still doesn't explain how the natives could have used this weapon to attack that part of the creature," Clien noted.

"No, but—" Trinh started, but then another thought occurred to her. "Wait," she said as she climbed back to her feet. "Computer."

"*Ready.*"

"Reset the simulation of the creature," Trinh said. "Place it lying on its side on the ground."

The image of the animal dissolved into thin air, as though it had never been, but then it reappeared as Trinh had commanded. She dropped to her knees once more, but instead of reaching for the creature's flank or the underside of its body, she placed her palm and fingers against the flat, circular bottom of its middle feet, first one and then the other. She peered up at her crewmates. "Feel this," she said. "It's soft." As proof of her claim, she pushed against one of the creature's soles, which dimpled beneath the pressure.

"I don't see it," Jeurys said. "They throw their weapons at the animal's feet?"

"No," Clien said, obviously understanding Trinh's point. He crouched down and ran a hand along the base of the creature's foot. "They don't *throw* the weapons at all."

Trinh took hold of the stone object with both hands and held it just above the ground, its shallow tip oriented upward, its long, tapering end pointing down. "Imagine a series of these set into the soil across the grassland," she said. "When the herds run through, some of them would inevitably step on them."

Jackie's mouth opened in an expression of sudden understanding. "They step on the protruding points and wound their feet," she said. "They effectively hobble themselves."

"And once they go down," Jeurys continued the reasoning, "they expose their vulnerable bellies."

"That's brilliant," Jackie said.

Trinh stood back up. "Well, it's a theory, anyway," she said. "One we obviously need to test."

Clien nodded. "We'll have to reset the parameters of our simulation so that—" The up-and-down call of a boatswain's whistle interrupted him.

"*Bridge to Ensign Trinh*," came the voice of *Enterprise*'s first officer.

Off to her left, a flat section of bulkhead appeared as if by magic in the middle of the grassland, putting the lie to the holographic trickery of the rec room. The bulkhead contained the doors that led out to the corridor, along with a control panel and an intercom. Surprised, Trinh looked to her colleagues, as though they might explain why Commander Spock wanted to speak with her. In her few weeks aboard ship, she had never been summoned from the bridge. Jackie, Jeurys, and Clien simply gazed back at her in silence, until Jackie finally said, "Shouldn't you see what he wants?"

Trinh blinked, then turned and hurried over to the bulkhead, where she reached up and activated the intercom with a touch to the button there. "This is Ensign Trinh."

"*Ensign, you have been assigned to a landing party,*" Spock said. "*We will be visiting an alien city, evidently abandoned, on the first planet of star system R-Seven-Seven-Five. The air temperature at our landing site is nine degrees Celsius. Outfit yourself accordingly.*"

"Yes, sir," Trinh said. "When, sir?"

"Report to the transporter room at once."

"Yes, sir," Trinh replied, feeling ridiculous for having posed the question. "Understood, sir." She wondered to which of the ship's transporter rooms she should report, but she didn't want to ask. Fortunately, she recalled that only one personnel transporter remained regularly active, and that the turbolift would automatically take her there when she specified her destination.

"Bridge out."

Trinh thumbed the intercom off, then turned to face her team. "I guess I have to go," she said.

"Looks like the new girl gets to have all the fun," Jackie said, smiling.

"I guess that's why they made me an officer," Trinh said. All of the personnel in the departments she headed carried enlisted ranks. "While I'm away, contact Specialist Hardy and see if she can help you reprogram the simulation." Trinh realized she still held the copy of the stone object from Drissana II. She held it up and said, "Let's see if we can verify our theory about how the natives use these."

"Yes, sir," said Clien, the most senior of the three scientists.

Trinh dropped the stone object to the simulated ground leading up to the bulkhead, then tapped a button on the control panel. The doors slid open. She dashed out into the corridor and to the nearest turbolift. After briefly stopping by her quarters to retrieve her field jacket and specially configured tricorder, she headed directly for the transporter room.

As Trinh arrived there, she felt both exhilarated and anxious about participating in her first *Enterprise* landing party. She relished the opportunity to explore the unknown, but in her month aboard ship, she'd grown unsettled about her choice to join Starfleet. She had come to understand that she might have been motivated primarily by a desire to run away from her own past, rather than by her stated aspiration of seeing more of the galaxy. Despite Trinh's Starfleet training and the service's conviction that she could function within a strict command hierarchy, she worried about that. As a scientist, she cooperated with peers, rather than issuing or taking orders. She'd so far found it awkward and even unsatisfying to lead people with far more shipboard experience than she, even though her professional expertise justified her position.

Trinh felt more concern, though, about how she would handle acting in a subordinate role. During her month on the ship, she'd met Captain Kirk just once, when he'd greeted her in the transporter room after she'd beamed aboard with three other new crew members. He seemed strong and confident to her, projecting the sort of self-assurance she expected in a person who commanded one of Starfleet's most advanced vessels, who regularly took that vessel into the unexplored reaches of the galaxy, and who maintained responsibility for the lives of more than four hundred people while doing so.

The captain intimidates me, she thought, and then had to admit more than that: the first officer daunted her as well. She'd met with the commander several times since arriving on board. In his capacity as the ship's exec, Mister Spock had informed her of her precise duties on *Enterprise,* and as the chief science officer, he'd introduced her to the staffs of the archaeology and anthropology departments, briefed her about their current research and analysis efforts, and doled out her assignments.

Trinh understood that Spock possessed a mixed parentage—his mother had apparently been human—but his comportment matched his appearance, both of which seemed one hundred percent Vulcan. Cold and stoic, the science officer did not joke or smile, nor did he respond to such behavior, a fact that had led to several uncomfortable moments for Trinh, who tended to keep the atmosphere light around the labs. More than his Vulcan demeanor, though, Spock wore his long service of nearly two decades in Starfleet like a second skin. He spoke and acted with precision, did not appear to make even the smallest mistakes, and set an incredibly high standard, both by expectation and by example, for the personnel in *Enterprise*'s science division.

I'd be a fool not *to be intimidated,* Trinh thought. At the same time, she recognized that the discomfort she felt reached far beyond her place in Starfleet's command structure, beyond her reactions to the exemplary records and strong personalities of *Enterprise*'s top officers. She had not discovered all of the issues with which she struggled once she'd arrived on board; she'd hauled many of them along with her from what she had begun to think of as her "former life."

The doors to the transporter room parted before Trinh and she hastened inside. She expected to find the room empty but for the operator; after all, she'd nearly sprinted through the corridors to get there. Instead, she had to pull up short, almost running into the broad back of a man wearing a red uniform shirt. Peering past him, she saw the room filled with people, including Commander Spock and the ship's chief medical officer, Doctor McCoy. Captain Kirk stood on the other side of the small room, facing them all.

The captain appeared to be in midsentence, but after the door whisked closed behind Trinh, the transporter room fell quiet. Then Captain Kirk said, "Nice of you to join us, Ensign." When all eyes in the room turned toward her, Trinh felt her heart begin to race.

"Y-y-yes, sir," she stammered. "Sorry, sir. We—the anthropology department—we were conducting an experiment." Although it registered in the next instant that the captain had made his remark with one side of his mouth curled up in a half smile, her obvious tardiness embarrassed her.

Captain Kirk looked to the man in front of Trinh.

"Mister Lemli," he said. The crewman held a hand out to Trinh. It took her a second to understand that he meant her to take the phaser pistol clutched in his fingers. She quickly pulled the strap of her tricorder up over her shoulder, then accepted the weapon and, as she'd been taught to do at the Academy, attached it to the belt of her pants, at her right hip.

"Mister Kyle?" the captain asked, peering toward the man stationed behind the transporter console.

"All set, sir," Kyle said. "I've targeted an open area that appears designed as a community square. It's in the center of the city, so you should find out quickly just what you're dealing with."

"And you continue to read no life signs there?" asked Commander Spock.

"No, sir, none," Kyle responded.

Captain Kirk pulled on his field jacket, an oversized tan garment sporting a number of pockets. As the other members of the landing party did the same, Trinh followed suit, first removing her tricorder's strap from her shoulder and then resettling it there atop her jacket. Then the captain turned to Doctor McCoy. "Well, Bones, shall we?"

"Bones"? Trinh thought. Had she heard Captain Kirk correctly? After her initial assignment to *Enterprise,* she'd been required to undergo a physical, which the doctor had conducted. He introduced himself at the time as *Leonard* McCoy, leaving Trinh to speculate that the captain had just called him by a nickname.

She couldn't imagine a less appropriate sobriquet for a physician, and surmised some form of black humor at work.

As Captain Kirk and Commander Spock mounted the two steps to the transporter platform and turned to face forward on the front pair of pads, the doctor grumbled a reply. "Shall we what?" he said. "Shuffle the atoms of our bodies all over the damn galaxy just so we can go visit a deserted city?"

Despite his complaint, though, the doctor stepped up onto the platform as well, moving onto one of the two side pads. Mister Lemli and a second red-shirted man followed, planting themselves on the rear pair of pads. That left a single empty space for Trinh, beside Doctor McCoy. She took it.

"Mister Kyle," the captain said, "energize."

The lieutenant worked the console before him, and a high-pitched hum rose in the room. As it did, Trinh considered the doctor's complaint about shuffling the atoms of his body. She'd never encountered anybody who suffered from transporter phobia, but she'd heard such people existed. Doctor McCoy's complaint, though, seemed like something different from an irrational fear, and she wondered if he fell into another category of individuals who resisted travel by transporter, namely those concerned about an essential loss of self in the process. Trinh understood the metaphysical debate about beaming from one place to another, including the argument that when somebody rematerialized, they became a *second* person, identical to but distinct from the person they'd been when they *de*materialized. As a matter of course, artists often cited a similar claim when delivering their work from one location to another; they wanted their original art to remain original, and not dismantled atom by atom and then reconstructed in the same fashion.

Trinh couldn't tell, though, whether Doctor McCoy genuinely disliked the transporter or whether he played at it for effect. During her interaction with him in sickbay, he'd come off both as a charming gentleman and as a bit of a curmudgeon. Whatever the case, Trinh felt the reverse of the doctor's protest: she relished the opportunity to have her body disassembled and reassembled at the molecular level. She had come to appreciate the notion that, each time she traveled via transporter, she distanced herself from the life she had lived to that point, perhaps even becoming a new person—perhaps becoming many new people, another with each successive beaming.

Golden motes formed across Trinh's field of vision, and Lieutenant Kyle and the *Enterprise* transporter room faded from view. Did consciousness slip away from her, for even the briefest time? Or, perhaps of more importance, did her mind lose the thread of continuity that tied her from the moment of her birth in Hoi An to her present self? Trinh didn't know—it certainly didn't feel as though any of that had happened— but when she appeared on the surface of the first planet in the R-775 star system, she liked to think that she could proclaim herself "the new Mai Duyen Trinh."

As she looked about, though, all such thoughts faded from her mind. Commander Spock had told her that the landing party would be visiting an abandoned city, and she'd envisioned empty buildings, no doubt decaying after an unknown period of neglect. Instead, she saw a scene of utter devastation.

In front of her, the captain and first officer turned in place, examining their surroundings. Trinh did the same. The six *Enterprise* crew members stood in the middle of a cobbled square, perhaps a hundred meters on a side. At one point, buildings had clearly bordered the space, but they had all been left in ruins. Here and there, a ragged portion of a wall reached skyward, as though still struggling to stand up to whatever force had laid the city low. Stone and mortar spilled across the ground like heaps of mangled bodies. The blackened lines of burned timber formed twisted geometric shapes, the skeletal remains of what had once marked the achievement of a people no longer in evidence.

As Trinh gazed around, her breath puffing from her mouth in transitory clouds of white, she saw that the annihilation reached in every direction. Even into the distance, nothing rose above the swells of wreckage save for the occasional half-collapsed wall. An eerie silence pervaded the area, and a layer of gray dust coated the dead city like a shroud. Based on appearance alone, Trinh estimated that the debris had stretched essentially unchanged across the landscape since before she'd been born, since before the Federation had been born, and for potentially far longer even than that.

Ahead of her, Trinh saw Commander Spock take hold of the tricorder hanging on a strap across his shoulder. He activated the device, and she heard its sharp whine as the first officer scanned their surroundings. The city, she knew, would read as lifeless.

"It's like Cestus Three," Trinh heard Captain Kirk say, but she didn't understand the reference.

"Are you suggesting that the Gorn might have had something to do with this?" Commander Spock asked.

"No," said the captain. "The Hegemony is on the other side of the Federation. I was speaking about the scale of the destruction."

"Then I concur," said Commander Spock.

Captain Kirk began to walk forward, and the first officer fell in step beside him. Trinh looked to Doctor McCoy, who nodded in the direction of the two men. Trinh, the doctor, and the pair of security guards started after them.

Realizing that she had been brought down to the planet for a reason, Trinh found her own tricorder where it hung at her side. She opened its cover and initiated her own scans, searching not for signs of life but for those of death. The captain would want to know the details of the city's loss, of its population's demise. Had they escaped whatever had flattened the place where they lived, or did their remains hide beneath the tonnes of rubble? Trinh wanted to know too.

As Captain Kirk and Commander Spock led the landing party across the square, a sudden gust burst across the open space, lifting a steel-colored curtain of dust fluttering above the cobblestones. A chill gripped Trinh, and she closed her field jacket about her. Off to one side, the wind howled through some piece of wreckage, a low moan that added to an atmosphere that already felt haunted.

In front of Trinh, Captain Kirk stopped. She looked up from her tricorder to see that they had walked almost to the end of the square. The captain squatted down to inspect a pile of fractured brick and stone. Something must have caught his attention, because he reached forward and began clearing away chunks of broken matter, not throwing them aside, but carefully placing them on the ground beside him.

Trinh watched the captain so intently that when he called her name, it startled her. She hied forward. "Sir?" she said.

"What do you make of this, Ensign?" Captain Kirk asked.

At first, Trinh didn't understand the question. What could she possibly tell simply by looking at a mound of shattered building materials? She would have to study the composition of the ruins, painstakingly searching for clues about the people who had

built the city and what had become of them. Archaeological investigation required time and patience, and
often enough, a fair amount of good fortune.

As Trinh's gaze passed over the area the captain
had uncovered, though, she saw, among the ragged
shards, bits of smooth, gently contoured surfaces,
mostly covered by grime, but showing through in
enough places to reveal a lustrous finish. The captain
had pulled only brick fragments away, Trinh saw, and
she quickly surmised that those reddish blocks had
once formed a straight-sided base, atop which—

"It was a statue," she said.

"Yes," the captain said. He pulled away two more
hunks of brick, then with both hands hefted one of
the larger pieces of silver-white chalcedony. It measured perhaps forty centimeters long and a dozen or
so through its circumference. It looked very much like
a section of an arm. "And maybe a statue depicting a
humanoid," Captain Kirk said.

"Maybe," Trinh allowed. She pulled open a compartment on her tricorder and retrieved a small,
fine-tuned scanner. She passed it over the polished
stone in the captain's hands, made an adjustment on
the tricorder to isolate the marble's physical structure, then scanned for it in the mass from which
he'd extracted it. Trinh saw representations of numerous other pieces appear on the small display on
her tricorder. "I'm reading a large quantity of this
tooled stone," she said. "I've also got software that

will attempt to virtually fit it all back together into a unified whole." She keyed in a control sequence on her tricorder to initiate that program. On the screen, sets of pieces began flying together as the software searched for matches in the surface geometry of the sculpture's fragments. They aggregated slowly at first, and then with greater frequency as the reproduction took shape, leaving a smaller and smaller population of unplaced segments.

When the figure became recognizable enough, Trinh offered her tricorder to the captain. He set the stone scrap back down, then took the tricorder and stood back up. Trinh stood with him, leaned in, and pointed at the top of the display. "It appears that the head and the bottom of the left leg have been pulverized," she said, "but this is essentially what the statue looked like." The image showed a female form, with a neck, a torso, two arms and most of two legs. Given its proportions, the sculpture captured more than just a humanoid form: it appeared *human*.

"Spock, take a look at this," the captain said. He held out the tricorder so that the first officer could see its monitor.

A single eyebrow rose on Spock's forehead. "Interesting," he said.

"There are no known human colonies out this far," said Captain Kirk.

"No," Spock said, "but we have encountered a number of alien races whose outward appearance mimics that of humans: the natives of Sarpeidon, the Scalosians, the Fabrini, to name just a few."

"Could the settlement here be the work of the Preservers?" the captain asked. Trinh recognized the name as that given to an advanced alien race who had rescued failing cultures in danger of extinction and relocated them to other planets to allow them to survive. Nearly two years earlier, the *Enterprise* crew itself had found the first evidence of the Preservers' existence. Trinh knew of the incident because of the shock waves it had sent through the world of anthropology.

"Possibly," Spock said. "If so, it could account for our finding only this single settlement on the whole of the planet."

"But . . ." the captain said. He handed Trinh's tricorder back to her, then turned and looked around at the devastated city. "What happened? Were the people here attacked? Did they do this to themselves? Was it some sort of natural disaster?"

"There may be no way of knowing," Spock said. "The thoroughness of the destruction suggests the use of energy weapons, and yet we read no heightened levels of radiation. However, if the city was destroyed long ago, which is at least what cursory observation suggests, the radiation levels could have returned to normal by now. At the same time, if the city had been deserted that far back in the past, weather and environmental forces could also be responsible for the extreme state of decay we see."

"Any thoughts, Bones?" the captain asked. Trinh looked over and saw that the doctor too had put his own tricorder to use.

"I don't have much to add," said Doctor McCoy. "I'm reading virtually no life signs inside the limits of the city—" He glanced around. "Or inside what used to be a city. That's somewhat surprising, as you'd expect more encroachment by both plants and animals over time, particularly along the borders."

"What could account for that?" the captain asked.

"It could be that the soil here's been rendered toxic to the local life-forms in some way I obviously can't measure," Doctor McCoy said. "Or there could be something on the perimeter—a force field or something like that—that's keeping most of the plants and animals out."

"Spock?" the captain asked.

"Sensors have detected nothing of the sort in or around the city," the first officer said. "Nor have we identified any artificial power sources anywhere on the planet."

Doctor McCoy shrugged. "I don't know what to tell you, Captain."

Captain Kirk nodded. He looked around again, but this time, he seemed to consider what he and the landing party should do next. "Spock, Ensign Davis discovered the city when he saw large quantities of refined metals on the surface. Where are they?"

The first officer once again worked his tricorder,

the device's shrill call slicing through the square. "I am reading significant amounts of aluminum, gold, silver, and iron, mostly in the form of steel," said Commander Spock. "It is buried within the fallen buildings."

"Household appliances," offered Trinh. "Computers, ovens, refrigeration and freezing units."

"Quite likely," said Commander Spock, his concurrence with her assertion providing her a moment of professional pride.

"What about the tritanium and rodinium?" the captain asked.

The first officer continued to consult his tricorder. "They do not appear to be within the confines of the city," he said. "But I am reading both in considerable amounts to the east, one-point-six kilometers beyond the city, and in smaller but still significant amounts half a kilometer to the southwest. The latter appears to be several dozen meters belowground, in a complex of caves."

"Explanations?" Captain Kirk said. "Theories?"

"Insufficient data," said Commander Spock. "We will need to investigate."

"Then let's investigate." The captain reached to the back of his belt and collected his communicator. He flipped it open and said, "Kirk to *Enterprise*."

"Enterprise. *Scott here, Captain*." The ship's chief engineer and second officer spoke with a rich but understandable Gaelic accent.

"Scotty, we need a site-to-site transport here on the planet," the captain said. "Details from Mister Spock."

The first officer opened his own communicator and spoke with Lieutenant Commander Scott, detailing their new destination for him. As he did so, the captain reached a hand up to Trinh's elbow and led her several paces away. Doctor McCoy followed along. "What's your take on all this, Ensign?" he said.

"Commander Spock is right," Trinh said. "We just don't have enough information right now."

"The captain's not asking for an answer, Ensign," the doctor said. "He's looking for intuition." Trinh looked to Captain Kirk for confirmation.

"Mister Spock has little taste for speculation," he said. He lifted both his eyebrows in an expression that seemed to say, *That's all well and good, but*— "I find that speculation makes for a nice snack every now and then."

Trinh understood the first officer's preference to avoid conjecture. Given her chosen fields, Trinh had considered numerous explanations for the things she'd seen since transporting down from the ship, but she too resisted drawing any conclusions until she had collected compelling evidence to lead her to one. "There are several questions I think we can ask here," she told Captain Kirk. "Who are the people who once called this city home? Are they native to this world? Regardless, what became of them? Did they perish along with this place, or did they abandon it prior to its demise, and if they deserted it, then where are they now? And for me—" Trinh looked away from the captain for a moment and eyed their surroundings. "—perhaps the question of greatest import is the one you asked a few minutes ago: what happened here?"

Once again, Trinh saw the side of the captain's mouth curl up in a look that didn't quite rise to the level of a smile. "I asked for speculation, Ensign," he said. "All you gave me were questions."

"You've only been aboard a month," Doctor McCoy said, with no hesitation in his broad smile, "and yet Spock's got you trained already."

Trinh looked at the doctor, then back at the captain. Despite their obvious good humor, she realized that she had just failed to provide her commanding officer with what he'd requested of her. Although she thought that the moment had passed, she decided to try again anyway. "Ağdam," she said.

"What?" the doctor asked, but Trinh kept her attention focused on Captain Kirk.

"Ağdam," she repeated. "You asked for my intuition, sir," Trinh said. "This city puts me in mind of Ağdam."

"What the devil is Ağdam?" asked Doctor McCoy, a reaction Trinh had more or less expected. Before she could respond, though, the captain spoke up.

"Ağdam was a village in the Republic of Azerbaijan, in the Caucasus on Earth," he said, his voice low and even. "In the late twentieth century, forces of the Artsakh Republic assaulted the town, causing its entire population to flee. Once the natives had abandoned their home, the attackers chose to destroy what remained of Ağdam in order to prevent its recapture."

"Yes," Trinh said, impressed by Captain Kirk's knowledge of history. "It existed for several decades after that as a buffer zone between military factions, and subsequently as little more than a ghost town."

"I see," Doctor McCoy said, his earlier smile replaced by a sober mien. The three officers stood together quietly for a moment, saying nothing more.

At last, Commander Spock announced Lieutenant Kyle's readiness to beam them to their next location. The captain acknowledged him, then stepped to one side, where every member of the landing party took up a position beside him approximating the format of the transporter stage aboard ship. Raising his communicator once more, the captain said, "Kirk to transporter room. Mister Kyle, energize."

And in the next moment, the latest version of Mai Duyen Trinh disappeared.

The landing party materialized in darkness, which Trinh found unnerving. With her last thoughts before beaming away from the city about becoming yet another new iteration of herself, her sudden awareness in a lightless environment made her question her existence. At the very least, she feared that something had gone terribly wrong with the transporter—maybe even that it had reassembled her body within solid rock. She opened her mouth to disprove the possibility, and to confirm the presence of the other members of the landing party about her, but instead, she found herself choking back a scream.

Calm down, she thought, and not kindly. She rebuked herself for having such a strong emotional reaction. She considered that perhaps she actually might learn something of value—something beyond science, beyond her duties aboard *Enterprise*—from the quite Vulcan Commander Spock.

Although Trinh had time for those thoughts to cycle through her mind, only a few seconds passed before a light bloomed in the darkness. Set on a tripod a meter or so high, the lighting panel glowed dimly at first, before intensifying to its full output, allowing the eyes of the landing party personnel to adjust easily. It illuminated the uneven, rocky patch of ground beneath it, as well as the six *Enterprise* crew members, but little else.

Captain Kirk turned and surveyed the landing party, as though to ensure that everybody had materialized safely. He then stepped over to the tripod, bent down, and retrieved one of a half-dozen handheld beacons sitting beside it. Even as Commander Spock and Doctor McCoy and the two security officers also moved in that direction, the captain said, "Everybody take one." Trinh suspected that he issued the order strictly for her benefit, owing to her relative newness aboard ship and her inexperience with planetary missions. The transport from *Enterprise* of the lighting panel and the beacons must have fallen into the category of standard procedure when beaming members of the crew into a dark environment, a likelihood not only because of its good sense, but borne out by the speedy reactions of the others.

As Trinh reached the tripod, Doctor McCoy handed her the last of the beacons. She thanked him with a nod. She felt cold, and noted that the fog of her breath seemed denser and lingered a bit longer than it had out in the city square. A deeper chill permeated the setting, though the stagnant air tasted stale.

As the members of the landing party clipped their beacons around their wrists and switched them on, Trinh did so as well, then turned to follow the lead of the captain. She saw him shine his beam upward, and so she peered in that direction. Far above them—though in the surrounding black, Trinh had difficulty estimating just how far above them—hung the roof of the cave. She noticed no reflective spots that would have indicated moisture, the dry character of the underground cavity also demonstrated by the lack of stalactites hanging down.

The captain lowered his beacon, and its beam—and several others—reached out horizontally to the cave walls a good distance away. Trinh perceived the considerable size of the chamber, and she turned around to check its dimension in the opposite direction. The bright white cone of light from her beacon settled not on the irregular surface of a cave wall, though, but on a surprisingly smooth surface. Trinh ran her beam up and down, left and right, and saw numerous flat surfaces connected together to form what looked like the hull of a vessel several times the size of a shuttlecraft. "Captain," she called at once.

She heard the scrape of boots along the cave floor as the others joined her, the beams of their beacons mingling with hers to better illuminate the ship. It had a bronze-colored finish, though she supposed that could have been the result of an accumulation of dust settling on it through the years—or through the decades, or the centuries. It tapered from a wide end aft to a smaller, blunt nose at the front, where several murky ports peered out like unseeing eyes. It rested upon a pair of abbreviated nacelles that depended amidships, one on either side of the craft.

With the additional beacons, Trinh had a better opportunity to study the details of the vessel. She saw that layers of dirt did indeed coat its surface, and also that it had undergone a physical assault: dents, many quite deep, littered its hull, and in one place, a fracture traced a jagged path up toward the overhead. Likewise, several fissures had compromised the engine structures.

"Spock," said the captain from beside Trinh. "Can you identify it?"

"The design is unfamiliar," said the first officer.

"As are these markings." Trinh peered at the various circles of light on the hull, until she saw one centered on a row of complex, blocklike ideograms. She recognized the flavor of the written language—in her archaeological work, she'd run across similar sorts of characters—but not its particulars.

"Ensign Trinh?" the captain asked as the whine of Commander Spock's tricorder rose in the chamber, its usually piercing tone somehow rendered thinner in the huge cavern.

"The *type* of writing is familiar," she said, "but not its content. It appears ideogrammic, but we can infer very little from that about the people who used the language."

"Captain," said Commander Spock, "the nacelles encase warp engines, but they are inert. They appear to have been drained of antimatter. The entire vessel is completely without power."

"I don't think it matters, Spock," said Captain Kirk. "Even if it had power, the ship doesn't look spaceworthy."

"Sir," called out one of the security guards, Crewman Lemli, from where he'd circled around the bow of the vessel. "There's a hatch open on this side."

Captain Kirk peered over at Commander Spock with an inquisitive look, and then the two headed around the front end of the vessel. Trinh and the others did so as well. They stopped two-thirds of the way to the stern, where Crewman Lemli held the beam of his beacon on a wide, rectangular opening in the hull. On the far bulkhead, Trinh saw, panels had been ripped out and the circuitry within smashed.

"Spock? Bones?" the captain said, and both men immediately began working their tricorders. Trinh noticed how few words Captain Kirk needed to convey his orders to his exec and chief medical officer. The men had clearly worked together for a long time.

"I detect nothing dangerous within the vessel," said Commander Spock. "It should be safe to board."

"I'm reading some minute biological matter," reported Doctor McCoy. "Epithelial cells, strands of hair . . . the sort of residual physical detritus likely left by whatever beings used the ship."

"Can you tell anything about them from your scans?" the captain asked.

"Only that they had skin and hair," the doctor said. "I'll need to take samples to determine if I can extract any DNA and sequence it. Depending on the age of the biological material—and it seems like all this happened a very long time ago—I may not have much success."

Doctor McCoy's words—*it seems like all this happened a very long time ago*—resonated with Trinh. So much of her work, at least on the archaeological side, involved civilizations lost centuries or even millennia in the past. She had spent much of her career sifting through the vestiges of societies unknown to the modern age, in places that had turned to ash.

Like the city on this world, she thought. Except that she had made no effort to date the ruins during the few minutes that the landing party had walked through the community square. Such tasks typically came later, at the time of site excavation and the collection of artifacts. With only a single, isolated set of ruins, though, Trinh lacked a frame of reference for the people who had built, lived in, and possibly perished in the city. Any attempt to pinpoint the era when they had resided there would require an absolute technique, such as radiogenic dating, which would in turn necessitate studying the planet's atmosphere and geology, as well as the output of cosmic rays by its star.

Unless, Trinh thought as a hunch grew in her mind. She knew the luminosity and spectral classification of system R-775's sun, and the Class-M status of its lone terrestrial world. Those general facts would narrow the parameters for radiogenic dating. *Especially if—*

The captain had spoken of the value of intuition, and so Trinh decided to act on hers. She worked the controls of her tricorder, recalling the data from the scans she had accumulated from the broken pieces of the statue in the square. In addition to their geometric shapes, the tricorder had recorded their composition, which Trinh began to analyze.

As she initiated several different programs, she heard the ring of an impact against metal. Trinh looked up to see that Captain Kirk had stepped onto the nacelle of the alien spacecraft. She also observed that, despite his first officer's assurance of safety within the vessel's interior, he had drawn his phaser. Still, even with the caution he demonstrated, he hadn't required either of the security guards to enter the cabin before him.

After Captain Kirk entered the vessel, Commander Spock trailed him inside. The doctor moved to follow, but then turned and held out a hand toward Trinh. "Ensign?" he said.

Realizing that Doctor McCoy expected her to enter the ship as well, Trinh walked to the open hatch. Though she declined to take his hand, she climbed up onto the nacelle and then into the alien vessel. The doctor stepped inside after her.

Trinh peered to her left, shining her beacon toward the stern of the ship. Just as she'd already seen across from the hatch, control panels in a rear bulkhead had been shattered, and their internal circuitry spilled out onto the deck and destroyed. Spatters of silver covered the deck there, as though some of the metal within the ship had melted under great heat. The implied violence felt palpable.

Gazing to her left, Trinh saw rows of empty seats marching along on both sides of a central aisle. Near the bow, another hatch stood open. Beyond it, visible in the combined glow of several beacons, more consoles had been demolished.

"Looks to me like somebody didn't want this ship going anywhere," offered Doctor McCoy.

"Despite the obvious paucity of our knowledge about precisely what transpired here, and under what circumstances," said the first officer, "I am forced to agree with Doctor McCoy."

"Really, Spock?" asked the doctor. "I thought that Vulcans practiced logic, not common sense." The lilt in his voice betrayed his lack of seriousness.

"For all our sakes," Commander Spock replied, "I can only hope that your actual use of *sense,* Doctor, grows more *common*." The comment, filled with unconcealed sarcasm, startled Trinh. Not only had she never heard the first officer joke in such a way—or in *any* way—but the familiarity with which the two men delivered their exchange told her that they had sparred in such a manner before, and likely on many occasions.

"Bones, collect whatever biological samples you can," the captain said, apparently ignoring the byplay. "Spock, I want you to see if there's anything at all intact in this vessel, and to learn whatever you can about the level of technology in use here." After both men acknowledged their orders, Captain Kirk turned to address Trinh. "Ensign," he began, but then her tricorder emitted a two-toned signal.

Trinh looked down at the device's display and saw that the analysis she'd run had completed. She quickly glanced through the readout until she spied the information she sought. It did not surprise her to see that her instincts had been correct. "Captain," she said, "it occurred to me that I could execute a series of rough radiogenic dating routines on the pieces of the sculpture we saw in the city square. Fortunately, the statue was formed from the equivalent of cultured marble, meaning that it contained synthetic resins, which I was able to date."

"How accurate would such a process be?" the captain asked.

"Depending upon the age of a particular artifact and various other factors, the margin for error could reach into the thousands of years," Trinh said. "In this case, though, the estimate is considerably more exacting than that."

"Spock, the ensign's already starting to sound like you," said the doctor.

"Bones," Captain Kirk said, clearly admonishing the doctor, and then, "How old is the statue?"

"The material it's composed of was manufactured within the last year," Trinh said.

"What?" Doctor McCoy said, his voice rising. "That means . . ." He didn't finish his statement, but the captain did.

"It means that the city was only just destroyed," he said.

Three

In the distance, the gray-white form of an *Enterprise* shuttlecraft banked to port above the planet and began its descent to the surface. Beyond *Mitrios,* the curve of the alien orb shined in denial of the depthless night of space. Through the viewports of *da Gama,* the shuttle he piloted, Sulu allowed himself a moment to appreciate the beauty of the scene unspooling before him: a living world rising like a paradisiacal way station along mankind's journey through the mostly barren universe, and a small ship carrying some of his crewmates to that world on their continuing quest for knowledge.

As *Mitrios* descended toward the cloud cover, Sulu raised his hands to the main console and tapped at the controls to execute *da Gama*'s own voyage to the surface. "Beginning our trip down," he announced.

"Acknowledged," said Lieutenant Hadley, *Enterprise*'s third-shift navigator. Sitting beside Sulu at the main panel, he touched a button, which chirped in response. "Approach vector set."

Outside the ports, the gleaming disk of the planet seemed to reel around and then grow larger. Sulu lost sight of *Mitrios* somewhere ahead. The cabin jolted mildly as the hull came into contact with the atmosphere. A gauge showed the increasing pull of the planet's gravitational field as *da Gama* streaked downward, and Sulu verified that the shuttle's artificial gravity net adapted appropriately.

As *da Gama* dropped through the sky, Sulu glanced back over his shoulder at the other six members of the team he led. After transporting down to the planet himself, Captain Kirk had returned to the ship with more questions than answers. Once back aboard, the captain consulted with his senior officers about how best to proceed. Guided by Mister Spock and Doctor McCoy, *Enterprise*'s command staff reached an easy consensus: send a scientific contingent to the planet, both to perform the regular research and analysis on an unexplored world, and to learn as much as possible about the ruined city there.

Sulu and his fellow senior officers had all reviewed the reports of the initial landing party the captain had taken down to the planet. Most agreed that whoever had constructed the city had come from another world; the singular nature of the settlement pointed to that conclusion, and the discovery on the surface of several warp-capable ships—all of them battered and rendered inoperative—seemed to support that view. Opinions divided, though, on what had taken place after the city had been built. Some, including Captain Kirk, believed that the city had been attacked from without; others thought that the inhabitants had fought among themselves. Still others envisioned a natural catastrophe, and some, a calamity brought about by scientific or military experimentation.

More than any other possibility, that of an external attack concerned the captain. Starfleet had scheduled *Enterprise* to explore that region of space over the course of the following six months, and it certainly mattered if a hostile alien species already claimed those sectors as their own. The expeditions, sent down to the planet aboard the shuttles *Mitrios, da Gama,* and *Christopher,* would focus on determining just what had befallen the city.

Peering back at the shuttlecraft's main cabin, Sulu checked on the rest of his landing party. Along with Hadley, a security guard and five of the ship's scientists had been assigned to *da Gama.* The team included Veldaclien ch'Gorin, an archaeologist and one of the few Andorians serving aboard *Enterprise.* Under his tutelage, Sulu had recently begun learning *vershaan,* a martial art invented and practiced as sport on Andoria.

Sulu knew all but one member of the landing party. The ship's new A-and-A officer had joined the crew only recently, and he'd seen her around *Enterprise* on only a couple of occasions. Until her detail to *da Gama,* he'd never even spoken to her.

As Sulu glanced at the crew members he had been chosen to lead down to the planet, he saw Ensign Mai

Duyen Trinh studying the readout of her tricorder. Petite, she stood not much more than a meter and a half tall. She had dark brown eyes, and her black hair hung down to just below the line of her jaw, framing her face the way a pair of quotation marks frame a sentence.

Lifting her gaze from her tricorder, the ensign saw Sulu peering in her direction. She offered him a tight-lipped smile, perfunctory and professional. Sulu nodded, then turned back to the main console.

The helmsman checked his display, then looked out again through the front viewports. He studied the highest layer of clouds and trimmed the shuttlecraft as it approached the troposphere. The bow bobbed up and the cabin leveled as *da Gama* continued toward the surface.

As the shuttle broke through the cloud cover, Sulu beheld for the first time what had once been an alien city. From above, it looked as though it had been flattened, as though a tremendous force had pressed down all at once, splintering buildings and toppling them in pieces to the ground. He could not imagine the terrible end the inhabitants must have suffered.

Nothing at all moved among the wreckage, underscoring the lifelessness of the tableau. Struck by the grimness of the static, crumbled place, Sulu could not look away. As *da Gama* flew toward the square at the center of the city, though, he caught sight of *Mitrios*, just ahead of and below *da Gama*. As Sulu watched, the lead shuttle rolled to starboard, off toward the northwest. The three *Enterprise* shuttlecraft would each alight at different points around the outskirts of the city, allowing the three landing parties to spread out their investigations. A fourth team would transport down to the community square and study it in detail.

At the point where *da Gama* tracked over the city center, Sulu pulled the shuttle around to port. A wooded area stretched away from the city along its southern edge, leading westward almost all the way to a deep canyon of considerable extent. The mission briefing had mentioned the natural formation, which reached several kilometers across and stretched for hundreds more along the surface.

Sulu eyed a clearing in the trees near the southwest corner of the city, the location that had been chosen for him to set down. While the scientists of his landing party would enter the city from that direction, he and Hadley would make their way to the cavern where the first alien spacecraft had been found. The third shuttle, *Christopher,* would land east of the city, not far from where the remains of several other ships had been located aboveground, although those had been left far less intact than the one Captain Kirk and his team had discovered.

"I'm reading the clearing just beyond the city," reported Hadley. He pressed a button, then twisted a wide control knob. "Making a minor correction to our projected course," Hadley said. "Our landing trajectory is set."

Sulu prepared for the switchover from thrusters to the antigrav generators that would take the shuttle to touchdown. He also checked the internal gravity net to ensure its continuing operation. "Taking us onto our final approach," he said.

As *da Gama* slowed its forward momentum and settled downward, the vast canyon disappeared from view behind the line of tall pine trees that bordered the clearing. The shuttle touched down gently. Through the front ports, Sulu saw a field of dark soil, punctuated by clusters of yellowish grass.

"Contact by all landing pads," Hadley confirmed. "Shutting down the antigrav generators." He worked his side of the control panel, while Sulu saw to his own responsibilities.

"Shutting down the thrusters," the helmsman said. "Taking the engines off line." The low hum that enveloped the cabin since it had powered up in *Enterprise*'s hangar bay diminished until it faded into silence.

Hadley touched a final button. "Main console is secure," he said.

Sulu nodded to Hadley, then turned in his chair to face the rest of the landing party. "The city lies just north of our location," he told the group. "Lieutenant Josephs—" Sulu motioned to the rear starboard seat, where an officer in red stood up and regarded the others. "—will stay with the shuttlecraft. Check in with him every two hours. You'll have eight hours on the surface before we return to the *Enterprise.*" Captain Kirk had made it clear that he wanted none of the crew on the surface past nightfall. They would have at least three days to make sense of what they'd found in system R-775, though the captain had indicated to the command crew that some leeway existed in the ship's schedule should they not find satisfactory answers in that time.

The scientists all voiced their understanding, then rose from their seats, some of them moving into the shuttle's rear compartment, where they had stowed various equipment. Sulu stood up as well and moved to the hatch, which he opened with a touch to the control panel set into the bulkhead beside it. The trapezoidal doors split and withdrew left and right into the bulkhead with a whoosh, while the panel below them folded outward to form a ramp across the portside engine nacelle. A warm, dry breeze wafted into the cabin. The surface temperature had risen since the captain had brought the first landing party down to the planet, and as the scientists filed to the hatch of *da Gama,* none of them donned the field jackets they'd brought with them.

Once all of the scientists had exited the shuttle, some of them hauling their equipment on antigravs, Sulu turned to the security guard. "You ready for your watch, Mitch?" he asked. They had known each other for three years, since Lieutenant Josephs had first transferred to *Enterprise* from space station KR-1.

The tall, broad-chested officer moved toward the bow of the shuttle. Holding up the tricorder in his hand, he said, "I've got two new collections to help me pass the time." A xenophilatelist, he had introduced Sulu to the pastime a while back. The helmsman had enjoyed learning about and searching for extant examples of alien postal stamps, but shortly after he'd taken up the hobby, he'd developed an interest in genealogy, which quickly grew to consume many of his off-duty hours.

"Anything interesting?" Sulu asked. He paced toward the aft end of the shuttle, peering back over his shoulder as Josephs responded.

"Somebody on Berengaria claims to have a four-hundred-year-old double-printed Andorian Presider stamp," he said.

"I thought that was a fabrication," Sulu said. He remembered reading that, when an Andorian collector had first produced an example of such a misprinted stamp several decades earlier, it had been unmasked as a forgery.

"Everybody thought he not only faked the stamp," Josephs said, "but even the story about the erroneous creation of such a stamp." The security officer shrugged. "I *still* think it's all a hoax, but I'm interested to see what sort of proof this Berengarian purports to have."

Sulu moved through the archway at the rear of the main cabin and into the shuttle's rear compartment.

Skirting the remaining scientific equipment, he withdrew from a locker there a tricorder and a portable engineering kit, along with his and Hadley's field jackets. Although the current weather seemed temperate, he'd been warned that the interior of the cave would likely feel considerably cooler. He started back through the arch and toward the front of the cabin. "You'll have to let me know whether or not the Presider stamp turns out to be legitimate," Sulu told Josephs.

"I will," said the security officer. When Sulu handed Hadley his jacket, Josephs leaned in and glanced at the shuttle's main console. "I'll expect you two to check in by twelve-eleven hours," he said.

"Will do," Sulu said. Then, of Hadley, he asked, "Are you ready, Bill?"

"Let's go," said the navigator.

Sulu led the way outside. Ahead of them, the scientists made their way across the clearing toward the edge of the city, pulling their equipment on antigrav sledges that floated along behind them. Sulu started after them, with Hadley at his side. Once the two reached the city, they would cut west, toward the canyon, to where the damaged alien spacecraft sat in a subterranean chamber. While another team investigated the vessels found east of the city, Sulu and Hadley would study the ship that the first landing party had found. Captain Kirk hoped that one or the other of the groups would learn something meaningful from the vessels; in particular, he sought to learn the identity and origin of those who'd flown the ships to the planet in the first place. Sulu would bring to bear not only his experience at the helm of a starship, but also his training as a mathematician. In addition to Bill Hadley's position as a navigator, he also held an A5 computer journeyman classification, one of the highest such ratings among the *Enterprise* crew. Armed with their various levels of expertise, they would do their best to coax some information out of the ruined spacecraft.

Sulu heard a hum behind him. He glanced back in time to see *da Gama*'s hatch fold closed. Then he turned back around and continued with Hadley toward the city. Sulu had no way of knowing that he would never board the shuttle again.

Sulu reached up and dragged his bare arm across his forehead, wiping away the sweat that had formed there. Reports of the chilly environment within the cave had been accurate, but after Sulu and Hadley had worked for some time inside the alien spacecraft, their physical efforts had combined with the enclosed space to create an oppressively stuffy atmosphere. They had peeled off their jackets first, and then later had pushed up the sleeves of their gold uniform shirts.

In front of him, bathed in the glow of four lighting panels that the *Enterprise* crew had beamed down, Hadley lay prone on the deck of the alien vessel, his arms and head buried inside its inner workings. They had just succeeded in prying off an access plate, below which sat several complex systems. According to the sensor scans they'd executed with their tricorder, those systems remained intact.

That'll be a first, Sulu thought. He and Hadley had scoured both the exterior and the interior of the vessel. Though the drive components had been compromised, they explored the possibility of reintroducing antimatter into the engines in order to establish a minimal level of power. When simulations to do so failed, they investigated the ship's backup batteries, wondering if they could recharge or even replace them. When even that scheme proved unworkable, they moved inside.

There, Sulu and Hadley had begun their efforts by searching for any equipment even remotely whole, without success. They then changed tack and pored over the remnants of the smashed control panels, recording symbols in an attempt to decipher the language in which they had been written. They attempted to link their tricorder up to the few existing computer pathways recognizable as such, hoping to secure access to any intermediate memory caches. Nothing worked.

At last, they'd taken to dismantling the vessel. Sulu and Hadley scanned the bulkheads, the overhead, and the decking, mapping the internal apparatus. Many had been disabled, their circuitry evidently overloaded by something akin to a high-wattage pulse. The vessel's deflector screens, shields, and weapons had all been compromised. Finally, though, Sulu and Hadley detected three unbroken systems: artificial gravity, atmospheric recycling, and temperature control. They didn't expect to find hiding within those systems an anatomy text describing the aliens, or an interstellar map pointing the way to their native planet, but even the subtlest of clues might suggest what had taken place there, and who had been involved. Although Starfleet had never before explored R-775, that didn't necessarily mean that the Klingons—or the Tholians or some other species already known to the Federation—hadn't done so. As Captain Kirk had pointed out, with the *Enterprise* crew set to survey that region of space over the course of the next half year, it would pay to know sooner rather than later who else traveled those skies—particularly if they were capable—militarily and morally—of laying waste to a populated city.

"It won't work," Hadley called from where he'd lowered his head and hands into the guts of the alien ship. His voice reverberated in the narrow space. Hadley pulled his arms from below the deck, and Sulu reached down to help him scamper all of the way back out.

Hadley removed the beacon from his bare wrist and dropped it to the deck without even switching it off. He took in a deep breath, then let it out slowly, his cheeks puffing in the process. "It won't work," he said again. "There's just no way to get at the power conduits." Their intention had been to run their own supply of energy through the undamaged systems, record their output, then search for any embedded firmware. The force of the artificial gravity net, the composition of the reprocessed atmosphere, and the temperature settings all could tell the *Enterprise* crew something more about the aliens—especially if they turned out to be a species familiar to the Federation. Sulu found that possibility unlikely, though, given the unfamiliar design of the ship.

Hadley pushed himself backward on the deck until he could sit back against a bulkhead. Sulu stood back up and peered down at him. "What if we remove the systems?"

Hadley chuckled. "Yeah, I thought of that too," he said. "I think that's what we'll have to do." He gazed down at the open panel from which he'd just extracted himself. "We're going to have to rip up the whole deck."

"Using a phaser torch?" Sulu asked.

"I'm not sure what else we could use that would do the trick," Hadley said.

"Right," Sulu agreed. "As though it's not hot enough in here already." In response, Hadley looked around and found one of the metal water bottles they'd transported down from *Enterprise*. He upended it and took a long pull. "What do you say we take a break? We can walk back to the shuttle and get some lunch."

Hadley shook his head. "You know, I'm not even hungry right now," he said. "I'd just like to sit here, or maybe out in the cave where it's cooler. I just want to sip my water and not think about anything for a half hour or so."

"We can transport back up to the ship and take a breather there," Sulu suggested.

Hadley seemed to consider this, but then shook his head again. "Nah, that's all right. I'll probably get my second wind before too long."

Sulu reached over to one of the nearby seats and picked up the tricorder he'd set there. He checked the chronometer and saw that they'd been working on the alien ship for nearly four hours. "We're coming up on our next check-in with *da Gama*," he said. "I think I'll stretch my legs and head back to the shuttle, get a report from Josephs on the progress of the scientists. And I *am* hungry, so I'll get some lunch too."

"All right," Hadley said. "I'll contact engineering and have them send down a phaser torch."

"Good," Sulu said. He draped the strap of the tricorder across one shoulder, then retrieved his communicator and phaser from where he'd set them aside while working. "I shouldn't be much more than an hour or so." The walk from *da Gama*, through the corner of the city, out to the cavern had taken only about fifteen minutes, and Sulu didn't intend to spend more than half an hour at the shuttle.

Sulu started for the outer hatch. Before heading

out into the cave, he peered back at Hadley. "If the aliens show up while I'm gone," he said, "just let them have their ship back."

"What if the aliens who *destroyed* the ship show up?" Hadley asked in mock seriousness.

Sulu shrugged. "Then say hello for me," he said.

Hadley smiled. "How about I just have them wait for you to get back so you can tell them yourself?"

"You're so thoughtful," Sulu told him. He stepped down onto the engine nacelle, and then down to the cave floor. He activated the beacon attached to his wrist, then marched toward the shaft that led up to the surface.

Sulu had already trod at least a hundred meters when the coolness of the cavern overcame the heat of his earlier exertions. He considered going back for his field jacket, but decided against it, instead simply rolling his uniform sleeves back down. He reached the mouth of the cave just two minutes later.

The city lay directly ahead, with the woods abutting it to the right. Sulu thought about trying a more direct route back to the shuttle, through the trees, but he had no idea how the footing would be there, or how passable the vegetation. Instead, he tramped back the way he'd come.

As he walked along the city's edge, tracing his way through the hulking mounds of fallen buildings, Sulu found the experience different than he had earlier. He and Hadley had held a conversation while making their way to the cave, but traveling alone along the same path, he heard only the rap of his own footsteps, the susurrus of his own breathing. Those sounds seemed somehow disrespectful, as though an intrusion on the memories of so many who had likely died there.

Sulu quickened his step. He reached the clearing in only twelve minutes. Although he didn't enter it with a sigh of relief, the disquiet he'd felt dissipated. His ease of mind did not last long.

As Sulu made his way across the field, the ground suddenly rumbled beneath his feet.

Four

Jim Kirk couldn't stop thinking about the Klingons.

The captain sat in the command chair on the *Enterprise* bridge, his gaze fastened on the main viewscreen, where the graceful curve of the world he had come to think of as Ağdam hung in the void like a jewel. He mused that perhaps the people who had settled upon it had seen it that way as well, with a romance and a poetry that promised a shining future. In the end, though, it hadn't turned out that way for them.

Had the Klingons spoiled that vision? Kirk wondered. Their empire comprised scores of conquered worlds and decimated peoples. They took what they wanted, aggressively seizing planets and resources they deemed of strategic importance. They lived in a state of perpetual war with their neighbors, and practiced a form of institutionalized violence that Kirk had never quite been able to understand.

They're not all *like that,* Kirk reminded himself. The captain had on a number of occasions found it possible to deal reasonably and effectively with his counterparts in the Klingon Imperial Fleet. Captain

Koloth had demonstrated an ability to negotiate and even compromise, as had Commander Kang. Still, the military nature of the Klingon leadership allowed for—and even rewarded—savagery.

Kirk knew that his last experience with the commander of the Klingon vessel *Klothos* probably colored his thoughts. Not all that long before, Kor had attempted to lure the *Enterprise* crew into a firefight with three Klingon D7-class heavies. When *Klothos* and *Enterprise* inadvertently became ensnared in a pocket within the fabric of space-time, though, Kirk and Kor worked together to save both crews and return the ships to their reality. But that success apparently didn't satisfy the Klingon commander, who planted an explosive aboard *Enterprise*—an explosive that came within seconds of detonating aboard the Starfleet vessel.

It's more than that, Kirk thought. *More personal than that.* Although it had taken place three years earlier, he had not forgotten his experience on the planet Organia. Kor had threatened to employ Klingon mind-sifter technology on Kirk, and he *had* used it on Spock. The Empire's soldiers utilized the brutal device to extract information from captives reluctant to talk, ripping through an individual's thoughts, potentially crushing their very essence. Only Spock's Vulcan heritage and mental discipline allowed him to withstand the interrogation, but he'd suffered lingering effects from the incident. Kirk knew that his first officer had spoken with a Starfleet psychiatrist about the terrible event, and once, Spock had discussed it with Kirk, revealing that vestiges persisted of the attempt to invade his mind and tear apart his consciousness.

So I have good reason to hate the Klingons, Kirk thought, *but the truth is that it just doesn't make any sense that they were involved here.* Although the Klingons often acted out of territoriality and expansionism, Ağdam lay nowhere near the Empire. In fact, given the great distance of R-775 from both the Federation and the Empire, as well as from the other known powers in the Alpha and Beta Quadrants, the star system didn't measure up as a target of value. Moreover, even if the Klingons had found a reason to attack, wouldn't they have occupied the planet? And if they *had* attacked, wouldn't the *Enterprise* crew have detected the energy signatures of Klingon disruptors?

No, not the Empire, Kirk concluded. And not the Romulans or the Gorn or the Tholians, either, for many of the same reasons. In truth, the *Enterprise* crew hadn't even determined with any degree of certainty that the city on Ağdam had been destroyed as the result of an external attack.

But it was, Kirk thought. He could feel it. The implications of that would—

"Captain," Chekov called from where he manned the primary science station. In his dense Russian accent, the word came out as *Keptin.* Spock had transported with a landing party to the center of the city to continue searching for answers about what had taken place there, and in his absence, Chekov had substituted for him at his console. "I'm reading a massive energy surge on the planet's surface."

Even as a jolt of anxiety coursed through Kirk, he took action. Rising quickly to his feet, he brought the side of his fist down on the right side of the command chair, onto the intercom control. "Bridge to transporter room," he said, his voice steady but containing a note of urgency. "Lock onto all landing party personnel and prepare to beam them aboard."

"Aye, sir," replied Lieutenant Kyle. *"We've been monitoring the locations of the shuttle crews and Mister Spock's party, so it won't take long to establish locks."*

"Do it and stand by," Kirk said. "Keep this channel open." He then turned toward Chekov and asked a question for which he feared the answer. "Was the energy surge in the city?"

Before Chekov could respond, Kirk heard a soft but unmistakable tone. He turned toward the console that stood before the command chair and that housed the helm and navigation stations. In the middle of the console, at the front, a large indicator flashed red in sync with the tone. "Deflector contact," reported Lieutenant Naomi Rahda, one of the ship's relief helm officers. Without waiting for an order, she worked her controls, and the sensor and targeting scanner began to quickly unfold from within the station.

"Chekov?" Kirk asked, glancing over at the ensign.

The captain needed more information. Considering the presence on the planet of a wrecked city, he wanted to raise *Enterprise*'s defensive shields, but doing so would make it impossible to transport the four landing parties—thirty crew members—to safety.

"I'm now reading several energy surges," Chekov said, leaning over and peering into the hooded viewer at the science station. Kirk could see a pale blue glow fluctuating across the line of the ensign's eyes. "Two surges near the city, but several others much farther away. There seems to be—" Chekov suddenly bolted upright and spun toward the center of the bridge. "Captain, sensors are tracking two missiles headed for the city."

Kirk didn't hesitate. "Transporter room," he said, looking toward the intercom in the arm of the command chair. "Beam up the landing parties at once."

Kyle said something in response, but Rahda spoke over him. "Captain, there are missiles closing in fast on the *Enterprise*."

"Transporter room, belay that order," Kirk said at once. "Shields up."

"Raising shields," said Rahda, but as her hands flew across her controls to translate the captain's order into reality, the alien weaponry pounded into the hull of *Enterprise*.

Trinh watched what looked like a rocket for only a few seconds before it disappeared from view, and then she saw a fireball roiling up into the sky out beyond the edge of the city. Standing amid the scraps of a settlement driven into the dust in an unknown set of circumstances, the A-and-A officer feared for her life. Even more than that, though, she worried about the safety of the people she led.

"What was *that?*" Clien wanted to know. The archaeologist had raced up beside Trinh, peering out to where something terrible had clearly happened.

With an effort, Trinh tore her attention away from the yellow-red flames. She turned toward the Andorian, grabbed the tricorder he held in his hands, and forcefully lifted it to his face. "Find out," she ordered, although she already thought she knew. "Scan for the *da Gama.*"

For a moment, Clien only stared at her. She didn't know if the situation had stunned him or if it had simply been her stony manner, but Trinh suspected they would have little time to secure their own safety. Before she had to say anything more, though, Clien appeared to emerge from his trance. "Yes, sir," he said, and started operating the tricorder.

As the whine of a sensor scan rose in the still air, Trinh turned to the rest of her scientific team. She saw Jackie Trieste between heaps of rubble that had once been buildings. The scientist stood looking toward the site of the explosion, her mouth agape. Trinh hurried over to her. "Where are Martha and Noah?" she asked. But she already knew. Martha Hunt and Noah

Ontkean, archaeologists specializing in architecture and urban settings, respectively, had split from the group in order to collect as much data as they could in their survey of the downed structures within the city.

"It doesn't matter," Trinh said, more to herself than to her colleagues. She reached to the back of her uniform pants and retrieved her communicator. The device chirruped when she flipped it open. "Landing party to *Enterprise*," she said. "This is Ensign Trinh."

She expected an immediate response. When she didn't receive one, she glanced at the communicator to make sure it still functioned. Seeing that it did, she tried again. "Landing party to—"

"Enterprise *here*," came the voice of Lieutenant Uhura. "*What's your status, landing party?*" The communications officer spoke in a rush, and Trinh thought she heard a commotion in the background.

"We just witnessed a rocket in the air and an explosion out past the edge of the city," Trinh reported. "I think the *da Gama* might have been hit, and that we might be under attack. Request an immediate transport of all personnel currently on the surface."

A burst of static issued from Trinh's communicator, and she thought she would hear nothing else. But then Uhura's voice resumed, apparently in the middle of a sentence. "*—struck the ship. We've just raised the shields, and so we cannot beam you aboard at the present time.*"

Trinh's heart sank. As the ranking officer and

leader of the scientific team, it would fall to her to keep the others safe. She had trained at Starfleet for such eventualities, but never before had such an event been anything more than an exercise for her.

Except that Lieutenant Sulu leads the full landing party, she realized. Into the communicator, she said, "Understood. Trinh out." She reached up and closed the channel with a touch to a control, then said, "Trinh to Lieutenant Sulu." She waited through another silence, but unlike her contact with the ship, she anticipated an eventual response.

It never came.

Instead, Clien ran over to her. The pale blue flesh of his face had flushed a deeper hue, an autonomic Andorian response, she understood, that accompanied fear or anger. "The shuttle . . ." he managed to say, but he needed no additional words to convey what had happened. Trinh knew that *da Gama* had been destroyed.

And how many of the landing party with it? she asked herself, and then didn't even try to formulate an answer. She needed to concern herself not with the dead, but with the living. Again, she spoke into her communicator. "Trinh to Lieutenant Sulu."

Again, she received no reply.

Maybe communicator signals can't reach him inside the cave, Trinh thought. She clung to the idea, trying to allow it to push away the image that formed in her mind of the rocket they'd seen moments earlier. Still, she imagined the missile streaking with violent force into the body of *da Gama,* reducing it to slag.

But then another image rose in Trinh's mind: the cave. She quickly returned her communicator to its place at her hip and took hold of her tricorder. She scanned for the complex of caverns that stretched beneath the surface near the great canyon. When she located it, she searched for the opening closest to her scientific team. Finding it, she turned to the other scientists. "Follow me," Trinh told them. "Quickly." Using her tricorder as a guide, she started through the city at a trot. On the way, she would contact Martha and Noah and order them to do the same, to identify the nearest cave entrance and make their way to it.

And if we're lucky enough to get there safely, Trinh thought, *maybe taking cover underground will be enough to protect us from whoever launched an attack against the shuttlecraft.* Trinh didn't like relying on an *if* and a *maybe,* but she didn't see any other reasonable choice open to her.

The second brace of missiles landed on *Enterprise.* Kirk felt the deck buck beneath him, but he kept his balance with a hand to the back of Lieutenant Rahda's chair. "Report," he said, though not to the helmswoman.

"One missile struck the underside of the primary hull," called Chekov from the science station, "and the other detonated against the engineering section."

He paused a moment, then said, "Minimal impact on ship's systems. Shields are down to ninety-five percent."

"What about our weapons?" Kirk asked Rahda.

"Engineering crews are working to replace the phaser couplings, and should have at least one bank available before too long," she said. "The photon torpedo tubes have been compromised at multiple points, though, and will take considerably longer."

"Understood," Kirk said. The first set of missiles had assaulted *Enterprise* when its defensive shields had been down. Although the weapons showed no particular degree of sophistication, the high-yield warheads caused considerable blast damage. A pair of hull breaches cost the lives of three crew members, and a hit on the port nacelle made faster-than-light travel impossible. The attack also compromised the sensor net, overloaded the phasers, and knocked both the impulse drive and life support off line.

Kirk had prioritized the repair of the latter two systems over all others, including the phasers. The crew required the impulse drive to maintain—or break—orbit, and they obviously needed heat and water and atmosphere to keep themselves alive. It helped to know that, with the shields raised, *Enterprise* risked no further damage, at least not in the near term.

The captain turned and made his way past the command chair, then climbed to the outer circle of the bridge. At the communications station, he peered down at Uhura. "Lieutenant," he asked quietly, "what about our personnel on the ground?" During the first moments of the attack on *Enterprise,* Kirk had directed Uhura to field messages from the members of the crew who had transported down to the planet.

"I've had contact with all four landing parties, sir," Uhura said, looking up from her console. She matched the captain's tone, also speaking softly. "All three shuttlecraft have been destroyed, and at least four of our people are unaccounted for."

The captain's face froze into an emotionless mask. *Already three dead on the ship,* he lamented, *and now four missing down on the planet.* Nothing troubled him more than losing members of his crew. Over the course of his four years in command of *Enterprise,* dozens—*scores*—of Starfleet officers had perished while carrying out his orders. Kirk loved his position as a starship captain, but his responsibility for so many lives—and so many deaths—wore on him. Because of his decisions, husbands would not return to wives, mothers to sons, children to their parents.

Kirk wondered if one of those missing on the planet was Spock, a man who in four years had become not only his trusted right hand aboard ship, but also the best friend he'd ever had. That thought led him to recollect another friend: Gary Mitchell. He and Kirk had met at the Academy and had quickly grown close. Fifteen years after that, upon his promotion to captain, Kirk had requested Gary's assignment to *Enterprise*. Though Starfleet approved the transfer, his friend's tour of duty neither lasted long nor played out in a way Kirk had expected. Only months into Gary's posting to the ship, exposure to an astronomical phenomenon gave him superhuman abilities and a callous disregard for his crewmates. Not only did he die while serving aboard *Enterprise,* but Kirk ended up having to kill him. That bitter memory had never left him, and he couldn't imagine that it ever would.

For the second time during his shift, the captain realized that he had lost his concentration, that he had fallen into a pit of tragic remembrance. He looked to Uhura, who sat silently at her console. When they made eye contact, she began speaking again, and Kirk understood that she knew he'd stopped listening.

"I've let the landing party personnel know we'll be beaming them up as soon as possible," Uhura said. "They're taking cover as best they can."

"Very good, Lieutenant," Kirk said. At the moment, without benefit of sensors, he couldn't risk lowering the shields to transport up the crew members on the planet. Before leaving the communications station, he thanked Uhura. She offered him a fleeting but seemingly genuine smile.

The ship suddenly rumbled again, and Kirk reached out to the station beside him to keep from falling. He righted himself, then looked to the science station. "Report, Mister Chekov."

"Another missile has crashed into the primary hull, and another into engineering," the ensign said. "Shields down to ninety-one percent, other ship's systems unaffected."

The captain returned to the lower portion of the bridge and reached to the right arm of his command chair. After activating the intercom, he said, "Bridge to engineering."

Several seconds passed before Kirk received a response, but he knew how busy his chief engineer must be. *"Aye, Captain, Scott here."*

"Scotty, what's happening down there?" Kirk asked.

"Captain, we've restored life support," Scotty said. *"We're now in the process of rerouting impulse power around the damaged section."*

"Do you have an estimate?"

"Seven minutes," Scotty said.

"I'm going to hold you to that," Kirk said.

"Aye, sir," Scotty said. *"You always do."*

"Bridge out." Kirk climbed back into the command chair. He glanced at the main viewscreen without really seeing it. Instead, he focused on the steps he would have to take to pull the landing parties out of harm's way. Once the impulse drive had been repaired, the crew could move *Enterprise* out of range of the missiles launching from the surface. Scotty and his engineers could then work on restoring the sensors. When the crew could detect incoming weapons, that would in turn allow them to safely drop the shields so that they could beam up the crew from the planet.

Kirk doubted that another Starfleet engineer could accomplish in a shorter amount of time what Scotty and his team would. *Enterprise* could not have been assigned a more capable chief engineer. As long as members of his crew remained in danger, though, Kirk knew that those seven minutes would not pass quickly enough to suit him.

Trinh paced inside the mouth of the cave. In her hands, she held her tricorder, its sensors reaching out across the nearby landscape in search of life signs. She spied just one, in the wood to the southwest.

"Anything?" Clien asked from over her shoulder.

"One person moving in this direction," Trinh said.

"One of *our* people?" Clien asked.

Trinh nodded. "They're human," she said. "They're approaching through the wood, on a direct line, I think, from the *da Gama*." She thought, but didn't say, *Or from where the* da Gama *used to be.*

Trinh felt the vibration in the floor of the cave before she heard it, but then a deep drone emerged from the surrounding rock. Dust trailed down from above like a dry mist. She turned toward Clien and saw his face flushing. She wondered if he could see the fear that she felt.

"Another rocket?" Clien asked.

Trinh consulted her tricorder, but she didn't want

to interrupt her scans for members of the landing party. While Martha and Noah had reached the cave shortly after Trinh, Clien, and Jackie, and Lieutenant Hadley had already been there, Lieutenants Sulu and Josephs remained elsewhere, though one of them clearly headed for the caverns. "I can't tell," she said, "but yes, I think it's another rocket. I think we're feeling the effects of a launch from somewhere in the vicinity of the city."

Clien lifted his tricorder and worked its controls. "I'm going to try to determine its target," he said.

Trinh wanted to ask him why he would bother to do so, since the scientists could do little more to protect themselves even with new information. But then she reconsidered the truth of that judgment. Perhaps if they made their way farther into the cave, deeper underground, they would stand a better chance of surviving a nearby—or even a direct—strike.

"Clien, don't wait," Trinh ordered. "Take the others and head as far into the cavern as you can."

"What about you?"

"I—" Trinh started, but didn't know exactly what to say. *What* about *me?* she thought. She needed to protect herself as well as the people in her charge. "I have to stay here right now," she finally told Clien. "Lieutenant Sulu and Lieutenant Josephs are still out there."

"And your staying here won't help them get here any faster," Clien insisted.

"Go," Trinh said. She felt tired, as though she lacked the strength to argue. Fortunately, as uncomfortable as she'd been issuing commands to *Enterprise* personnel with far more shipboard experience than she, she appreciated the fact that she didn't have to explain herself. "Clien, you have your orders. Follow them." She hiked a thumb back over her shoulder for emphasis.

Clien didn't move, but simply stared back at her. For an awkward few seconds, Trinh felt challenged, and she thought that he might not do as she'd bidden him. At last, though, he dropped his gaze, but before he moved off, he reached up a hand to her upper arm and gave it a squeeze—an act beyond the borders of professionalism or propriety, and one that surprised her. "Stay safe," he told her.

Trinh watched him retreat deeper into the cavern, until at last he reached the other scientists. She saw him speaking, and then motioning past them. She wanted to make sure that he indeed obeyed her orders, but then she glanced at the display on her tricorder. There, she saw that the person racing toward the cave had nearly reached it, but had unaccountably stopped moving. Suddenly, the life signs of a hundred humans and as many Andorians appeared on her readout.

Then Trinh heard the missile soar past.

The tumult of the explosion surrounded Sulu, and the earth quaked beneath him. His fingers scrabbled at the terrain as he desperately attempted to halt his slide toward the fissure that sliced into the cliffside. The hard ground resisted his efforts, though, and Sulu felt the earth run out beneath him as he tumbled over the edge of the canyon.

His stomach reeled as gravity sought to claim him. The realization of falling shocked him, the innate fear gripping him tightly. He saw a tremendous torrent of flame below him, and out beyond it, the vast floor of the canyon.

Sulu slammed back against the wall of the fissure. In an eyeblink, he visualized his plunge not as a long fall from a great height, but as a series of crashes, his body fracturing as it struck over and over against the rock face. He would eventually reach the ground broken and battered, a bloodied rag doll twisted into an inhuman posture.

But then Sulu didn't fall. Profoundly relieved but also confused, he tried to look up. The back of his uniform shirt had been pulled up, though, and the tautly stretched garment prevented him from turning his head. He thought his clothing must have fortuitously caught on an outcropping in the side of the fissure, but then he heard a voice calling over the rolling sound of the blast below. He couldn't make out the words, but in his peripheral vision, he saw a hand gripping the collar of his shirt.

"Give me your hand!" the voice called.

Sulu reached up with his right hand. A ripping

noise suddenly filled his ear, and his body dropped another handful of centimeters. The terror of falling to his death clutched at his heart. He waited to plummet to the canyon floor.

But then a hand grabbed his raised arm, and then a second hand did so as well. They pulled Sulu upward, his bare back scraping against the rock. He felt his shirt slacken, and then two more hands wrapped around his left biceps. Sulu felt himself yanked up, then hauled back over the edge of the cliff and onto the ground.

He lay there for a long moment with his eyes closed. It seemed to Sulu that he could feel nothing. He considered the idea that he had actually fallen—perhaps even continued to fall—and that his mind had invented a different perception, protecting him from dying of simple fright on the way down. By degrees, though, he became aware of his chest heaving in great, desperate breaths and of rills of perspiration slipping down his face.

He heard something—*A voice?*—as though from a distance. He thought he would open his eyes and look around, but then the sound began to fade. Everything began to fade.

And then Sulu passed out.

Five

On the *Enterprise* bridge, Spock spun the control wheel on the side of the hooded viewer projecting from the primary science station. As he studied the device's internal display, he manipulated an increase in the magnification, bringing into sharp focus a region of R-775-I's surface. He had already attuned the scanner to process the data collected by a pair of probes that the crew had directed down to the planet. Both of those probes had been lost to the alien missiles, but not before gathering vital information.

Planetside when the *Enterprise* had been attacked, Spock learned upon his return what had taken place. The first pair of missiles that struck the ship caused significant damage, including to the engine and weapon systems. Chief Engineer Scott and his staff quickly restored the impulse drive, though, allowing the captain to order the ship out of orbit, with the intention of escaping the range of the missiles. That effort succeeded approximately two hundred thousand kilometers from the planet, and the engineering staff then effected repairs to the sensor grid and phasers; work on the damaged warp nacelle continued.

Bringing the ship back into range, Captain Kirk tested the effectiveness of the phaser banks against the alien weaponry. Once satisfied that the missiles could be destroyed before they reached the *Enterprise,* the captain ordered the shields down and the members of the four landing parties back aboard.

Pulling away from the scanner, Spock reached for a control on his console. "Switching to the main viewscreen," he said. He turned toward the forward portion of the bridge to confirm his handiwork, then looked to the captain.

"That's the city in the lower left-hand corner?" Kirk asked from the command chair.

"It is," Spock said. He reached for a button on his console, one of several he'd programmed as context-sensitive graphics tools. On the main viewer, the image of the city appeared to lift from the scene and pitch upward, providing an edge-on view. Lacking an intact metropolitan skyline, the profile of the mounds of broken buildings revealed the completeness of the destruction there.

The first officer pressed the button again, and the city returned to its overhead representation. He then tapped another control, which highlighted three areas on the screen. "The red circles indicate the launch sites of the missiles," Spock said. "As you can see, one is proximate to the ruins of the city, while the other two are spread out across the same continent, but some distance away."

"Are there others?" the captain asked.

"Not that we have yet been able to find," Spock said, "but we have reason to believe that there may be."

"Explain," Kirk said.

Working his console once more, Spock caused the picture on the viewer to shift, the point of view zooming in to one of the red circles and displaying in detail a portion of the planet's landscape. "This is one of the known launch sites," he said. The image on the screen showed rolling hills covered by uncultivated vegetation—and nothing else.

"Camouflaged?" asked the captain.

"It would appear so," Spock said. "Before the *Enterprise*'s sensors were damaged, they recorded the physical coordinates on the surface of the energy surges, which marked the precise locations from which the missiles were launched. The probes scanned those areas. It would appear that a three-dimensional projection hides each site, and that some form of shielding prevents it from being detected by sensors."

"So we have no notion what's inside the missile complexes," Kirk said.

"That is correct," Spock confirmed.

"And there's no way of beaming through the shielding?" Kirk asked.

"Negative," Spock said. "Without being able to scan within the launch site, it will not be possible to target the transporter."

Kirk lifted an elbow onto the arm of the command

chair and dropped his chin onto his curled fingers. As the captain continued to regard the image on the main viewscreen, Spock noticed his features harden and a distant look come over him. The first officer had spent enough time with Kirk through the four years of their association to surmise what occupied his thoughts. When the landing parties had returned to the ship, the captain had learned that four of the crew had been killed, each of them dying as the result of a missile strike on an *Enterprise* shuttlecraft. Kirk clearly understood the dangerous nature of their mission of exploration, and within that context, he acted as best he could to safeguard the people he led. Although he never let it cripple him, the captain clearly felt deeply the loss of any crew member.

Spock knew that he could say little that would ease his commanding officer's burden, and certainly nothing on the bridge, in front of the crew. He took note of the captain's reaction, though, and resolved to say something later, in private, if it seemed necessary. More than simply their relationship as shipmates, as captain and first officer, the two men had become friends.

Lifting his head back up, Kirk said, "Analysis, Spock."

The first officer placed his hands behind his back, the fingers of one hand wrapping around the opposite wrist, and made his way down to the lower portion of the bridge. He stopped beside the command chair. "It would appear that there are sensor mechanisms on the planet that monitor alien visitation," he said.

"Sensor 'mechanisms'?" Kirk said. "You don't think that there are beings on the planet who are scanning the ship and making these attacks?"

"No, sir," Spock said. "We have not been contacted or warned away, and the fact that the attacks cease when the *Enterprise* moves beyond a specific distance from the planet suggests automated defenses. Since the ship was not immediately fired upon when first we arrived, it is also reasonable to assume that the defensive emplacements respond either after the prolonged presence of a ship in orbit, or after visitors appear on the surface."

"We can notify Starfleet to keep Federation vessels away from this system," Kirk said, "but I don't want to leave other ships and crews who might visit here in danger."

"Understandable," Spock said.

The captain stood from the command chair and made his way around the combined helm-and-navigation console, his eyes regarding the seemingly benign setting on the main viewer. He appeared to study the scene for a few moments, and then he turned to face Spock. At their stations, Lieutenant Rahda and Ensign Chekov looked up at him. "Spock, whatever projections and shields protect those sites from our scans, they must come down when missiles are launched."

Spock considered the statement, but he could not

entirely agree with it. "Possibly," he said. "But physical objects can readily pass through light, and it is possible that the missiles can travel through the shields."

"Yes," the captain said, "but even so, the shields would not remain totally intact when a missile passed through them; there would be a gap at the point of contact."

"A gap occupied by the missile itself," Spock pointed out.

"Yes, but would it be possible to perform a sensor scan *through* the missile and into the emplacement below it?"

Spock contemplated the captain's question. "It is possible," he decided, "especially given the lack of technological sophistication in the missiles themselves. They were able to destroy the shuttlecraft and damage the *Enterprise* primarily as a result of the element of surprise, but with our phasers and shields intact, their effectiveness has waned. That suggests that the concealment of the launch sites may not easily resist our attempts to penetrate them."

Kirk nodded, then peered down at the navigation console. "Mister Chekov, lay in a course to return us to the planet." After retrieving the members of the landing parties, the captain had ordered *Enterprise* back out of orbit, beyond the range of the missiles.

"Aye, Captain," replied the navigator, who began operating his panel.

The captain turned his attention to the helm. "Ms.

Rahda, same drill as before. Shields up, fire phasers as necessary to destroy any missiles headed our way."

"Yes, sir," said Rahda. Like Chekov, she immediately worked her controls.

Finally, Kirk looked back over at Spock. Understanding what the captain's plan required, Spock did not wait for an order. Instead, he headed back to the science station. There, he started to calibrate the ship's sensors, in preparation for the mission to come.

The view of the launch site had cleared from the main screen, and Kirk watched from the command chair as the orb of Ağdam grew in its stead. If the sensors could penetrate into any of the lairs from which the missiles had been fired, he had no intuition of what they would discover there. He suspected Spock would prove correct—as he typically did—in his estimation that they would find only automated installations. In that case, Kirk at least hoped that the crew could shut down the facilities, protecting any other ships that might enter the system and explore the planet.

But Kirk also wanted more than that. *Seven of my crew were killed,* he thought angrily. He did not wish to let that harsh fact stand without explanation. The captain did not want vengeance, but he wanted answers.

"Sir, we are crossing the two hundred thousand kilometer threshold en route to establishing orbit about the planet," reported Lieutenant Rahda. Kirk saw her lean left and peer into the sensor and targeting scanner on the helm. "I'm reading two energy surges on the planet's surface, one from each of the sites away from the city," she said. "Two missiles are headed directly toward the ship."

"Spock?" the captain asked, wanting to ensure his first officer's readiness.

From his position at the main science station, Spock said, "I have directed the ship's sensors toward those sites. The next time missiles launch, I will endeavor to scan beyond them."

"Understood," Kirk acknowledged. "Lieutenant Rahda, you may fire at will."

"Waiting for the missiles to enter optimal firing range," Rahda said. She waited, her hands poised to take action at her controls, her gaze glued to her scanner. After a few moments, she began counting down from five. When she reached zero, her fingers moved swiftly atop her console, unleashing *Enterprise*'s firepower.

Kirk watched the screen as twin streaks of brilliant red light leaped from the ship's circular primary hull. The audio effect providing confirmation of the use of *Enterprise*'s phasers, almost like the short blast of a hydraulic pump, sounded on the bridge. The beams sliced through space and disappeared from view as they hurtled down toward the planet. Kirk could not see the two missiles racing toward *Enterprise*, but he saw the fiery explosion in Ağdam's atmosphere that claimed them.

"Direct hit," said Rahda. "Both missiles have been destroyed."

"Well done," Kirk said.

Rahda continued looking into her scanner. The bridge quieted, with the background hum of the impulse drive a steady rhythm beneath the intermittent beeps issuing from various consoles. The captain sensed expectation growing around him, and he felt it himself.

When Rahda announced the detection of two more energy surges, Spock said, "Scanning." Kirk waited a moment, then found himself rising and padding over to the steps on the starboard side of the bridge. There, he climbed to the outer deck and took up a position near his first officer, who peered into his viewer.

"Sensors are penetrating into the launch sites," Spock said. "I'm reading sizable spaces, a considerable amount of equipment . . . and dozens of missiles." He stood up and turned to face the captain. "I detect no life-forms."

Kirk spun toward the main viewer again. As *Enterprise* had dropped into orbit about Ağdam, he saw, the image of the planet had grown until it covered the bottom half of the screen. He imagined the complexes Spock had just scanned, automated defense centers filled with destructive weapons, dormant until an unknowing crew arrived to explore.

At her station, Lieutenant Rahda detailed the flight

of the latest two missiles to take aim at *Enterprise*. Once more, she used her scanner to target them. The captain heard the familiar sound of the phasers firing, and again saw an explosion far below, inside the planet's atmosphere.

Had the people who'd founded the city also constructed the missile facilities? Kirk wondered. And if so, had they then destroyed their own city, either intentionally or in some sort of colossal accident? Kirk didn't know, but he resolved to find out as much as he could about what had resulted in the loss of the city— and in the loss of seven of his crew.

The captain turned back to his first officer. "Spock, if you can make sensor contact within the launch sites, would it be possible to transport inside?"

An eyebrow rose on Spock's forehead in one of the Vulcan's characteristic expressions. "It would be possible, yes," he said. "But it would also involve unknown, and therefore potentially dangerous, risks."

"Which is why you need to stay aboard the ship," the captain said. "Have Scotty and four security guards meet me in the transporter room." Kirk felt his heart beat faster in his chest, not from fear, but in anticipation of heading into the unknown. He looked at the planet on the viewscreen and thought of the single lost city on its surface, and the missile installations that still functioned even with nobody in them. Determined, he said, "I'm going down there."

• • •

When Scotty's vision cleared from the materialization effect, he found it almost impossible to tell it had done so. Above him, to the sides, and below, virtually all surfaces gleamed a radiant gold. It made it difficult for the chief engineer to estimate the dimensions of the space, though it felt large. *I'll bet it's three or four times the size of my engine room,* he thought, but then he recalled an old Scottish maxim: "Nane but fools and knaves lay wagers."

The landing party had transported into one of the launch sites on the first planet in the R-775 star system. They did so by waiting for a missile to lift off, then utilizing the momentary breach in the shielding to beam down. With communication to *Enterprise* limited to those same brief moments, the captain had decided to have the landing party automatically recalled to the ship during the first launch to take place after thirty minutes had passed; they would have that long to explore the complex.

Beside Scotty, Captain Kirk gazed all around, and the engineer did the same, attempting to locate something upon which he could accurately focus. Gradually, he picked out various structures, despite their reflective gloss and uniform hue. Numerous conduits ascended the walls, then snaked their way across the ceiling in a tangle of straight lines and angles. Catwalks hung not only above, but also along the walls, with many of them connected by ladders and stairways.

"What do you make of it, Scotty?" the captain asked. His voice echoed thinly in the enormous area.

"It doesn't look like any missile complex I've ever seen," Scotty offered. "Of course, it doesn't really look like *any* sort of facility I've ever seen." He took hold of the tricorder strapped across his shoulder and activated it. "I'll take a closer look." The engineer glanced behind him and saw the four security guards assigned to the landing party. All of them had their phaser pistols conspicuously drawn, and one—Ensign Vanelia Fessey—had raised her own tricorder, which she deftly operated with her one free hand. The whine of its operation reached out into the huge chamber, but seemed to lose itself among the various constructs.

As Scotty worked the controls of his own tricorder, Captain Kirk began walking cautiously forward, toward the nearest wall. The chief engineer went with him, scanning the various surfaces, and *through* them. Without looking up, he said, "I'm seeing a muckle of equipment and circuitry on the other side of these walls, Captain."

"Is there anything you can tell about it at first glance?" Kirk asked.

"For one thing, it's active," Scotty said. He studied some of the components, noted the scale of miniaturization, and measured the extent of the power consumption. "I'll need more time to inspect it before I can make any definite determinations," he went on, "but my initial impression is that there *is* a level of sophistication in the design. Even so, I'd say that it doesn't rise to our level of technological advancement."

Scotty and Kirk reached the wall. Although it appeared smooth and straight, their reflections stared back at them in distorted forms. The captain slowly reached out and placed his hand on the shining surface. "It's warm to the touch," he said.

"Aye, it does not surprise me," Scotty said. "There's a lot of activity going on here. It's bound to generate some heat."

"Can you distinguish a control room anywhere?" the captain asked. "Or a main operations console?"

"I'll need to trace the circuitry for that," Scotty said, directing his tricorder to do so. As he awaited the results, he saw other details that demanded mentioning. "As far as I can see here," he said, "the only shielding is external. There is no internal shielding within this chamber, or anywhere within the complex."

"Good," Kirk said. "That should make our work here easier to manage. And it'll be even more helpful if we can identify the controls for the external shielding so we can shut it down."

On the display of his tricorder, Scotty followed the flow of energy through and around the chamber. He turned slowly as he did so, like the needle of a compass finding magnetic north. He eventually settled facing a point on the right-hand wall, about a third of the way along. "I think there's something there,"

Scotty said, and he headed in that direction. Having adjusted to the peculiarities of the setting, he moved more quickly and with greater confidence than he initially had. His bootheels rang against the golden floor, as did those of Captain Kirk and the security guards, who trailed along behind him.

When Scotty arrived at the spot indicated by his tricorder, he saw nothing but the flat, featureless plane of the wall. He looked up and saw several sizable conduits and a scaffold hanging beside them, all colored the same lustrous gold. Not quite knowing what else to do, he reached out and placed his fingertips on the wall. As the captain had just observed himself at the first wall, it felt warm. Scotty applied a small amount of pressure, but to no effect. He verified the readings on his tricorder, then tried again, exerting a greater force.

When nothing happened, he moved his hand to the right, also without result, and then to the left. Beneath his touch, a large panel—perhaps three meters tall and twice as wide—shifted to the side, dark edges appearing around it where, previously, none had been visible. Scotty looked to the captain. "Sir?"

Captain Kirk drew his phaser and stepped up to the panel. "Go ahead," he said. "Open it."

Scotty ran his hand farther left. He felt no resistance at all. The panel glided silently to the side, moving easily, as though carried along by antigravs.

Scotty had expected to see a new, smaller chamber

abutting the first, but instead, the relocated panel revealed what looked like a control board. Buttons, dials, toggles, and slides filled it, interspersed with a handful of small display screens and meters. Unlike everything else in the chamber, the board was not gold, but jet black. Lines of white script, rendered in extremely small but fluid characters, adorned the controls.

"Well done, Scotty," the captain said. He raised a finger and drew it along a spate of writing. "These characters aren't the same type as those we found on the ship in the cave. That might well answer the question of whether—"

The floor suddenly began to tremble, lightly at first, and then more dramatically. Scotty saw the captain bend his knees and lower his center of gravity, holding his arms out from his sides like a man walking a tightrope. Scotty had more or less done the same thing, as had the security guards. Around them, a deep, amorphous noise rose up. *It almost sounds like the* Enterprise *going to warp,* he thought.

"Is that a missile launching?" Kirk asked, raising his voice over the roar.

"Yes, sir, it is," called out a voice from behind Scotty. Both he and the captain turned to face Ensign Fessey. She examined the display of her tricorder, then motioned with her other hand—still carrying a phaser—off to the right. Having acclimated somewhat to the surroundings, Scotty estimated that wall at least twenty meters distant, and the ceiling at least that high. "Sensors indicate that a closed panel in that wall opens onto a tunnel," Fessey said, "which stretches seventy-five meters to a subterranean launchpad." The ensign continued to scan, and as the missile launched and the chamber quieted, the whine of her tricorder once more became audible. "I'm also reading another compartment," she said, turning to her right to face the wall opposite the control board. "It's directly adjacent to this compartment, and it looks like . . ." Her voice trailed off to silence, and she held out her tricorder toward the chief engineer. "Mister Scott," she said, "what does that look like to you?"

Scotty inspected Fessey's display, then worked the controls of his own tricorder. He searched for anything that resembled a connecting corridor. When he found it, he crossed the chamber to the wall opposite the control board. The rest of the landing party went with him, their collective footfalls sending up a torrent of sound echoing in the space.

At the wall, Scotty again reached out and pushed against it, then moved his hand to the left. As before, a panel, approximately half the size of the first, shifted to the side, its outline suddenly visible. The captain stepped up to the wall, his phaser again held at the ready.

Scotty eased the panel aside. Beyond it, a short, featureless corridor led to another wall. It did not surprise Scotty to see it lined in polished gold. He looked around for the light source illuminating the space, but could not see it.

The captain peered back and nodded to the security guards, then started forward. Scotty followed him into the corridor. At its far end, Kirk lifted his hand to the wall. Scotty watched him try unsuccessfully to move the panel to the left. When he attempted to push it in the other direction, though, it slid away easily.

A great, discordant racket immediately emerged from the newly revealed chamber. Captain Kirk stepped forward out of the corridor, and Scotty did so as well. Both men stopped together, their eyes darting about as they took in the tumultuous scene. The clash of sounds that filled the space, and the tremendous amount of active machinery that gave rise to it, transfixed the engineer.

As in the other chamber and the connecting corridor, glossy golden surfaces abounded. Unlike in those mostly empty spaces, though, huge masses of equipment marched from wall to wall and climbed from floor to ceiling. Scotty thought that the compartment measured at least as large as the first, although given the lack of open areas, it seemed more confining than a Jefferies tube. Everywhere the chief engineer looked, he saw something in motion: phasers—or, more likely, lasers—cutting through sheets of metal, massive presses bending those sheets into new shapes, manipulator arms fastening objects together, injectors installing some form of circuitry into various components.

"It's an assembly line," the captain said.

"Aye," Scotty agreed. "And it's not making tea and crumpets."

Fessey walked up beside the captain and offered him her tricorder. Scotty glanced at its display and saw a linear diagram depicting rows of long, cylindrical objects. "There's a chamber beyond this one," the security guard said. "There are hundreds of missiles stored there, and room for hundreds more."

The captain nodded, then almost absently thanked Fessey. She withdrew, and Kirk peered at Scotty. "How badly is the port warp nacelle damaged?" he asked. The question seemed to Scotty like a non sequitur.

"I've got my engineers working on it," he said, "but it's going to take some time."

"How much time?" the captain wanted to know.

"It'll take the better part of three full days to make her spaceworthy again," Scotty said, and he could hear the forlorn tone of his voice. "And even then, it won't be a permanent fix, and I cannot promise how long she'll last."

"We just need it to last long enough to get us to the nearest starbase," Kirk said.

Scotty's mouth widened in a mirthless smile. "Nearest from *here*?" he said. "That's still quite a distance. We're not exactly on the Federation border."

"If you can't repair the nacelle, Scotty, I need to

know," Kirk said. "I'll contact Starfleet Command, and we'll have to wait out here until another vessel can be routed out this far to tow us in."

"*Tow* the *Enterprise*?" Scotty said, his voice rising with indignation. "I'll not have that, sir. We'll get her ready."

In response, the captain smiled, but just as Scotty had, he appeared to do so without humor. "I know you will," he said. "You always do." Then the captain raised his head and peered about their surroundings. "In the meantime, while you're repairing the warp drive, see if you can spare an engineer or two to study this place. When we return to the ship, I'm going to send Spock and the A-and-A officer down here to see if they can learn anything about the people who built it—and *why* they built it."

"They must be protecting something," Scotty said.

"But what?" Kirk asked. "There's nothing of any unique value on this world—or even in this entire system."

Scotty's shoulders rose in a small shrug. "They masked their missile sites," he said. "Perhaps they've also masked whatever it is they're protecting."

"Perhaps," Kirk said. "But I'm not sure that makes sense. If they can effectively hide something valuable to them, then why the need for missiles?" When Scotty offered no reply, the captain continued. "We've got three days," he said. "We'll see what more we can learn in that time, but when the nacelle has been made functional, we're heading to Starbase Twenty-Five, where you'll oversee permanent repairs. When we depart this system, though, I'm not leaving these installations intact so that they can attack other visitors who might happen upon this world."

"I understand," Scotty said.

"Can you destroy these facilities?"

Scotty looked around at the active machinery and the walls that enclosed it. "Aye," he said. "I'm not entirely sure about the properties of these surfaces, but we can detonate explosives in each compartment, and at the launchpads. I'll have my engineers run some simulations, but I'm certain we can find a way to leave these emplacements in ruins."

"Good, Scotty," the captain said. "Right now, let's see what else we can learn before it's time to beam back to the ship."

"Aye," Scotty said, and he returned his attention to his tricorder. As he gathered readings about the machinery working to construct missiles, he specifically sought out any data he could gather about the building of the warheads. When the time came, he suspected that he would be able to use the alien weaponry as a tool to destroy their own place of manufacture. He considered it a clever solution, perhaps even poetic, but it also saddened him in a way. Scotty would do what he had to in order to protect the *Enterprise* and her crew, and to rid the galaxy of threats to others, but he had not joined Starfleet to blow things up.

He had joined it to build.

Doctor McCoy lingered beside the command chair on the *Enterprise* bridge, his gaze not on the tight view of the planet's surface on the main viewscreen, but on the ship's captain. McCoy saw a hardness in the expression on Kirk's face, and he thought he recognized it. For a man willingly taking on the responsibility for the safety of more than four hundred lives in dangerous circumstances—an accomplished, successful man—the *Enterprise* captain never stopped asking questions of himself, and never completely put to bed the doubts and fears that the best leaders feel.

"Are you all right?" McCoy asked quietly.

The captain offered a curt nod without looking away from the main viewer. McCoy turned to look at it himself. There, he saw an overhead view of a verdant landscape, an undulating terrain covered almost entirely by wild growth. In the center of the display, though, a large hole in the ground gaped. To McCoy, it looked almost like a wound, a dark cavity in an otherwise bright, healthy scene.

As the doctor understood it, the view on the main screen showed one of several sites from which alien missiles had been launched. Over the prior three days, *Enterprise* personnel had visited each of them, learning whatever they could about the installations and who had constructed them. Scotty's engineers had come to understand enough both to deactivate the shields employed to mask their existence, and to allow a search via ship's sensors to confirm that no other hidden sites existed on the planet.

More than that, teams of *Enterprise* security and engineering personnel had readied the missile emplacements for destruction. McCoy suspected that the captain had not rested well since making his decision to obliterate alien property on a world far beyond Federation borders. While it might seem at first blush the proper action to take, it also risked potential enmity— or worse—with an unknown species.

From the communications console, Lieutenant Uhura said, "Captain, Ensign Fessey reports that preparations at the last site have been completed." McCoy peered over at Uhura and saw her raise a hand to the silver earpiece she used. The lieutenant appeared to listen for a moment, then said, "She reports that her team is the last one on the planet, at any of the sites. She'll notify you when they have beamed back aboard the *Enterprise*."

"Very good, Lieutenant," Kirk said without inflection.

McCoy glanced past the captain and over at Spock. The first officer sat at his regular station, his attention on the instruments before him. The doctor wondered what Spock thought about the captain's intention to eradicate the alien facilities. He couldn't imagine the

Vulcan falling on the side of such willful destruction, but if Spock had counseled against it, he had proven less than persuasive.

"Jim," McCoy said, his voice barely more than a whisper, "are you sure you want to do this?"

At last, the captain's attention diverted from the main viewscreen. He spun his head quickly toward McCoy. "Am I sure, Doctor?" he asked, his voice loud enough for the entire bridge crew to hear. "Those installations down there attacked both the *Enterprise* and our landing parties down on the surface. We lost seven of our people, three of our shuttlecraft, and we came perilously close to suffering the loss of this ship."

"But we don't know what those facilities were meant to protect," McCoy said. "Perhaps by destroying them, we're leaving somebody vulnerable."

"Perhaps," the captain agreed. "But we've taken three full days to search for any living beings on the planet, and we haven't found anybody. I'm unwilling to risk the possibility of any other passing vessels being attacked in the way that we were."

"Surely there must be other remedies," McCoy said. "Marker buoys, general alerts—"

"Doctor," Kirk said loudly, the single word like an unexpected phaser blast. The captain seemed to gather himself before continuing, and when he did, he spoke again in a normal tone. "Bones, I've considered the arguments you're making," he said. "I don't have a desire to be out here on the frontier and firing our phasers at any life-forms we meet, or at the things that they've built. But we were attacked without provocation or explanation, and *Enterprise* crew members lost their lives."

McCoy dreaded asking the question that rose in his mind, but felt that he had to do so. "This isn't about vengeance, is it?"

Rather than angering the captain, it somehow managed to evoke a close-lipped smile from him. "No, it's not about vengeance," he said. "It's about having the ability to prevent what happened to us from happening to some other ship and crew. And you're right, we could take other steps. But marker buoys can be destroyed, and alerts can go unheeded or fail to reach the people they're meant to save." Kirk looked back at the main viewscreen. "I'd be lying if I said I didn't want retribution for the people taken from us. I'm human. But I'm not an officer of the law, or a jury, or a judge; I'm an explorer. And my sole aim here is to ensure as best I can the security of other explorers who pass this way."

"That's a reasonable explanation, Captain," McCoy said gently. "I'm sorry for questioning your decision."

Kirk's lips parted as he smiled again. "No, you're not, Bones," he said. "You're aboard this ship so that you *can* question my decisions. I trust you to do that. I *need* you to do that."

"Yes, sir," McCoy said, pleased at the turn the conversation had taken. He took pride in providing the

captain with what he needed to ably lead the crew: a
sounding board, a shoulder to lean on, a confidant,
a devil's advocate, and a source of honest opposition
when necessary. McCoy also felt his life richer for having Jim Kirk as his closest friend.

The boatswain's whistle sounded, followed by a female voice. *"Transporter room to bridge. This is Ensign
Fessey."*

Kirk leaned to his right and pressed the button on
the arm of his command chair to activate his intercom. "Bridge here," he said. "Go ahead, Ensign."

*"Captain, all personnel have beamed back up to the
ship,"* Fessey said. *"All preparations have been made,
and control of the operation has been turned over to the
weapons subpanel."*

"Lieutenant Rahda?" Kirk asked, looking to the officer at the helm. Since his ordeal on the planet, Sulu
had yet to return to duty. McCoy had diagnosed the
lieutenant with a dislocated shoulder, an intracerebral
hemorrhage, and a grade-two concussion. The doctor
had reset Sulu's shoulder and surgically repaired the
bleeding in his brain, but his full recovery from the
trauma to his head would require rest and time.

"Transfer of control confirmed, Captain," Rahda
said.

Into the intercom, Kirk said, "We're all set here,
Ensign. Kirk out." He thumbed the channel closed,
then turned toward the port side of the bridge. "Mister Scott," he said, "are we ready for warp drive?"

"Aye, sir," said the chief engineer. "The *Enterprise* will get us home."

Shifting his attention to the other side of the bridge, he said, "Mister Spock, execute one more sensor sweep of the missile sites. Verify that they are clear of life signs."

Spock responded at once. "Scanning," he said, standing up and bending over his hooded viewer. McCoy and the captain and the rest of the crew waited as the first officer swept the ship's sensors across each of the three installations. He announced the results with the completion of the first scan, and then the second. Finally, he stood up fully, descended to the lower, inner section of the bridge, and took up a position opposite McCoy across the command chair. "Sensors confirm no life signs at any of the sites," he informed the captain.

"Thank you, Mister Spock," Kirk said. Then: "Lieutenant Rahda, you may commence ignition."

"Commencing ignition," she said. McCoy watched as she pressed a button on her panel, which caused an indicator light to change from amber to green. Then she used the index fingers of both her hands to toggle two switches set apart from each other. A second indicator light burned green. "Signal initiated," she said as she peered up at the main viewer.

McCoy followed her gaze, but for a moment, nothing happened. He thought to say something, but then a brilliant cone of fire rushed upward from the underground missile silo. The flames burst into the sky as though erupting from a volcano. It lasted just seconds, though, and McCoy wondered if the destruction the captain sought had been so quickly completed.

Suddenly, the ground beside the silo jumped and shifted, then collapsed in on itself. Flames rose and licked at the sky from the newly widened hole. An explosion sent a fireball curling upward above it, and then another. More of the earth failed, tumbling down into the fresh abyss. More flames revealed themselves, and then another red-hot cloud swirled up to join the others. Nearby trees caught fire.

The missiles, McCoy realized. The crew must have armed the warheads, or removed the safeties, or otherwise rigged the alien weaponry to detonate in a chain reaction. As he watched the screen, more and more of the ground near the silo collapsed beneath the conflagration. Devastation on such a massive scale disturbed him, and yet he could not look away.

It took nearly ten minutes for the sequence of destruction to exhaust all of its ammunition. When it had, Spock headed back to the science console, and Rahda leaned left to peer into her scanner. "It's over," she said.

After a moment studying his own instruments, Spock said, "Confirmed. All of the existing missiles and warheads have been destroyed at all sites. The launchpads, the assembly machinery, all command and control equipment are gone as well."

"Acknowledged," Kirk said.

Not Very good *or* Well done, McCoy thought, though it seemed abundantly clear to him that the security and engineering teams had accomplished the task the captain had set them. *Jim really didn't want to do this,* thought the doctor. *He felt he* had *to do it.* McCoy could have kicked himself for so badly misreading the captain's motivations. *I was wrong even to question him about it.*

In the command chair, Kirk turned to McCoy. They regarded each other without saying anything, and then the captain sighed slowly, heavily. McCoy thought he looked tired, and he marveled—as he often did—at how Jim could do the things he did without exhausting himself completely.

"I'm, uh . . ." the doctor began, thinking that he should visit Sulu's quarters to check on the lieutenant's condition. But then he thought beyond that, to when he would return to sickbay. "I'm going to go check on Sulu," he told the captain, "then I'm going to head back to my office." He leaned in over the arm of the command chair and, sotto voce, said, "Come see me if, you know, you feel you might need a prescription."

Kirk smiled again, but it did nothing to mitigate how tired he looked. "Thanks, Bones," he said. "One of your special potions?"

"On my last shore leave," McCoy said, "I picked up a bottle of Saurian brandy that I have yet to crack open."

"Ah," Kirk said. "Well, we'll see."

McCoy started away, but then the captain called him back. "Let me know how Sulu's doing," he said.

"I will, Captain." As McCoy headed toward the turbolift, he heard Kirk's next orders.

"Mister Chekov, set course for Starbase Twenty-Five," he said. "Ms. Rahda, best and safest possible speed that we can get out of Mister Scott's repaired warp drive."

McCoy entered the turbolift and turned to face forward in the car. Just before the doors closed, he saw that the image on the main screen had switched from a view of the missile site to one of the planet hanging in space. The doctor thought not only of the destroyed launch complexes, but also of the wrecked city the crew had found there. And as McCoy heard and felt the ship come to life around him, he saw *Enterprise* leave that dead world behind.

Six

Sulu slowly reached up to the shelf above the head of his bed. Over the previous few days, he'd learned not to move too quickly. He'd spent much of that time in sickbay, relocating to his own quarters only the day before. Although he'd gone through surgery and treatment for his injuries, the symptoms of his concussion had yet to fully subside. Doctor McCoy had told him that a full recovery could take weeks, perhaps even months. Sulu had initially scoffed at the notion that it would require so long for him to get well, but the vertigo he continued to feel, and the general fogginess of his thoughts, all bound together by an overwhelming sense of fatigue, had subsequently convinced him otherwise.

The tips of Sulu's finger brushed against the cool side of a glass—the medical staff had urged him to drink a lot of water—and then against a narrow, triangular shape. He pulled the wedge-shaped data slate from the shelf and onto his lap. He sat with his back against a pillow and his knees up, and he propped the slate up against his thighs. Prior to his mission to the surface of R-775-I, Sulu had begun reading a history

of the later Sengoku period in Japan, and specifically
about that nation's first invasion of Korea by Toyotomi
Hideyoshi. Sulu's genealogical research indicated that
one of his ancestors might have taken part in the military action, and so he wanted to familiarize himself
with the event.

Sulu activated the data slate with a touch to its
small, black button at the top left of its face. Lines
of text immediately appeared on the screen, and the
middle of the three indicator lights above it blinked
on, burning white. The slate displayed the page Sulu
had been reading when last he'd used the device.

Sulu read the chapter title, which marched across
the top of the screen: *The Siege of Busan.* He'd reached
that section of the book prior to suffering his injuries down on the planet. His gaze moved across the
first couple of sentences, and though he recognized
the name of Konishi Yukinaga, a territorial lord and
military leader, he realized halfway through the first
paragraph that he wasn't grasping the sense of what
he read. That might have concerned him had Doctor
McCoy not explained in detail the nature of concussion symptoms to him; instead, his inability to read
simply annoyed him.

"What am I supposed to do?" Sulu asked the
empty room. He might have liked some time off from
his shipboard duties if he were able to indulge in some
of the leisure pursuits he enjoyed, but he'd never cared
much for idle relaxation. So many activities piqued

his interest, and he knew that no matter how much energy he put into them, he'd never in his life have enough time to try everything he wanted to do. Because of that, he eschewed inactivity; he couldn't lie out on a beach, taking in the sun, or go for long, contemplative walks. He needed goals, and he needed to take actions to achieve them. Having Doctor McCoy prescribe rest, for days or even weeks, felt like a kind of torture.

Sulu glanced at the words on the display of his data slate. He wanted to try again to read, but understood the futility of doing so. Already, a low-level ache had formed in the back of his head. Much as he disliked the idea, he would have to take it easy. He thought about downloading a vid to his slate from the ship's library, but then decided even that might tax him too much. He'd nearly needed a nap after donning his uniform that morning, an unnecessary act, since he would not see duty that day, but it had made him feel better to do so.

Maybe just a little music, Sulu thought. He reached to bring up a menu on his data slate, but then the buzz of his door signal sounded. Over the past day and a half, several of Sulu's friends had called on him, though none had stayed long, heeding the advice of Doctor McCoy. Pavel Chekov had come by the previous night, as had Captain Kirk. Sulu suspected, though, that a member of the medical staff—perhaps Nurse Chapel or Nurse Luxon—had come to check on him, since he so far that day had yet to see any-body from sickbay. Regardless, he would be grateful for even that distraction. "Come in," he called. The instant that he raised his voice, it felt as though a vise squeezed the sides of his head.

The single-paneled door to his quarters glided open—Sulu could just see it past the room divider—and when he saw the sky-blue uniform shirt, he thought that he'd been correct in predicting a visit from a member of the medical staff. The woman walked partway into the office half of Sulu's quarters, then stopped when she saw him in the other half. "I hope I'm not disturbing you, Lieutenant," she said.

"No, not at all," Sulu told Ensign Trinh, unsure why the ship's A-and-A officer would stop by to see him. "I've been so bored," he went on, "I was prepared to welcome a visit from Doctor McCoy." He smiled as he spoke, and Trinh laughed at the comment, a light, trilling sound that Sulu found quite appealing. He re-membered noticing her—*really* noticing her—on the landing party's excursion down to the planet aboard *da Gama*.

"I'd say that qualifies as bored," Trinh agreed. "When I asked the doctor for permission to come see you, he emphasized that you'd had a concussion, and that I therefore shouldn't stay long or overtax you with too much conversation. I can't imagine that he'd be good company for you right now."

"No, definitely not," Sulu agreed. "Forgive me for

not getting up, but I'm having some trouble with my balance these days."

"Oh, of course," Trinh said. "I completely understand."

Sulu smiled again, but then felt self-conscious when he didn't know what else to say. He wanted to blame the perpetual fog that had clouded his mind since his concussion, but he also thought some other force might be at work.

The ensign returned Sulu's gaze, but quickly seemed to grow uncomfortable as the silence between them lengthened. She looked away, then made a show of peering around his quarters. Her eyes stopped darting about when they found the wall opposite her, to Sulu's left. "Do you fence?" she asked.

Sulu glanced up at his display of crossed épées hanging on the bulkhead. "I do," he said. He felt the urge to mention the championships he'd won while at Starfleet Academy, but thought better of it. "Actually, I haven't had a match, even an assault, in quite some time. When I've been in the gym lately, I've spent most of my time learning vershaan."

"Vershaan?" Trinh asked. "Is that Andorian?"

"Yes, it's a martial art," Sulu said. "I'm learning it from one of your colleagues."

"Clien," Trinh said. "I mean, Crewman ch'Gorin."

Once more, Sulu smiled. "When we're off duty, I call him Clien too." The statement didn't seem to ease Trinh's apparent awkwardness. She twisted her fingers together with what seemed like nervous energy. Attempting to put them both at ease, Sulu forged ahead, trying to find something to say. "I guess he and I won't be sparring for a while. I'm pretty much relegated to bed rest until my symptoms disappear."

"Even after that," Trinh said, "I doubt that Doctor McCoy's going to want you to be taking any blows to the head."

"No, probably not," Sulu said. He felt embarrassed to be speaking to Trinh while she stood and he lay propped up on his bed, and so he decided that he should offer her a chair. He realized, though, that he didn't know the purpose of her visit, which he had so far treated with a lack of formality. "So is there a duty-related reason you wanted to see me, Ensign?" he asked.

"Oh . . . no," Trinh said. "I just . . . I wanted to check on your recovery."

Sulu wondered if she had been sent to do that by McCoy, perhaps in the hope of checking on his condition without causing him too much stress. He thought that the doctor probably wouldn't resort to such subterfuge, but it also didn't really matter to him. He liked that she had come to see him, regardless of the reason. "Why don't you have a seat?" Sulu said, motioning toward the far corner, where a chair sat just across from the foot of his bed.

"Oh, that's all right," Trinh said. "I can stand."

"Please," Sulu insisted. "It feels rather ungentlemanly

for me to be talking with you while I'm lying down and you're standing up."

Trinh offered him a smile that carried little more than an acknowledgment of what he'd said. "Of course." She entered the inner half of his quarters and crossed to the chair. When she sat down, Sulu noticed that her fingers twined together in her lap.

"What are you reading?" she asked, briefly freeing one of her hands and pointing to his data slate.

"Oh, it's a history of feudal Japan," he said, taking the slate from his lap and tossing it onto the bed next to him. "I've been chronicling my ancestry, and I was trying to get some context."

"One of my ancestors was a prince in old Vietnam," Trinh said.

"Really?" Sulu said. He thought the ensign's mention of a member of her lineage as royalty interesting, but the deep knowledge of her family history impressed him even more.

"Um," Trinh said, her expression growing blank. "No, not really," she said. "I don't even know if they've ever had princes in Vietnam. I just thought it sounded good."

Sulu stared back at Trinh, unsure how to react. When she raised her hands, palms up, and contorted her face into an obviously counterfeit smile, though, he threw his head back and laughed. He felt his temples begin to throb at once, though, and he quickly cut short the physical manifestation of his amusement.

When he lifted a hand to massage his forehead, Trinh stood from her chair and took a step toward the bed, her comic expression replaced by one of concern. "Are you all right?"

Sulu stopped her with a wave of his free hand. "I'm okay," he said. "It's the concussion. I'm suffering from headaches and dizziness and fatigue. Doctor McCoy says I should make a complete recovery, but he's not sure how long that'll take. In the meantime, I just need to take it easy."

"I should go," Trinh said, and she took a step toward the office half of Sulu's quarters.

"No," Sulu said—perhaps a little too enthusiastically, he thought. He genuinely wanted the ensign to stay, though, and not just because of the monotony of his medical seclusion and forced inactivity. "If it's all right, I'd like you to stay a little while longer."

Trinh looked at him uncertainly, but then she sat back down in the chair. "Doctor McCoy *did* warn me not to tire you out."

"I won't tell him if you won't," Sulu said. Then, wanting to move past the incident so that Trinh wouldn't be compelled to leave, he said, "Can I ask you something?"

"Sure," Trinh said. "Of course, I can't promise that I'll answer you."

"Your name is Mai Trinh?"

"Yes," she said. "My full name is Mai Duyen Trinh." Though she spoke unaccented Federation Standard, the ensign pronounced her name *Mī Dwin Tring*, with a distinctly foreign inflection. Sulu assumed that resulted from her Vietnamese origin, but he hadn't heard enough native speakers in his life to know for sure.

"I thought that in Vietnamese names," he said, "the first name listed was the surname."

"It is," Trinh said. "Mai is my family name, and Duyen Trinh is my given name."

"But I've heard Captain Kirk and Mister Spock call you Ensign Trinh," Sulu said.

"That's right," Trinh said. "But they were correct when they did. The captain actually asked about my name when I first came aboard, and I explained that, in the Vietnamese culture, the formal form of address combines a title with the final part of the given name."

"So if we were friends," Sulu said, "I wouldn't call you Mai?"

"You'd call me Trinh."

Sulu nodded his understanding. Then, before he could stop himself, he blurted, "I'm Hikaru."

Trinh's lips widened into what seemed like an involuntary smile. "It's nice to meet you, Hikaru."

"It's nice to meet you, Trinh." He returned her smile, and even felt a rush of heat begin to crawl up from his uniform collar.

"I suppose we should be on a given-name basis," Trinh said with a chuckle, "since I'm now responsible for your life."

Sulu's brow furrowed, and mercifully, he felt his flush abate. He had no idea what Trinh meant by her comment, and he told her so.

"Oh, you know," she said. "That old concept— Asian, I think, maybe Chinese—that when you save somebody's life, you become responsible for them."

Sulu didn't understand. "Wait," he said. "Are you saying that you saved my life?"

Trinh's mouth dropped open. "You didn't know?"

"I don't remember anything after I saw a missile strike the *da Gama*," he said. "When I asked Doctor McCoy in sickbay what had happened, he told me that I'd taken a bad fall, which is how I hit my head and dislocated my shoulder."

Trinh's eyebrows rose. "I guess the doctor didn't read my report," she said. "I can't tell you exactly what happened to you after the *da Gama* was destroyed, but when my team couldn't beam up to the *Enterprise* be- cause the ship was under attack, we took cover in the cave system out by the canyon. From there, I scanned the area for life signs, and I saw a human moving toward the caves, through the woods. That turned out to be you."

Sulu shook his head, and a wave of vertigo made him regret it. "I don't remember any of that."

"You'd almost reached the caves when you stopped," Trinh said.

"I *stopped*?" Sulu asked. "Why?"

"I believe that you set your tricorder to emit the

life signs of two hundred humans and Andorians," Trinh said. "A rocket was bearing down on the area, so I think you must have been hoping that it would target those false life signs. I ran out of the cave to try and help you, just in time to see you throw your tricorder into the canyon. The rocket followed it down, but then the force of the explosion sent you tumbling down a slope toward the canyon rim." Trinh hesitated and looked down at the deck, as though she didn't know what else to say.

"What did you do?" Sulu asked, fascinated by an episode in his life about which he recalled nothing.

"I ran," Trinh said, still peering down. "I reached you just as you went over the edge, and I managed to grab you by the neck of your shirt as you did."

"You caught me?" Sulu said. "But . . . how? I mean, you're—" *So little,* he thought, but then refrained from saying the words because they might sound pejorative.

"I'm petite," Trinh said, finally peering back over at Sulu. "I know. It must have been an adrenal effect. It didn't last long, though. I managed to prevent you from falling, but you were still hanging precariously over the edge of the cliff, and I couldn't pull you up. Fortunately, Clien saw what was happening from the mouth of the cave—against my order, by the way— and he raced over to help. When you reached up, he grabbed your arm and, together, we heaved you back onto solid ground."

Sulu lifted his left hand to his right shoulder, as

though the revelation of what had taken place had injured his arm anew. "That's an incredible story."

"It was . . . memorable," Trinh said. With a grin, she added, "Well, at least it was for me."

"I don't how to respond to that," Sulu said, still rubbing his shoulder. "I mean, other than to tell you how grateful I am."

Trinh waved a hand before her, as though she had done nothing out of the ordinary, but still, Sulu could see that his appreciation pleased her. "That's just life on a starship, right?" she said.

"Sometimes," Sulu said. "But that doesn't take anything away from what you did. Thank you."

Trinh looked away again, and Sulu saw a flush creeping up her cheeks. She abruptly stood up and nervously straightened the creases in her uniform pants. "I really didn't come here to regale you with my 'heroic deeds,'" she said. "I just wanted to see how you were feeling."

"I'm glad you did," Sulu said. "And thanks to you, I'll be fine."

"Thanks to Clien too."

"Yes, thanks to Clien too," Sulu said.

Clearly uncomfortable with the turn of the conversation, Trinh said, "Well, I should let you get your rest." She started toward the door.

"Trinh?" Sulu said. She stopped and turned back just past the divider that separated the two sections of his quarters. "Since you're responsible for my life now," he said, "maybe, when I get better, you should have dinner with me." He paused, then added, with what he hoped would be amusing effect, "You know, so you can make sure I'm getting the proper nutrition."

"What about Clien?" she asked. "He helped save your life too."

"That belief about being responsible for a life you save? You said it was Asian, meaning *human*, not *Andorian*," he said. "I think it should be just you and me for dinner."

Trinh smiled again, not quite as freely or as broadly as earlier, but with a degree of bashfulness that added to her charm. "I'd like that, Hikaru." With a bounce in her step, she turned and left Sulu's quarters.

But she did not leave his thoughts.

The small, circular table sat in one of the two spaces Kirk could reasonably call corners in the crescent-shaped bar. He had chosen it for its relative privacy, tucked away from the few other patrons in the long, curving establishment. Other than with the man sitting across from him, the captain hoped to avoid conversation with any Starfleet officers who might stop in to The Roadhouse, the oddly named watering hole on Starbase 25. Not only did no roads pass by the Starfleet facility, which orbited the planet Dengella II, but with its location on the edge of the Federation, few space lanes led there either.

Kirk peered through the run of transparent

deck-to-overhead ports that lined the outer side of the dimly lighted bar, to where *Enterprise* floated against the magnificent blur of the Milky Way. Several power and communications umbilicals tethered the ship to the cone-shaped starbase. A repair framework enclosed the port nacelle, and from his vantage, Kirk could see workbees and spacesuited engineers swarming about it.

Enterprise had arrived at the starbase a week earlier, limping on its functioning but wounded warp drive. Scotty had been true to his word and had gotten the starship to its destination, but not without complications. Along the way from Ağdam, the port nacelle faltered twice, necessitating additional repairs. The captain came close to contacting Starfleet Command for assistance, but Scotty somehow inveigled *Enterprise*'s warp engines back into service. In his imagination, Kirk pictured his chief engineer sitting astride the damaged nacelle, holding it together with his bare hands and cajoling it to work. Scotty's success impressed even Spock.

The captain turned from glancing out into space when the waiter arrived back at the table. In one hand, he held aloft a circular tray, from which he plucked a tumbler showing two fingers of an amber liquid. "Irish whiskey," he said, his sturdy musculature and blue flesh distinguishing him as a Pandrilite. The nametag on his crisp, white shirt read *Garo*. He deposited the drink in front of the other person at the table,

Commodore Robert Wesley, then followed it with a second glass. "And a water back," the waiter said.

Nearly two decades Kirk's senior, Wesley had a long, well-lined face that seemed serious even when it wore a smile. For a time, he had colored his hair back to the dark brown of his youth, but he'd apparently abandoned such vanity. His short but full locks, worn in a squarish cut, had gone completely gray.

The commodore thanked Garo, who lifted the final item from his tray. The waiter set down the etched cordial glass, filled with a crimson liquid, in front of Kirk. "And for you, a Denebian liqueur." Garo then collected the empty glassware from the table and refilled his tray. He'd ably served the captain and the commodore for the previous hour, when the two men had arrived in the bar from their respective starships.

"Thank you," Kirk told the waiter. The captain reached forward and took the stem of the glass between two fingers. Though he had initially resisted getting together with Bob Wesley, he felt glad that he'd eventually changed his mind. The commodore had arrived at the starbase in his ship, *U.S.S. Lexington,* two days prior, and had sent several messages to Kirk inviting him to meet for drinks. Even though the captain had known Wesley for some time, he hadn't wanted to see anybody, least of all one of his peers. Kirk still struggled with the impending culmination of his crew's five-year mission, something he knew he needed to deal with, but that he had no desire to discuss with anybody. After the commodore's fourth invitation, though, he finally capitulated.

As the waiter left the table, Wesley nodded toward Kirk's liqueur. "I've watched you drink that stuff, but I just don't know how you can do it." He held up his glass and swirled its contents. "*This* is a drink for a man."

Kirk scoffed at the assertion. "You sound like my chief engineer," he said.

"Scotty?" Wesley asked. "He might have a better taste for alcohol than you do, but the Scots don't even know how to properly spell *whiskey.*"

"I'll be sure to tell him you said so."

Wesley raised his glass high in salute, then knocked back a healthy gulp from his glass. "Be sure to tell him what you were drinking," he said. "That stuff is so minty. It's like liquid candy."

Kirk lifted his own glass to his lips and savored the ambrosial aroma before taking a sip. The strong flavor, containing both sweet and peppery components, tasted fine, and when he swallowed, a spreading warmth flowed down his gullet. "Minty on the tongue and fiery in the throat," he told Wesley. "When you're a starship captain and travel the galaxy, you get exposed to all sorts of new experiences. But you wouldn't know about that, would you, Bob, stuck out on Mantilles?" He set his glass back down on the table, as though punctuating his question with it.

In the time they'd so far visited over drinks, Kirk

hadn't until that moment brought up the peculiar detour that the commodore had taken in his career. After three decades in Starfleet, Wesley resigned his commission and settled in the Pallas 14 star system, on Mantilles, at the time the most remote inhabited planet in the Federation. Knowing the commodore as he did, Kirk believed his departure from the service out of character; Bob Wesley loved Starfleet, and he loved commanding *Lexington*. Even though Wesley became the governor of Mantilles, Kirk thought the position a peculiar fit. He never doubted the commodore's ability to do the job, but he also never understood his decision to take it on in the first place.

Wesley lifted a finger from around his glass and pointed at Kirk. "Jim, I think maybe you've had enough of that stuff," he said. "You know I'm back on the *Lexington*."

"I do," Kirk admitted. He hadn't intended to broach the subject at all with Wesley—the commodore had a right to his privacy—but Kirk felt intensely curious about the sequence of events. And maybe he *had* begun to feel the effects of the alcohol he'd imbibed, because he then said, "I guess you weren't exactly cut out for a life in politics, were you, Bob?"

"As if the upper echelons of Starfleet aren't filled with politicians," Wesley returned. If he took offense at Kirk's comments, he hid it well. "But no, I guess it wasn't for me."

The captain considered changing the subject, but

since Wesley didn't seem bothered by it, Kirk continued. "To be honest, Bob," he said, "despite your impressive service record, I'm surprised that Starfleet Command made it so easy for you. The admirals take a dim view of their best personnel resigning their commissions, and an even dimmer view of commanding officers changing their minds so drastically."

"Who said they made it easy?" Wesley asked.

"Come on, Bob," Kirk said, not accepting the implied denial. "They put you right back in the big chair aboard the *Lexington*."

The commodore stared askance at Kirk for a moment, actually tilting his head to one side. "Are you putting me on, Jim?"

"What?" Kirk asked, not really understanding the question. "No, of course not."

"Then you really don't know?"

"Know *what*?"

Wesley quaffed the remainder of his whiskey— Kirk noted that he hadn't even touched his glass of water—and put the tumbler back down on the table. He then glanced around the bar, as though satisfying himself that none of the few patrons present would overhear him. "What's your security clearance, Jim?"

Kirk hadn't anticipated the question, but he answered it anyway. He suspected that Wesley already knew his clearance level, otherwise the commodore wouldn't have asked about it. Wesley leaned in over the table and dropped the volume of his voice to a conspiratorial tone.

"Jim," he said, "I didn't choose to go to Mantilles. *Starfleet Command* put me there."

"What?" Kirk said. "Why?" He couldn't think of a good enough reason to remove an officer of Wesley's caliber from the command of a starship.

"We were having a problem out that way with the Tholian Assembly," the commodore said. "Pallas Fourteen is a long way from everywhere, without much backup in the neighborhood."

"Surely the Tholians wouldn't attack a Federation world," Kirk said. "They can be punctilious and arrogant, but they don't want war."

"They might not *want* war, but they've been preparing for it," Wesley said. "Starfleet Intelligence discovered that the Tholians enlisted the help of the Remalla to plant spies on Mantilles."

"But why?" Kirk asked. "Mantilles is so remote, it doesn't possess any strategic value, and it doesn't have any rare or unusual resources that the Assembly would want." He thought of the *Enterprise* crew's visit to the Pallas 14 system after a spaceborne entity had consumed the outermost planet and then set its sights on Mantilles. Spock had ultimately communicated with the being and convinced it to spare the planet and its population of eighty-two million. The captain wondered if the Tholians thought that they could somehow harness the entity for use as a weapon. Or perhaps they believed it part of a Federation threat.

The timing isn't right, though, Kirk thought. By the time the entity had appeared in the Pallas 14 system, Wesley had already left Starfleet and become governor of Mantilles, so clearly that hadn't motivated the Tholians to infiltrate the Federation world. "But if Starfleet Intelligence learned about the Remalla agents, maybe it was because SI was already keeping a close watch there," Kirk reasoned aloud. He looked his friend in the eyes. "Bob, was Starfleet using the planet for some purpose that might have jeopardized Tholian security?"

"All I can say," Wesley told him, not flinching beneath his gaze, "is that Starfleet Command considers Mantilles vital to Federation interests." The commodore didn't need to say more—and despite the high level of Kirk's security clearance, probably *couldn't* say more.

"Obviously, you must have succeeded there," the captain said.

"We rooted out the Remalla spies," Wesley said. "I don't know with certainty what happened after that, but my guess is that the Federation ambassador to Tholia delivered some potentially devastating news to the ruling conclave. The Klingons had just agreed to several substantial trade and diplomatic agreements with the Assembly, but if the High Council learned of the Tholians employing alien spies to infiltrate other powers—even the Federation—that could have brought a rapid end to those compacts."

Kirk shook his head when he considered the political machinations of the Tholian Assembly, as well as those of the United Federation of Planets. He remembered his own experiences with Starfleet Intelligence, including a particularly harrowing assignment into Romulan space to purloin one of the Empire's cloaking devices—an assignment Kirk had opposed because it had put his crew at tremendous risk.

Wesley seemed to want to say no more on the subject of his *mission* as governor of Mantilles, and so Kirk let the matter drop. Instead, he turned the conversation back to *Lexington*. "Well, I'm glad you're back to exploring now."

"So am I, and grateful for it too," the commodore said. Kirk thought that Wesley wore his gratitude more like relief. "What about you? How long before the *Enterprise* heads back out?"

"According to Scotty, we've got another three or four days here," Kirk said. He picked up his cordial glass and sipped at it. Suddenly, the flavor of the liqueur struck him less as refreshing and more as medicinal.

"So a total repair of ten or eleven days," Wesley said. "That's not bad for a damaged warp nacelle." The commodore hesitated, then added, "And I'm sure you want to waste as little time as possible with your mission nearing an end."

Wesley's mention of Kirk's five-year command of *Enterprise* coming to a close felt somehow like a betrayal. "We've still got almost a year left," the captain said, careful not to sound defensive.

"And then clear sailing to commodore," Wesley said.

Kirk hadn't previously heard any suggestions of an upcoming promotion for him, but he knew that rumors propagated through the fleet at warp speed. In his case, he thought such speculation made sense, considering the record of accomplishments his *Enterprise* crew could already boast. The possibility of an increase in rank meant little to him, though, and he told Wesley that. "The only thing that interests me is standing in the center of a starship bridge."

The commodore looked away from Kirk, first down at his glass, then out into space. The unspoken implication sent a shock through the captain. "Bob?"

When Wesley looked back, he wore an apologetic bearing. "Listen," he said, "I don't *know* anything."

"But you've *heard* something," Kirk said.

"Scuttlebutt," Wesley said. "There's probably nothing to it."

"Come on, Bob," Kirk said. "Of course you think there's something to it. Otherwise you wouldn't look like you just jettisoned an ion pod in clear space."

Wesley did not respond for a moment, and it seemed as though he wrestled with what more he should say. The commodore raised his glass again, but when he realized that he'd already emptied it, he set it back down on the table. "Yeah, I've heard a couple of things," he finally said. "Including that you might skip commodore altogether and move directly into the admiralty."

The statement dumbfounded Kirk. He'd never heard of anybody in the service being promoted two levels in rank. More than that, he knew of nothing in the regulations that even permitted it; upward movement, as far as he knew, required not only an exemplary record, but minimum service time at each stratum within Starfleet's hierarchy. "That sounds to me like idle gossip," he managed to say. "I mean, I'd be honored—"

"They'd want you to be," Wesley said gravely.

"But the truth is that not everybody at headquarters is . . ." Kirk cast about for the right word or phrase, and as he did so, he even allowed a grin to play across his features. ". . . *enamored* of my command style."

"I'm afraid I can't argue with you about that," Wesley said.

Even though Kirk had made the assertion in the first place, it troubled him to hear it so easily confirmed by a fellow starship captain. In fact, the entire turn of the conversation troubled him. Choosing to put the matter to rest, to quash a rumor assuredly spurious, he said, "They couldn't vault me over the rank of commodore anyway. It's not as though there are any admirals out there commanding starships."

Wesley cast his gaze down at the table, where he wrapped both hands around his empty whiskey tumbler. His glass of water still sat untouched. When he looked back up, his expression had become severe. "Jim," he said, "from what I hear, your days on the bridge of a starship may be numbered."

Kirk could only stare back at Wesley. He wanted to scream his frustration, wanted to transport back to *Enterprise* and contact the commander in chief of Starfleet, wanted to demand that he be compensated for his years of service and lengthy list of achievements simply by being allowed to remain in the position in which he had enjoyed so much success. Instead, he sat there motionless, as though the strength had drained not only from his body, but from his will.

"There's a lot of talk about refitting the *Constitution*-class vessels," Wesley said, "and I think Command wants to use that as an opportunity to reassign you. I've heard that they might want you in charge of a starbase, or that they might even want you to oversee an entire sector."

A glut of thoughts spun through Kirk's head, and he settled on voicing one of them. "Basically, they want me somewhere they can keep a tighter leash on me," he said. "They want me to have less autonomy than I do on the *Enterprise*." Kirk could see in his memory the stern countenances of the admirals—not many of them, but apparently *enough* of them—who disapproved of the captain's methods and style. He wanted nothing more than to deny them their intentions for his career—for his *life*. "I don't have to accept promotion."

"No, you don't," Wesley said. "But your only alternative might be resignation."

Kirk felt as though he'd been slapped in the face. "Would they really force that on me? Would they that readily dispose of everything Starfleet has invested in me, of all my experience?" The notion seemed absurd on its face. Kirk leaned forward on the table, and his voice slipped down to a whisper, as though pleading with the commodore for an answer. "*Could* they do that to me?"

"Jim," Wesley said, "after three decades in Starfleet, with half of that time spent commanding starships, I ended up as the governor of Mantilles."

"But they brought you back," Kirk said, as though that excused strong-arming the commander of a starship into taking on a job he didn't want.

"And I hope I'm on the bridge of the *Lexington* to stay, at least until I'm ready to step down on my own," Wesley said. "But I know now that I can't really count on that."

"Bob . . . I'm sorry," Kirk said. "I had no idea."

"Thanks, but it's all right," Wesley said. "I've made my peace with it. Plus I've earned some favor in Starfleet Command for being a good soldier, for going where they wanted me to go, for doing what they needed me to do." The commodore paused, but clearly wanted to add more. At last, he said, "It's not as though Starfleet Command is a villain or an enemy. They weren't trying to hurt me by asking me to go to Mantilles. And I could have refused."

"But what would have happened if you had?" Kirk asked.

"Maybe nothing," Wesley said. "Maybe I would have continued as the captain of the *Lexington*. Maybe I would have been forced to resign. I don't know. But I understand that Command is doing the best they can to keep the Federation safe, and that means assigning personnel to do the jobs that need to be done. There were enough admirals who felt that I was the best choice for the Mantilles operation."

"So what you're telling me is that there are enough admirals who think I'd best serve Starfleet by being posted to a starbase," Kirk said, unable to hide his bitterness at the thought.

"Again, I don't know for sure," Wesley said. "Jim, everybody knows what you've done out here . . . the first contacts, the exploration of unknown space, the diplomatic missions. But you know as well as I do that some of your decisions, and probably even more of your methods, haven't set well with certain people."

Kirk glanced down at his cordial glass, still half-filled with its purplish red contents. "What am I supposed to do?" he asked quietly.

"Jim, I only mentioned this because I wanted to prepare you for what may be coming," Wesley said.

"What *may* be coming. For all I know, Command may ask you to re-up for another five-year mission. But I remember when we installed the M-5 computer aboard the *Enterprise*." The supposed next step in the evolution of processing technology, the M-5 had been the brainchild of the brilliant scientist Doctor Richard Daystrom. *Enterprise* had functioned as a test bed for the computer complex, which had been intended to replace the entire crew of a starship. "Starfleet didn't brief you about the M-5, didn't bring you into the decision-making process, until I showed up in your transporter room with the news. I thought that was wrong, and I hated being the one to spring the operation on you. Even though I'm not involved in the determination of where your career goes from here, I didn't want you to be blindsided."

"I appreciate that," Kirk said.

"I just thought that if you have enough time to think about it," Wesley said, "if you consider the situation from all angles, then you'll be able to make the choice that's right for you and for Starfleet."

Kirk understood the commodore's reasoning, but couldn't conceive of willingly agreeing to step away from the command of a starship. At the same time, just discussing the matter had exhausted him from an emotional standpoint. For the moment, he needed to stop thinking about it.

"Well, I already know what I'm going to do." Kirk raised his glass and upended it into his mouth.

Preparing to lighten the mood and move the conversation in a different direction, he said, "I'm going to have another drink." He motioned over toward the bar and caught the waiter's attention. Garo immediately hurried over to the table.

As Kirk ordered another round—not another Denebian liqueur, but a Saurian brandy—he knew that he would have that next drink, complete his visit with Bob Wesley, and then head back to *Enterprise*. And once Scotty and his staff completed the repairs to the warp nacelle, the captain would take the ship back out beyond the borders of the Federation and, with his crew, explore the unknown for the next year.

After that, though, Kirk had no idea what would come next.

Dresden

II

Seven

Sulu retreated slowly across the greensward, measuring his steps carefully so that he didn't lose his footing on the uneven ground and damage the delicate cargo he carried. He headed toward the middle of the grassy expanse, away from the coppices that intermittently bordered the open area, and away from the other people out in the park. When he reached a distance of twenty-five or so meters from Trinh, he stopped and waved back to her. "How's this?" he asked, raising his voice so that she would hear him. She'd instructed him on what to do, but as an utter novice, he wanted to make sure he made no mistakes.

"That's good," Trinh called. She pulled back on the cord in her hands, and Sulu felt the line tauten. "Okay," she said, "let's launch."

Sulu raised his arms, lifting the kite as far up as he could reach, careful to keep it properly aligned with Trinh. About three meters wide and in the form of a symmetric lens, the main body curved up at the ends, creating a gentle, sweeping curve, almost like the wingspan of a large bird in flight. A flat rectangle emerged backward from the center of the body, attached to two more lens-shaped figures, also flat, that formed a tail. A light, bright-red fabric covered the frame of polished, lightweight wood.

"Okay," Sulu called, stretching as high as he could. Even as he did, though, the kite gently slipped upward, a breath of air catching it as Trinh drew back on the line. Sulu watched the bridle—a network of cords designed to spread the force of the pull—and appreciated its combination of geometric beauty and engineering utility. The kite continued to rise, and so he started to sidle back across the grass to Trinh, his head turned so that he could follow the ascent.

By the time Sulu reached Trinh, the kite had climbed to a height of at least twenty meters. It flew almost as though floating, as if relying not on air currents but on antigravs. "You did it," Sulu said, his voice reflecting the enthusiasm he felt.

"*We* did it," Trinh said, and indeed they had. Over the course of the previous six months, the two crewmates had spent more and more—and recently, almost all—of their off-duty hours in each other's company. They socialized too with other friends—Pavel Chekov, Uhura, Jackie Trieste, Clien ch'Gorin—but usually together. As a consequence, Sulu and Trinh had gotten to know each other quite well.

Two weeks earlier, in anticipation of their first real shore leave as a couple, they had begun discussing what they should do. Unfortunately, with *Enterprise* outside of Federation space for the prior half-year, the ten-day furlough that the crew had earned would not coincide with a visit to a world like Risa or Pacifica or Allarin, but to Starbase 25. The facility possessed some features the ship did not—an elegant bar, several restaurants, a number of shops, a few sporting amenities—but it essentially equated to the same setting: a limited, closed environment, filled with recycled atmosphere and artificial lighting, hanging in the punishing void of space. Sulu and Trinh craved fresh air and sunshine—perhaps a beach, perhaps the mountains, perhaps something else entirely—but they sought the allure of nature.

Starbase 25 orbited Dengella II, a Class-M planet with little tamed wilderness. It hosted several mid-sized settlements, but beyond the borders of those populations, the Federation's Department of the Interior considered the land unsafe for visitation. That left Sulu and Trinh—and the rest of the *Enterprise* crew—with few options.

In the days leading up to their shared shore leave, the two had decided on a number of activities. Starbase 25 featured a ten-story climbing wall in one of its massive gymnasia, as well as a low-gravity flying chamber, both of which sounded like fun. They also wanted to try one of the base's eateries, Shadows, which had a reputation as a cozy, romantic bistro that featured soft music, warm candlelight, and exquisite desserts.

Trinh had also researched the inhabited areas

of Dengella II. She suggested a trip to the one art
museum on the planet, along with a picnic in one of
several parks on the surface. The latter proposal had
kindled another idea in Sulu's mind.

During the six months of their relationship, Sulu
and Trinh had asked each other about their lives,
and had relished telling and hearing the stories that,
when added together, had brought them into one another's arms. Trinh spoke fondly of her childhood in
Vietnam, a place she'd left at the age of ten, when her
parents had relocated to Bradbury Township on Mars.
With plenty of family still residing on Earth, though,
she returned there regularly, and she later stayed for
an extended period when she earned her baccalaureate and master's degrees in Hanoi.

When Trinh had proposed enjoying a picnic lunch
in one of the parks on Dengella II, it had spurred Sulu
to recall one particular set of memories that she'd
shared with him. As a young girl, she had learned
from her grandfather how to construct and fly kites,
including a traditional type called a *dieu sao*. Trinh
spoke of her time with her mother's father almost
with reverence, so important a place did it hold in her
heart.

Sulu had performed some basic research via the
ship's library-computer, after which he enlisted the aid
of some of the ship's engineers to help him fabricate
the materials required. Once he completed his preparations, Trinh arrived at his quarters one evening to

find the components for a kite scattered over the deck, chairs, desk, and bed. He would always cherish the moment she walked through his door, looked around, and realized what she saw; she actually gasped before running into his arms with tears spilling down her cheeks. They ended up clearing his bed so that they could make love, but in the days that followed, they shared their love in a different way, working together to assemble the dieu sao so that they could it fly on shore leave.

As Sulu watched the kite sailing above the park on Dengella II, he felt a happiness—a *joy*—that he'd never before known. "Yes," he echoed Trinh, "*we* did it." He watched as she played out the line a bit, then pulled some of that length back. The kite drifted higher into the air, the crescents of the planet's two moons a striking backdrop in the azure sky.

"Actually, we haven't done it, not yet," Trinh said. "The wind shifted."

At first, Sulu thought that she worried about being able to control the kite, but he saw that she had no difficulties keeping it aloft and steady. Then he felt the breeze at his back and realized her concern. With the currents of air moving away from them and toward the dieu sao, they couldn't experience the kite's full effect.

"Let's move around that way," Trinh said. Sulu looked away from the kite to see her point to the left. She began walking in that direction, turning her body as she did, essentially keeping the dieu sao in the same place in the sky as she moved around it.

Sulu did not immediately follow Trinh. Instead, he watched her. For their special day in the park—they'd planned a picnic, kite flying, a stroll to the small lake there, and a leisurely boat ride for two—Trinh had chosen to wear a traditional Vietnamese outfit, an *ao dai*. Made of silk, it consisted of a golden-yellow tunic, with a formfitting bodice, that split at the hips and hung front and back down to her shoes over white pantaloons. Embroidered florets adorned the torso of the ensemble. The ao dai flattered her petite figure and provided a dramatic contrast for her dark hair.

"There it is," Sulu heard Trinh say. She seemed gleeful. She turned to look at him, but then peered around when she didn't see him beside her. "Hey," she called over to him.

"I'm coming, I'm coming," he said, trotting over to join her.

"Were you woolgathering?" she asked as he caught up with her.

"I was *Trinh*-gathering," he said. "I just couldn't take my eyes off you. You're beautiful."

Trinh tilted her face down and looked up at him as though embarrassed by his attention, but the sly smile told him that it pleased her. As she stared into his eyes, he heard the sound she'd been seeking, but that the wind had carried away from them. Completing the dieu sao, Sulu and Trinh had mounted atop it five small flutes of varying length. As the kite hovered at the other end of the line, air currents passed through the simple, diminutive instruments, playing notes.

Trinh adjusted her hands and allowed the dieu sao more line. It dipped, and its music quieted. Trinh moved the line again, drawing it in, and the kite rose, the notes of the flutes gaining strength.

Then Trinh moved her arms left and right, pushed her hands out and pulled them back in, testing the wind. The dieu sao suddenly rolled and swept down, but she worked the line and righted it. As time passed and Trinh manipulated the kite, sending it gamboling about the sky, her movements became more and more certain.

"I thought you were concerned because you hadn't done this in such a long time," Sulu said, teasing her.

"I *am* still rusty," Trinh told him. "I can feel it." Sulu would have been hard-pressed to identify anything she could have done better. Her movements appeared artful, her hands and arms graceful. As she sent the kite swooping, climbing, diving, and arcing across the sky, all accompanied by the combined sound of the flutes, her actions seemed like a collective piece of performance art.

"Yeah," Sulu said, "you're about as rusty with the kite as I am at the helm of the *Enterprise*."

Trinh laughed, sweetly and cheerfully, and Sulu joined in. He watched her, and he saw that several other people had gathered around the park to look on as well. He felt appreciation and pride as he stood beside her, and far more than that too.

Finally, Trinh said, "My hands and arms are getting tired."

"Why don't you pull her in?" Sulu said, realizing that he had referred to the kite in the same way he referred to *Enterprise*: with a feminine pronoun. "We can go have our picnic."

"Don't you want to try?" Trinh asked. She reached her hands toward him, but he didn't take the reel and line.

"You know that I've never done this before," Sulu said. "After watching you fly it, it'd be easy for me to humiliate myself, especially now that we've got an audience."

Trinh glanced around at the spectators, but their presence did not deter her. "Come on, Hikaru," she said. "Take the helm."

Sulu laughed again, and when Trinh tried to hand him the reel and line once more, he took them from her. He felt the force of the wind on the kite at once, as though it wanted to tear it from him. He reflexively yanked the line toward him, and the dieu sao jerked upward. Attempting to compensate, he quickly extended his arms. The kite dipped back down, but then heeled around to the right and surged downward. Sulu exclaimed—more a sound than a word—and tried to guide the kite back up. Trinh had taught him how to use the line, but those lessons had been theoretical, not practical. While he managed to reverse the direction of the kite momentarily, its flight seemed neither steady nor smooth. "I think I need some help here," he said.

Trinh reached for Sulu's hands, presumably either to guide his movements or to take the line and reel from him, but too late. The kite swung around again and plunged toward the ground. Sulu tried to work the line, but it had slackened. Whatever small amount of control he might've had over the kite vanished. He watched helplessly as the bright-red dieu sao rocketed into the ground. The tones produced by the flutes abruptly ceased, giving way to the sounds of breaking wood and tearing fabric. Some of the onlookers added their own startled exclamations.

For a moment, Sulu and Trinh stood side by side, unmoving, staring at the wreckage of the kite they had worked together to create. He had intended the entire experience to have meaning for Trinh, to help her hark back to the wonderful days of her childhood when she'd shared such things with her grandfather, who had died while she'd been away earning her doctorates. Instead, he had destroyed what they'd built.

Turning to Trinh, he said, "I'm so sorry. I—"

"Are you sure you know how to steer a starship?" she asked. She appeared neither upset nor angry.

"I . . . I . . ." Sulu tried again, but he didn't know how he could possibly apologize.

Trinh regarded him, then threw her head back and laughed. She stepped up to him and put her arms around him. "It's all right," she said. "It's just an object. I mean, I know we built it together and that made it special, but we can always build another one. And even if we never do, so what? We still have each other."

Sulu hugged Trinh to him, grateful to the universe at large for allowing their paths to cross. He still held the line and reel in one hand. He kissed her urgently but softly on the lips, then pulled back and gazed into her dark eyes. "I love you," he said, telling her for the first time what he had just realized himself.

Then he kissed her again.

The door signal buzzed, surprising Kirk. He sat at the desk in his quarters aboard *Enterprise,* reviewing his recent log entries in preparation for submitting them to Starfleet Operations and Starfleet Command. Most of the crew had departed the ship on shore leave, heading either for Starbase 25 or for Dengella II, leaving behind only a skeleton staff.

Kirk had spent a few days off-ship himself, despite that he hadn't really wanted to do so. He knew, though, that if he shunned leave completely, his ever-vigilant CMO would have made an issue of it. Not that the doctor had much cause for concern. After Kirk's meeting with Commodore Wesley, the captain spoke with McCoy about it—about the upcoming end of *Enterprise*'s mission, about the possibility of being promoted away from starship command, about how to handle both potential and real changes in his life. Kirk strived to keep the future ahead of him and to hold his fears at bay. He reasoned that if Command would allow him only one more year as *Enterprise* captain, then he would not waste that time by indulging in self-pity.

"Come," Kirk called toward the door. The single panel withdrew into the bulkhead, revealing a Starfleet officer the captain didn't know, a member of neither the *Enterprise* crew nor, so far as he knew, the Starbase 25 staff. A human, the uniformed woman possessed a slim build, and though she probably stood a head shorter than Kirk, her ramrod-straight posture lent her the illusion of height. As she padded into the captain's quarters, he noticed an angularity in the movements of her arms and legs, almost like those of a fawn. She had thick, golden hair—blond almost to the point of being silver—that gave her a radiant, youthful appearance, though the merest beginnings of lines in her face suggested that she had lived perhaps five or ten years longer than Kirk.

The woman wore the braid of a vice admiral, as well as the starburst-shaped assignment patch of Starfleet Command. She stopped two paces inside the cabin, and the door slid closed behind her. Kirk stood from his chair, though he couldn't say whether he did so because of the flag officer who'd entered his company, or the beautiful woman.

"Captain Kirk," the woman said easily, her manner not nearly as staid as her bearing. "I'm Vice Admiral Lori Ciana."

"Admiral Ciana," Kirk acknowledged. He stepped forward and offered his hand. She grasped it firmly and shook, a single up-and-down pump. The captain became uncomfortably aware of the heat of her flesh, and when she did not let go until just an instant longer than he expected, he felt as though *he* had committed some graceless breach of decorum. He retreated behind his desk, hoping to cover his discomfort, and gestured to the chair opposite his own. "Please, have a seat."

Ciana crossed the cabin and took the chair offered. Kirk waited until she sat, then did so himself. "Admiral Ciana," he repeated, searching his memory for the names of the members of Starfleet Command. Ciana's name seemed familiar, but he didn't believe that he'd ever met her or that there had ever been any communication between them. "Are you a member of Admiral Nogura's staff?" he asked. A formidable officer, Commander-in-Chief Heihachiro Nogura held the highest position within Starfleet.

"I am," Ciana said. "Technically, I'm simply an aide to the admiral, but my training is in xenopsychology, and so Starfleet Command's relationships with non-human species fall under my purview."

"That sounds fascinating," Kirk said. His echo of a word that Spock so often used—*fascinating*—rang false in his ears. It made him realize that he hadn't even really thought about what Ciana had said before responding to her. *And that's what I'm doing,* he thought. Responding *to her.*

"It is fascinating, of course," Ciana said. "But then, many positions in Starfleet are."

The admiral hadn't quite put the lie to what he'd said, but she clearly noticed the speed with which he'd replied to her, and the blatancy of his esteem. *Who wouldn't notice?* Kirk thought. *I'm acting like a schoolboy.*

Determined to establish a professional tone, Kirk said, "May I ask the purpose of your visit, Admiral?"

"I'm here at Starbase Twenty-Five to consult with Commodore Cohen," she said, identifying the commander of the space station. "There are plans to begin colonizing out in this region, and I'm here to coordinate those efforts with the commodore."

"I'm sure he'll welcome an influx of settlers into the sector," Kirk said. "I know we're on the edge of Federation space, but the border here seems to have reached considerably farther out than our expansion has."

"That's certainly true," Ciana agreed. "At least in part, it's because Starfleet Command wanted to establish a beachhead for exploratory efforts out beyond this sector."

"And the *Enterprise* crew has been taking advantage of that," Kirk said. "Although we've ascertained that the sectors beyond Starbase Twenty-Five are nearly as empty as this one."

"Nearly," Ciana said, "but not entirely. I've read your reports on the first contacts you've made in the last six months: the Graym . . . the Ktarians . . . the Ellesant."

Kirk felt the features on his face freeze. The admiral's reference to the Ellesant, and the manner in which she'd mentioned them—dramatically last in her list—made him wary. Although Ciana had answered the question of her presence at Starbase 25, she hadn't yet articulated her reason for boarding *Enterprise* and calling on Kirk—but the captain believed she had just revealed it.

A month earlier, the *Enterprise* crew had entered an unexplored star system to find two of its planets—and one moon—occupied. The Ellesant had evolved on the third planet, growing to a global population of three and a half billion. Having achieved the capability of interplanetary flight, they had also settled one of their three moons, and had begun colonizing the fourth world.

When the *Enterprise* crew had first scanned the star system, they'd detected more than just the interplanetary vessels of the Ellesant, though; they had discovered a massive asteroid on a collision course with the fourth world and its one hundred thousand inhabitants. Spock programmed and executed simulations of the cataclysmic event, concluding that the fourth planet would be laid waste and rendered uninhabitable for a considerable length of time; of greater import, all of its residents would perish. The Ellesant had clearly forecast the approaching disaster, for they had started both an evacuation from the fourth planet and an attempt to destroy the asteroid. With time running out, though, both of those efforts failed to achieve the results necessary to prevent the deaths of the colonists.

Captain Kirk had taken action, in direct and willful contravention of Starfleet's Prime Directive, which forbade interference with pre-warp societies. Kirk ordered his crew to take *Enterprise* into the system, where they employed the ship's phasers and photon torpedoes to destroy the asteroid. Unable to hide *Enterprise* from detection by the Ellesant, the captain then had to decide whether or not to establish direct contact with them. Kirk chose contact.

If some of the admirals want to use the end of Enterprise's *five-year mission to remove me from starship command,* he thought, *I've given them more ammunition to make their case.* The idea upset Kirk, not because of his own self-interests, but because he had seen no moral reason to allow so many of the Ellesant to die when they could be saved. If Starfleet Command opted to cite that incident as grounds not to return him to the bridge of a starship, then maybe he needed to reconsider being part of Starfleet in the first place.

"Captain?" Ciana asked, clearly noticing Kirk's quiet deliberation.

"I'm sorry," the captain said. "You reminded me of something." Before the admiral could ask him about that, he quickly pressed on. He folded his hands together atop his desk and leaned forward. "You've told me why you're here at Starbase Twenty-Five, Admiral," he said, "but what can *I* do for you?"

"Actually, Captain Kirk," Ciana said, "this meeting is about what *I* can do for you."

For the second time, Kirk froze, though he recovered quickly. He thought he must have misunderstood the admiral. "Excuse me?" he said.

"As I told you, I'm here to discuss the colonization of the sector with Commodore Cohen," Ciana said. "But Starfleet Command knew of the *Enterprise* crew's shore leave here, of course, and so Admiral Nogura instructed me to pay you a visit."

"Forgive me for belaboring the point," Kirk said, but then he paused in order to modulate his tone and avoid sounding insubordinate. He parted his hands and laid them flat on his desk. "You've told me that you have orders to be here," he went on, "but that doesn't tell me *why* you were given those orders."

Ciana laughed. "I've been given to understand that

you sometimes question *your* orders," she said, "but now you feel the need to question *mine*?"

"I'm sorry, Admiral," Kirk said, "but—"

Ciana quickly sat forward in her chair and placed one of her hands atop one of Kirk's. Again, he felt the warmth of her touch, and when he peered across the desk at her, he once more saw the loveliness of her visage. The strength of his attraction to her surprised him. "It's all right," she said, patting his hand. "I was just teasing you." She sat back again, and Kirk did the same.

"I'm . . . not used to being 'teased' by Starfleet admirals," the captain said.

"Honestly, I'm not used to doing much teasing," Ciana said. "At least, not while I'm on duty." She smiled, and her behavior suddenly seemed less like teasing and more like flirting. Before Kirk could even begin to consider how to react, Ciana continued. "Anyway, Admiral Nogura is aware of certain . . . *speculation* would be the nice word for it . . . the admiral knows that there is speculation about how your career will proceed once you complete the *Enterprise*'s five-year mission. He doesn't know whether any of that scuttlebutt has reached you, but in case it has, he wanted me to assure you, on his behalf, that no decisions have yet been made. Admiral Nogura appreciates your service to the Federation, and respects all that you've accomplished during your command."

"That . . . doesn't sound like the admiral," Kirk said, regretting the words as soon as he'd spoken them. He had no wish to impugn Ciana's word or Nogura's reputation, but he'd said what he felt. Kirk had known the commander in chief to conduct himself only in the severest, most serious manner.

"No, I guess it doesn't sound like the admiral," Ciana said. "But if it helps, I can tell you that I heard him say those words myself."

"It does help," Kirk told her, "but I'm still at a loss. I thank the admiral for the vote of confidence, and I thank you for personally delivering it, but I don't understand what it means." He noted to himself that, in listening to Nogura's approbation, he hadn't heard a promise to permit him to continue his career in the position of starship captain.

"It means that Starfleet Command values you, Captain Kirk," Ciana said. "It means that we're all on the same team, and that you should continue to do what you're doing out here."

Kirk nodded, trying to process what Ciana had told him. As he thought about her words—and Nogura's—she rose from her chair. Kirk did the same, understanding that she meant to conclude their brief meeting. He wanted to ask her more questions, but he resisted, not knowing whether she would have the answers, or if she did, whether she'd be able to reveal them to him.

"Captain," Ciana said, holding her hand out just as

he had when she'd entered. "Thank you for giving me a few minutes of your time."

"My pleasure," Kirk said, taking the admiral's hand in his own. When he softened his grip, though, she tightened hers.

"I have to admit something to you, Captain," she said, holding his gaze. Ciana had unusually large eyes, Kirk saw, and it felt to him as though she could hypnotize him with little more than a glance. "I've wanted to meet you for some time now."

"I—" Kirk began, but then had no idea what to say. He settled on simply thanking the admiral.

"My pleasure," she said, echoing his words, a wry smile fluttering across her face. She released his hand, then turned and headed for the door. Kirk watched her go.

After the door to his cabin closed behind her, the captain remained standing. Although the conversation had been relatively short, it seemed to Kirk as though a veritable mountain of information had been revealed to him. He thought about Ciana's visit, about Nogura's message, about Ciana appearing to flirt with him. He didn't quite know what to make of it all.

Even after Kirk sat back down at his desk and returned to reviewing his log entries, his thoughts continued to drift back to his meeting with Nogura's aide. It seemed as though what had been said to him could tell him what he should expect when *Enterprise*'s mission ended in another six months, but he couldn't see it, not with any certainty. But even as Kirk's mind replayed the conversation, even as he recalled the generous words of the commander in chief, even as he tried to muddle through the various career possibilities he would soon enough face, his thoughts kept wandering elsewhere.

He couldn't stop thinking about Lori Ciana.

Eight

Alpha shift had nearly ended when the figurative ground seemed to drop from beneath Sulu's feet. A month out from their last shore leave at Starbase 25, the *Enterprise* crew continued their exploration of space previously unvisited by the Federation. Even as the helmsman monitored and adjusted the ship's orbit above a terrestrial world in an unknown star system, he looked forward to his off-duty hours—and particularly to that evening, when he would see Trinh.

As the first officer stood at the science console and recited his findings, Sulu peered across the bridge at him from his place at the helm. The lieutenant could hear the progression of the sensor readings that Spock detailed and knew the determination he would reach. It did not feel like déjà vu—the illusion of recalling an event when experiencing it for the first time—because Sulu actually *had* experienced the scene being played out on the *Enterprise* bridge. Unlike on the previous occasion, though, he dreaded where all of it would lead.

"In addition to those refined metals," Spock said, continuing his litany, "sensors are detecting processed woods and concrete. The materials appear to be arranged essentially in a large grid comprising numerous blocks and several open squares, all covering an area of approximately seventy-five square kilometers."

The first officer did not end up voicing the obvious conclusion, but the captain did. "A city," Kirk said, and he turned in his command chair to face Doctor McCoy, who stood beside him.

"Just the one, Spock?" the doctor asked. Sulu suspected that he already knew the answer to that question too.

"Yes, Doctor," Spock said. "And, as with the lone city on the first planet in the R-Seven-Seven-Five system, those materials of urban construction are in disorder, indicating some level of decay or destruction."

"Population?" the captain wanted to know, though Sulu understood that Kirk surely had his suspicions. The helmsman figured that, at that moment, every person on the bridge did.

"The area is uninhabited," Spock replied.

Kirk pushed up out of the command chair and crossed to the starboard steps, though he did not ascend them. Sulu watched Doctor McCoy follow the captain and take up a position next to him. Both men looked up at Spock. "I didn't hear you mention rodinium or tritanium in the list of refined metals," Kirk said. Sulu remembered that the two had been present on R-775-I, in the hulls of wrecked ships. "Can you confirm their absence from the area?"

"Sensors did not detect any within the confines of the city," Spock said, "but if you recall, that was also the case on the other planet; the incapacitated warp ships lay outside the de facto municipal borders."

"Widen the focus of the sensors to check in the surrounding areas," Kirk said. "I also want you to scan for anything resembling the hidden, subterranean missile installations we found on the other planet." Once the *Enterprise* crew had unmasked the launch sites, Sulu recalled, they had also discerned how to identify them even in their concealment.

"Aye, sir," Spock said. The first officer turned to his console, where he rapidly pressed a sequence of buttons, then bent to peer into his hooded viewer.

"You think it's the same situation as on the other planet?" Sulu heard McCoy ask the captain.

"I don't know, Bones," Kirk said. "We're in roughly the same region of space as when we surveyed the R-Seven-Seven-Five system, the sensor readings are exceedingly similar, and we're talking about a distinctive and unusual set of circumstances: a single, dead city on the surface of an otherwise untouched world. It seems too coincidental for there to be no connection."

"I agree," McCoy said. "What are you going to do about it?" At the helm, Sulu nodded to himself, both because he concurred with what the captain had said, and because he wanted to find out just how Kirk intended to proceed.

The captain peered past McCoy toward the main

viewscreen, and Sulu turned his head in that direction. The second world in a system that Starfleet designated R-836 filled the bottom portion of the viewer. It looked to Sulu perhaps a few shades bluer than its apparent counterpart in R-775, with differently shaped land masses, but otherwise, the two planets showed little difference.

The captain drew in a deep breath, then let it out slowly. Sulu looked back over as Kirk answered the doctor's question. "I think there's only one thing we reasonably can do," he said. "Investigate."

McCoy's brow knitted, and he tossed a thumb back over his shoulder toward Spock. "Aren't we already investigating?" he asked the captain.

"If it's safe," Kirk said, "if there are no missile compounds, or if there are and we can render them inoperative—"

"You mean blow them up," McCoy interjected. Though the doctor spoke the truth, Sulu didn't quite understand the point he intended his statement to make. The captain ignored the interruption.

"Once it's safe," he went on, "we'll need to send a landing party down to the surface to make sure we know exactly what we're dealing with."

At the helm, Sulu felt what seemed like a rush of adrenaline course through his body, as though experiencing a fight-or-flight response to danger. *I am having that response,* he thought, *just not to danger I'll be facing.* He knew that if Captain Kirk decided to enlist a landing party to examine the city on the planet below—or more likely, the ruins of a dead city—he would likely include the ship's A-and-A officer among its members. Sulu's stomach churned at the idea of Trinh heading into any situation that could potentially threaten her life.

"I don't know, Jim," McCoy said. "I'm not entirely sure how reasonable it would be to beam anybody down to that planet. Last time we did that in a similar situation, we ended up with a nonfunctional warp nacelle and seven dead crew members." Sulu appreciated McCoy arguing on the side of caution.

"Thank you, Doctor," Kirk snapped, clearly upset by McCoy's comment. "I'm not about to risk anybody's life unnecessarily."

The captain's declaration pleased Sulu, but the lieutenant also knew that in the more than four and a half years of *Enterprise*'s mission, dozens of the crew had died in the performance of their duties. He wondered how many of those lives Kirk believed had been put at *unnecessary* risk. Sulu assumed that the captain's answer would be zero, and yet none of those Starfleet officers had made it safely back home.

"Captain," Spock said from where he peered into his hooded viewer, "sensors have detected tritanium and rodinium outside the city, in quantities that would suggest several small spacecraft, just as we discovered on the other world. Also as before, I read no active warp engines."

"And what about any camouflaged missile complexes?" Kirk asked.

"Since encountering such installations on the other planet," Spock said, "we have added subroutines to the sensor protocols that will automatically recognize similar readings. We have not yet scanned the entire globe, but to this point, no such readings have manifested themselves."

"But obviously you've scanned the surface in relative proximity to the city," Kirk said. "Can we conclude, then, that there are no missile emplacements?"

"We can only state with certainty that, in the seventy-two-point-six percent of the planet we've scanned," Spock said, "there are no such facilities."

"Recommendations?" Kirk asked the first officer.

"Complete our scans of the surface," Spock said. "If we locate missile facilities, we can disable them. Once we have done that, or once we have ascertained that no such facilities have been constructed on this world, I recommend transporting a small landing party down to the city in order to learn more."

Kirk nodded. "It's important to know if we're dealing with the same situation on both planets," he said. "Did the aliens who settled the first city also settle this one? Did the same faction attack both? And why has this destruction taken place?"

"I agree," Spock said.

"Now wait a minute," McCoy said. Sulu felt grateful to the doctor for affirming his opposition. "I agree with you two that, since Starfleet's decided to traipse around this section of the galaxy, it's important for us to figure out what's been going on down on these planets, if for no other reason than the possibility that we might be able to prevent it from happening somewhere else. But it's also important to realize that we can't save this city or the first one, or anyone who might have died in them, and we certainly won't resolve anything by getting any more of our own people killed." Sulu wanted to stand up and applaud the doctor's sentiments.

"I would point out that the situations are different," Spock said, "in that we were surprised by the attacks at the first planet. The reason that the landing parties could not immediately be transported to safety in system R-Seven-Seven-Five was because the ship was attacked at the same time as our personnel on the surface. The unexpected attack on the *Enterprise* succeeded to the extent that it did because it happened without warning, and because our defenses were down. Once prepared for the attacks, we had no difficulty in protecting ourselves."

The captain turned toward the helm. "Shields up, Mister Sulu," he said. "Ready main phasers."

Sulu sent his hands darting across his panel. "Shields up full," he said once he'd raised the ship's defensive screens. "Main phasers on standby."

"Should you choose to send a landing party down to the planet, Captain," Spock said, "we can keep the shields raised to protect the ship. Recall what we learned at the first planet. Were the *Enterprise* to be attacked with similar missiles, we can employ the ship's phasers to destroy them. A measurable interval occurred between the attacks, and should this be true again, that would provide sufficient time to safely lower the shields, bring back the landing party, and renew our defenses."

"Agreed," Kirk said. "Still, I would be more comfortable confirming that there are no missile installations on the planet, or disabling them if there are. How long will it take to finish scanning the entire surface?"

"At the present rate," Spock said, "fifteen hours, forty minutes." He did not consult his console in announcing the duration of the sensor sweep, but Sulu did not doubt his accuracy.

"So we'll complete our scans by approximately zero-seven-thirty tomorrow," Kirk said. "What portion of the day will that be in the city?"

Spock turned back to the science station, pushed a button, then bent and gazed into his viewer. Sulu watched him work the circular control on its side, then stand back to his full height. "Zero-seven-thirty ship's time will coincide with early afternoon in the city."

"Good, then it'll be light out," Kirk said. "Pending the outcome of your scans, Mister Spock, we'll transport down a landing party at the beginning of alpha shift tomorrow morning." The captain regarded the doctor, and with a light tone, asked, "Bones, are you up for a little more exploring?"

"What if I said no?" McCoy replied.

"Then I'd order you to go anyway," the captain said with a grin. Sulu recognized Kirk's attempt to lighten the mood, perhaps in an effort to reassure the doctor—*Or maybe to reassure the entire bridge crew,* he thought—but it didn't ease the helmsman's concerns.

"That's what I figured," McCoy said, apparently capitulating. The doctor's sudden equanimity troubled Sulu, who had hoped for a continued protest against beaming a landing party down to the city.

"Spock, considering our experiences on the first planet, and allowing for potential danger here," Kirk said, "I want you to remain aboard the *Enterprise*. I'll take Doctor McCoy, Ensign Davis, Ensign Trinh, and two security guards." The mention of Trinh caused a wave of anxiety to break over Sulu.

"I shall see to it, Captain," Spock said.

"If sensors pick up anything at all on the planet—weapons, life signs, a power generator—I want to be informed at once," Kirk said. "Shields will remain up at all times."

"Acknowledged," Spock said.

Sulu saw the doctor glance toward the helm-and-navigation console. "Well, the day shift is almost over," McCoy said to Kirk. "Care to have a last supper together?"

"Very funny, Doctor," Kirk said, though clearly the comment had not amused him. He crossed the bridge and sat back down in the command chair, his demeanor serious. "I'm going to wait for the beta-shift duty officer so I can apprise her of the situation directly." The captain seemed to relent a bit then, telling McCoy, "I'll meet you in the mess hall."

"All right," the doctor said, and he headed for the turbolift.

Sulu knew that the moment alpha shift ended, he'd be right behind McCoy. Sulu hadn't had plans to meet Trinh until hours later—he'd scheduled a vershaan training session in the gym with Clien, and then after showering and changing, a dinner with the Andorian—but he couldn't wait that long to see her. He would postpone his plans with Clien and go find the woman he loved.

In that instant, Sulu wanted nothing else but to see Trinh, and to hold her in his arms as long and as tightly as he possibly could.

They walked through the city—*What remains of the city,* Trinh thought—for hours.

Before that, the landing party had materialized outside the urban expanse, in a mountainous region located to the south. In the cool shade cast by a tall peak, Captain Kirk led the group to three large fields of wreckage, each of them separated from the others by enough distance to indicate that it had required discrete attacks to cause all the destruction. The mounds of debris, charred blacker than the shadows draped across them, resembled nothing even remotely recognizable to Trinh. She could discern that whatever had occupied that space had been blasted apart and set ablaze; some pieces of metal, both large and small, showed signs of shattering, while others drooped and wavered, rigid surfaces that had obviously turned malleable under the influence of great heat.

Ensign Davis, one of *Enterprise*'s junior scientists, had detected with his tricorder substantial amounts of tritanium among the shards and fragments left behind. "A hull, then," the captain concluded, and no one disagreed. They all knew that a number of disabled spacecraft—warp-capable vessels—had been discovered near the empty city on R-775-I.

"In that case, it looks like they might have been trying to hide them," Doctor McCoy had remarked. "Just like on the first planet." Trinh recalled that the ships there had been located in a large cave system, as well as in a low valley, both sites out beyond the borders of the city. The *Enterprise* crew had drawn the conclusion that the inhabitants had attempted to secrete the vessels away from their attackers, and examination of those ships had yielded a likely reason: they possessed only minimal weaponry. When the cities had been assaulted, the ships could not have substantially aided in defending them, only in providing a means of escape. Once populations had come under fire, they must have wanted to conceal the ships for that purpose—though it appeared that, in the end, their annihilation had prevented their flight.

When the members of the landing party had finished their investigation in the mountains, they transported to the outskirts of the destroyed city, where sensors indicated an easier passage along the thoroughfares that divided the area into blocks. The bright sunlight that shined down on the demolished landscape seemed to Trinh like an exposé, as though the star around which the planet orbited had laid bare the ruthless attack on the people who had once called the place home. She did not know who had dealt such viciousness to those who'd attempted to settle that world, nor did she know their reasons for doing so, but she found herself hating them.

Even before they'd begun exploring the city, Trinh had executed a scan of the materials employed in constructing it. An analysis of her sensor readings told her that, as on the first planet, the settlement had not existed for long. She estimated that it had been established less than a year earlier, and more than likely, not even half that far back.

At the periphery of the city, some buildings still stood, though not a single exterior door or window remained intact. Mostly one story, and never more than two, the structures appeared in Trinh's imagination as homes. Here and there, she could see patches of color on the outer walls, though most of the paint had been either singed or melted away. Many of the houses—*If that's what they were*—attached to small, open plots of land. Wild vegetation covered a few of those spaces, but most had become desiccated tracts of fallow soil. Trinh envisioned residents of the city tending small gardens, helping to feed themselves, and thereby contributing to the sustainability of their settlement.

Captain Kirk had wanted to enter some of the buildings, as had Trinh, but one of the security officers—Lieutenant Roger Stack—reported that the blasts that had totally destroyed many structures had also left those still standing extremely unstable. The captain contented himself with approaching some of the empty doorways and window frames to peer inside. Trinh accompanied Captain Kirk when he did so, but she saw little more than burned-out interiors.

As they'd walked through the city, taking readings and trying to learn all they could about what had taken place there, they searched in particular for some means of verifying that the alien species who'd settled there had also settled the lost colony in the R-775 system. To some extent, the two sets of ruins resembled each other, but what could distinguish between one collection of broken buildings and another? The degree of destruction in the two cities prevented any meaningful comparison of architecture.

At several points along their route, though, the *Enterprise* crew members had espied written characters.

They saw two rendered in wood, hanging off-center and askew, above an empty doorway that led through the lone standing wall of one building. Several more appeared on a metal sign lying on the ground, the top portion sheared away. The ideogrammic characters resembled those Trinh had seen on the first planet, on the hull of one of the spacecraft, but when she compared them, using the records on her tricorder, she saw that none of them matched up.

Later, though, Trinh had spotted an identifiable shape peeking from beneath a mass of crumbling concrete and twisted steel. She started to climb over a half-fallen run of fencing in order to retrieve the object, but because of the uncertain footing, Lieutenant Stack insisted on doing so himself. When he returned, he carried what Trinh had spotted: a hardbound book, with only one green corner of its back cover differentiating itself from the rest of its burned, blackened form. But it had landed open on the ground, as though a reader had set it down like that before stepping away, so that they could find their place in the text when they returned to it.

Trinh had opened the book as best she could, but most of its seared pages disintegrated in her hands. In the middle of the volume, though, she turned to four pages, parts of which had survived the inferno ignited by the attack. She juxtaposed the characters there with the writing she'd recorded on the first planet. A few of the ideograms matched precisely.

"We have our confirmation," Captain Kirk had said when she'd shown him her results. "The two cities on these two planets were built by people who communicated in the same language. That means there's a good chance that the inhabitants were members of the same species." The captain looked at Trinh. "Well done, Ensign," he told her, a small accolade that nevertheless pleased her greatly.

As the landing party had made their way toward the center of the city, the extent of the destruction increased. They saw larger building foundations, but fewer and fewer structures that had not toppled and burned completely. They ran into large chunks of pavement that had buckled upward, and still other sections that had collapsed into deep, wide holes. Rubble began to clog the thoroughfares over which they passed, and on more than one occasion, they had to backtrack and find another way forward.

Finally, as the sun made a run for the horizon, lengthening their shadows along the ground, the landing party reached the city center. The dimensions of the open space and the cobblestones that lined it seemed identical to those in the square at the heart of the first city. More than that, the two places *felt* similar to Trinh, as though each had been built by the same people, and as though each had been destroyed by the same enemy. But—

"It's worse here," Trinh said into a grim silence she hadn't realized had risen around the landing party.

Along their path through the city, the rap of their heels against the paved streets, the high-pitched wails of their tricorders, and the intermittent conversations had hardly filled the area with noise, but had at least prevented it from lapsing into the haunted quiet that had suddenly appeared. Trinh felt as though her voice, as quietly as she spoke, still desecrated the memories of those who'd died there. Doctor McCoy offered her a sympathetic glance, but neither he nor any of the others said anything.

While moving through the fallen city, Trinh had sensed the widespread nature of the devastation, but standing in the mostly empty square in the city center and peering all around its perimeter, she saw the terrible enormity of the violence that had been wrought there. On the first planet, and also along the rim of the city they'd been exploring, buildings and parts of buildings and segments of the municipal infrastructure still stood. *The bones of the dead,* she thought. The people had died—had probably been murdered—but some perceptible remnants of their existence remained.

Along the edges of the square that stretched before the landing party, though, almost everything had been flattened. The center of the vanquished city had been *crushed,* the vast majority of its physical components reduced to ash. In some places, one or two support beams clawed upward, like the hands of drowning men looking for something to grab hold of to save their lives. Beneath the darkening afternoon sky, though, the bulk of the detritus left behind looked more like low-lying sand dunes than the vestiges of a humanoid city.

"It's Dresden," said the captain. He stood slightly ahead of the rest of the landing party, gazing out across a place that, not that long ago, had been an active, living city. He didn't elucidate his comment, and nobody asked him to do so.

Trinh didn't require an explanation. During the Second World War on Earth, near the conclusion of hostilities, the German city of Dresden had been the target of a carpet-bombing campaign. In a series of air raids made over several days, almost the entire city center had been obliterated. Trinh knew that, after the war, historians had debated the morality of the attack; the cultural importance of Dresden to the Germans, the beauty of its architecture and layout, and the presence of a civilian population contrasted with its use as a communications and rail center, and as a site of munitions manufacture. For Trinh, such questions missed the point. In the end, the wasted landscape that resulted from the massive aerial bombardment of Dresden served her as a powerful symbol of the horror and senselessness of war.

Trinh started to say something about that, but then heard a pair of short tones. The captain immediately reached to the back of his waist, grabbed his communicator, and flipped open its gold metal grille.

Trinh clearly heard Commander Spock speak the name *Kirk,* but then a burst of static covered whatever might have come next. The captain reached up to the device and worked its controls, plainly trying to clear a channel to *Enterprise.*

As Captain Kirk made adjustments to his communicator and the rest of the landing party looked on, Trinh realized that she heard a new sound, some noise not created by the members of the *Enterprise* crew tramping through the blighted carcass of the city. She cocked her head to one side, then turned in place as she tried to follow the drone—*Is it getting louder?*—to its source. She saw awareness of the sound dawn on the others, including the captain, and they all peered around in search of the cause.

When Captain Kirk lifted his gaze skyward, Trinh saw his eyes suddenly widen. She quickly looked around to see what had caused such a reaction. Even as she spotted the blur up among the clouds and registered its rapid approach, Trinh heard the captain issue the last command she would ever heed in Starfleet.

"Run!"

Nine

The vessels appeared on *Enterprise*'s sensors as though a veil around them had abruptly lifted. A moment earlier, the proximity alert indicator had flashed red at the front of the helm-and-navigation console, causing Sulu to lean left and peer into the scanner on his panel. He'd seen at once that a swarm of ships—he counted half a dozen—had emerged from behind the planet's large natural satellite, which they had evidently used to obstruct their presence in the system.

"Mister Spock," he said, "six vessels have just shown up on sensors, from behind the moon." Sulu studied the profiles of the ships, but did not recognize them, and his display—automatically tied into the ship's library-computer—provided no identification for them. "Configuration unknown," he told the first officer. He checked the headings of the vessels, then worked his panel to project their paths. "They appear to be on an intercept course."

It pleased Sulu to see that the vessels did not measure up to *Enterprise* physically; each elongated hull had dimensions similar to a single one of the *Constitution*-class starship's warp nacelles. He didn't know if the aliens intended to attack, but they had clearly sought a tactical advantage by keeping themselves hidden until that point; they also clearly possessed an edge in terms of absolute numbers.

"Lieutenant Uhura," Spock said from the command chair, "hailing frequencies. Open a channel—"

Enterprise shuddered, a roar filling the bridge. On his scanner, Sulu saw that all six vessels had leaped forward, closing on the ship in an instant. He could only surmise that they'd engaged their warp drive, despite the danger of doing so across such a relatively short distance and while deep inside the gravity wells of both the planet and the moon. The readings that appeared on his scanner confirmed his supposition.

The ship continued to shake beneath an onslaught that did not relent. From the science station, Chekov announced that the six vessels fired versions of the missiles that the *Enterprise* crew had encountered at R-775-I—good news, at least in the aliens' apparent lack of advanced weaponry. Uhura called out that she received no response to her hails. Quiet and calm only seconds earlier, the bridge had grown loud and unsteady.

"Fire phasers," Spock ordered. "All banks."

Sulu's hands moved as if of their own volition, finding the proper controls and working them to enact the first officer's orders. Over the clamor of the missiles carrying their payloads and detonating against *Enterprise*'s shields, he heard the squall of the phasers' operation. In his scanner, he saw a number of the energy blasts finding their marks, but the alien ships pursued twisting, evasive courses, their movements extraordinarily agile. Many of the phaser beams missed their intended targets.

"Two direct hits," Sulu said. He glanced up at the main screen to see one of the vessels slice across the field of view above the planet. Matte black, the blade-like ship flew a serpentine path, firing missile after missile as it moved. *Enterprise* continued to pitch fiercely beneath the onslaught.

"Fire photon torpedoes," Spock said above the furor enveloping the bridge.

Enterprise rocked again and again, and Sulu had to set his feet widely against the deck to keep himself in his chair. He operated his console, unleashing a fusillade of the matter-antimatter casings into the battle. In his scanner, he saw one of the alien vessels take a hit, a torpedo detonating against its hull. It lost flight control, appeared to right itself, but then tumbled end over end away from the planet. He reported it to Spock.

"Shields are down to eighty-seven percent," Chekov called. The measurement seemed low to Sulu, considering the basic nature of the alien weapons. The incessant pounding by the missiles, though, had clearly begun to take its toll on *Enterprise*'s defensive screens.

"Still no response to hails," Uhura called out.

"Lieutenant Sulu, fire all weapons at will," Spock said. "Lieutenant Hadley, coordinate evasive maneuvers with the helm."

Sitting beside Sulu at the navigation station, Hadley acknowledged the order and immediately operated his controls to bring the ship about. Sulu glanced at the astrogation panel as *Enterprise*'s new course appeared on it, and then he pressed a button to feed it directly into his scanner readout. Consulting the display once more, he saw the ship drawing a path through the attacking vessels. Sulu activated every phaser bank mounted on the ship, fore, aft, and lateral, then launched a photon torpedo from every tube.

Peering back up at the viewer, the helmsman saw frenetic movement as the five remaining vessels buzzed about *Enterprise* like flies about a piece of carrion. Each discharged missile after missile in an unceasing hail of aggression. The bright red beams of Starfleet phasers screamed through the void of space, mostly missing the swift, nimble vessels, but occasionally landing on one of the black hulls. White flashes punctuated the combat as *Enterprise*'s photon torpedoes exploded.

On his scanner, Sulu saw a second vessel disabled and sent tumbling away into space. For a moment, he thought that *Enterprise*'s weapons had incapacitated a third as well. The vessel arced down and entered the planet's atmosphere. It flew straight and steady, though, and when Sulu plotted its course, its apparent destination horrified him.

"Mister Spock," he shouted above the din, "one of the ships is headed for the city."

Sulu did not hear the first officer push the communications button on the arm of the command chair, but knew that he must have when he said, "*Enterprise* to Captain Kirk." Spock paused, then said it again.

"Sir," Uhura said, "the ships out there are jamming local communications. I doubt our signal's getting through to the captain."

"Acknowledged," Spock said. Sulu heard him stand from the command chair, then felt his presence as the first officer stepped up between the helm and navigation stations. "Lieutenant Hadley," he said, "set a course directly away from the planet. Lieutenant Sulu—"

"Mister Spock," Sulu exclaimed, unable to keep his concern in check, "what about the landing party?"

"Lieutenant Sulu," Spock repeated levelly, "cease fire and prepare to match the velocity of the alien vessels. On my order, accelerate to that speed and follow Lieutenant Hadley's course."

Despite his fear for Trinh, Sulu said no more. He worked quickly to follow Spock's orders. "Course locked in," he reported. "Ready to match velocity with the aliens."

"Execute," Spock said.

Sulu brought *Enterprise* up to speed as it shot

through the remaining three vessels and away. He inspected his scanner, then told Spock that all three ships had turned in pursuit. Sulu could only hope that whatever the first officer had planned would not take more time than they needed to return to the planet and rescue the landing party.

Trinh saw the slender, black object cutting through the sky and assumed that a rocket, like one of those that had attacked them in the R-775 system, had targeted the landing party. Even as Captain Kirk yelled for all of them to run, she wondered what good that could possibly do. They could not outrun a rocket, and even if it did not strike the ground precisely at their location, how could they hope to escape the effects of its nearby detonation?

And yet she ran.

Trinh turned toward the point where the landing party had entered the square from their circuitous path through the city. She took to her heels at once, and saw that her crewmates did so as well. *Where can we hide?* she wondered, already knowing that they would find no safe haven within the city. Near the center square, none of the buildings—virtually no *section,* no *piece* of any building—remained standing. Even if one had, though, it would surely collapse from the concussion wave of an explosion rather than provide any real protection.

As Trinh neared the edge of the square, she saw

Captain Kirk looking at Doctor McCoy and pointing, then getting the attention of Ensign Davis and steering him in a slightly different direction. Trinh understood immediately: the captain wanted the members of the landing party to scatter as best they could, to offer multiple targets so that perhaps a single rocket would not kill every *Enterprise* crew member on the surface.

Trinh veered to her left as she neared the perimeter of the square. Once there, she picked out a narrow opening between heaps of ash and raced into it. The mounds around her blocked the light of the setting sun, throwing her into a trail of shadows. Her boots sent up muffled beats as she ran, telling her that she probably sprinted not on one of the many thoroughfares crisscrossing the city, but on unpaved land that had once lain between two buildings.

As she rushed on, she darted left and right when she could, as though she could somehow confuse the targeting mechanism of the rocket. She thought of how Hikaru had made a similar dash back on the first planet, cutting through the trees on his way to the caves—and she thought of his clever solution. He'd figured that the rocket closing on that location tracked the life signs of Trinh and the other scientists, and so he set his tricorder to simulate such readings, then hurled the device into the canyon.

And it worked.

Trinh stopped, skidding on a mixture of dirt and

ash. The sound of footsteps continued for a moment, disconcerting her, and then Lieutenant Stack ran into her from behind. He would have knocked her to the ground had he not taken hold of her by the arms and caught her as she started to fall.

"We need to keep going," the lieutenant told her.

"I know, I know," Trinh said around mouthfuls of air. It struck her as peculiar that, even in the midst of literally running for her life, she observed that Lieutenant Stack was not even breathing heavily. As she operated her tricorder to attempt what Hikaru had done, she quickly explained her plan to the lieutenant. When she'd finished, she handed him the device. He took it from her, exchanging it for his own, which she set about programming as well. Lieutenant Stack reared back and threw her tricorder, and when she'd completed preparing his, he tossed that one as well.

"Now, let's go," the lieutenant said, tapping Trinh on the elbow as he resumed fleeing the square.

Before Trinh followed, she peered up into the sky, in the direction that she'd seen the rocket. It had grown closer—*much* closer. She turned and ran.

Trinh had covered less than ten more meters when she heard thunder above her and felt the ground quake. The great roar seemed to pass over her, and then a tremendous explosion split the day. She staggered but somehow stayed on her feet and kept running.

Suddenly, a great wall of ash to her right erupted horizontally, sweeping her up within its mass. She felt her feet leave the ground, and then she wound sideways through the air—except that there was no air. Dry flakes of burned material found their way into her mouth and throat, and she inhaled them into her lungs. She coughed hard, uncontrollably, but when she breathed in, she still could find no air.

She ended up on her back, or at least she thought she did. In the darkness—she could see nothing, and didn't know whether she'd instinctively closed her eyes or she'd been buried alive—she panicked. Trinh tried to wave her arms, but found them pinned above her head. She continued to gasp for air, then frantically began turning her head from side to side as she hacked up the dried remains of the city. Terror consumed her, and she writhed against it.

When nothing happened, when Trinh could not free herself but she did not die, she stilled her movements and tried to gather herself. She found space on the right side of her body, where her head had pushed aside some of the material around her. She thrust her mouth against her shoulder, using her uniform shirt as a sort of filter, respiring against it, her lips pressing tightly enough against the fabric to keep the ashes out. Trinh heard nothing but the sounds she made trying to fill her lungs, and the too-rapid beat of her heart.

I'm buried alive, she thought. The wild alarm she'd

felt moments before threatened again, but she fought against it. Trinh struggled to slow her breathing. She smelled the sour tang of her own sweat.

Hikaru, she thought, seeing his face in her mind. He had saved her, not once, but again and again. On R-775-I, he had used his tricorder to direct the rocket away from the cave in which she had taken cover, a trick she had just used a second time to once more avoid—at least temporarily—her own death. Even if she could not free herself, she could at least make the claim that Hikaru had helped her elude death from another rocket's explosion.

And of course, he had saved her with his love. He had rescued her not from death, but from something perhaps worse: a life not fully lived. She'd had love before and lost it, and it had taken Hikaru and his bright smile and handsome face, his quirky sense of humor, his ridiculous amount of enthusiasm for so very many things—it had taken all that made him the person he was to pull her out of a stagnation that could have lasted for the rest of her life.

I'm going to miss him, she thought, and recognized immediately the ludicrous character of her thought. Dead, she would not miss him, *could* not miss anybody or anything. But she missed him at that moment, and felt deeply saddened that what they had begun to share would never come to fruition. They would not wed, they would not have children, even though they had recently started discussing such matters. They had loved each other for a time, and that would have to be enough.

No! Trinh thought. She hated the idea of doing to Hikaru what had been done to her. She loathed the prospect of leaving him in the most permanent way. He deserved more than that.

I deserve more than that, Trinh thought, and amazingly, she actually believed it.

Trinh tried to move again. She flexed one leg, then the other. The ash atop her gave slightly, but still pushed down on her and prevented her from trying to dig herself out. She shifted her hips and torso, and found them as tightly held as the rest of her lower body. She tried to get her left arm to stir, in vain, and then the right.

But then Trinh's hand opened and closed on nothing. Thinking she might have been imagining it, she tried again. Her fingers furled and unfurled into a fist easily, with no resistance.

My hand is free, Trinh thought, not knowing how that could be, but also not allowing herself to celebrate just yet. Concentrating, she turned her hand over and bent her wrist, reaching toward the ground. She felt it at once, a hard, granular sensation on the pads of her fingers.

Trinh walked her fingertips along the ground to one side. Nothing replaced the texture of the dry, wasted earth. Sending her fingers in the opposite direction, she began to think that she shouldn't even bother. She had no idea how badly her body had been mangled in the explosion and its aftermath. If she survived, would she even be the whole woman Hikaru had fallen in love with? She would not want—

Trinh's fingertips brushed against a smooth surface, cool to the touch. It felt like metal—like *rounded* metal. Trinh stretched her arm out as far as she could, tried to extend her reach even millimeters more. Beads of perspiration formed on her face, and a cramp tightened her muscles just below her rib cage. She ignored it. *If I can just—*

Her fingers closed around the object. She had no idea what it was, but it fit in her hand and she could grasp it firmly. Carefully, she pulled on it. When it didn't move, she increased the force she applied, and still the rod or whatever it was stayed in place.

Hope welled within Trinh. She paused for a few seconds to collect herself, to focus her mind on putting whatever strength she owned into what she had to do next. She had to concentrate, for herself, for Hikaru.

And that'll be all I think about, my love, until I'm free, she told herself.

Then Trinh began to pull.

More missiles crashed into *Enterprise.*

"Shields down to seventy-eight percent," called out Chekov. "We've lost shield generators around the starboard warp nacelle and the forward ventral section of the secondary hull."

Sulu monitored *Enterprise*'s velocity, then checked his scanner to match it against the three remaining alien vessels. He wanted to push the ship's velocity higher, thinking that they could draw their pursuers away from the planet, outrun them, then return to rescue the landing party. For the moment, though, he trusted that Spock had a viable plan.

"Viewer astern," the first officer ordered, and Hadley touched a control. The image on the viewer shifted, and the empty space ahead of the ship gave way to the receding form of the planet behind them. The three slim, black vessels continued to chase *Enterprise*, weaving evasively as they fired their weapons without interruption.

"Return fire?" Sulu asked over his right shoulder. Spock stood on that side of him and a step behind.

"Not yet," Spock said. "Have the alien vessels increased their velocity?"

Sulu consulted his scanner. "No," he said, but then corrected himself, knowing the precision with which Spock thought. "Yes, marginally, but they are not closing the distance." Even as he spoke the words, Sulu wondered how that could possibly be true. If the speed of the aliens vessels increased to a level greater than that of *Enterprise,* then they should obviously be shortening the distance between them.

But then Sulu saw the reason why: the alien vessels did not travel in a straight line. Even as they pursued *Enterprise,* they continued to make evasive maneuvers; they therefore traveled a greater distance than if they followed a linear path, and thus required a higher speed to maintain the gap. *Spock wants to straighten them out,* Sulu realized. It had been the ability of the aliens to avoid *Enterprise*'s weapons that had prevented the Starfleet crew from achieving a rapid victory.

"Increase speed," the first officer said. "If the alien vessels do so as well, then increase it again."

"Aye, sir," Sulu said, and he worked the helm to draw more power from the impulse engines. *Enterprise* flew faster, and the aliens matched the increased velocity.

"The alien vessels' sublight engines appear to be at their maximum output," Chekov said from the science console.

"Lieutenant Sulu," Spock said.

Sulu pushed *Enterprise*'s velocity higher. When he looked up at the viewscreen, he saw that the alien vessels had reduced the evasive component of their pursuit. He kicked the ship's speed up another notch, and the course of the alien ships hewed even closer to a straight line.

Spock crossed behind Sulu and over to the left side of the helm. "Lieutenant, bring all weapons to bear. I want a massive barrage, allowing those vessels no avenue for escape. Do not stop until all of them have been disabled."

Sulu nodded, then peered into his scanner. His

hands moved across his panel without him even looking at its controls. In his display, he saw targeting indicators for each of *Enterprise*'s phaser banks turn green and stay green, then watched as the photon torpedo tubes acquired their marks. "Firing all weapons," he said as his fingers pushed multiple buttons.

When the lieutenant peered up at the main viewscreen, the red fire of the ship's phasers had already begun to blaze from *Enterprise*'s stern. He saw the glowing bolts of photon torpedoes follow. In seconds, he learned that his aim had been true.

Sulu didn't realize that he'd been holding his breath until the first of the alien vessels blew up in a fiery cloud that quickly vanished to nothingness in the vacuum of space. The helmsman's breath hissed out in an expression that combined his sense of victory with one of relief. He grew concerned when the other two ships veered off, but their action came too late: they exploded in quick succession.

"Lieutenant," Spock said, and Sulu turned to look at him. "Best possible speed to the planet."

Sulu's hands flew across his panel.

Trinh didn't know how much strength she had left— nor how much air. She felt lightheaded, and suspected that she'd been breathing in as much of her own exhalations as the planet's atmosphere. Her muscles ached, and she wanted nothing more than to relax her body and drift off to sleep.

No! she told herself. *There is something I want more. Some*one.

Steeling herself, Trinh resumed pulling on the piece of metal her right hand had found outside the mound of ashes that had buried her. It felt as though hours had passed since she'd begun, but she knew that the perception of time behaved strangely in extreme circumstances such as hers. However long it had been, though, she'd succeeded in pulling herself closer to the metal piece gripped in her hand, and therefore closer to freeing herself.

If there's anything left of you to free, she thought. She had no idea how badly she'd been hurt. Her body ached everywhere, but she felt no bad pains, nothing that might have indicated a broken limb or a massive cut, or something worse.

PULL! she thought, actually visualizing the characters in her mind, seeing bright, red letters, capitalized, complete with an exclamation point. She pictured her right hand, her fingers clenched around the stray piece of metal that might save her life. And she pulled.

Something cold touched the top of Trinh's scalp, and she thought that she'd somehow cut herself, that she'd wounded her head and it had begun to bleed. But then she felt a rustling movement, and then a slight variation in the chill on her skin.

It's a breeze, she realized. *I feel a breeze.* She had pulled herself far enough along that her scalp had cleared the heap that had fallen on top of her.

A strong urge to reach her free hand to her head rose within her, a desire to try to dig herself out that way, but she resisted. If she did, she feared that she might never find the piece of metal again. And so, once more, she pulled.

When her nose emerged from the ash and she could breathe in unused air, tears spilled down the sides of her head. She let go of the piece of metal and brushed her face clean—or at least clean*er*—then opened her eyes. Great heaps of ash rose high on either side of her, with fragments of debris sticking out of them. Directly above her, the sky looked only slightly darker than when she and the rest of the landing party had bolted from the city center. She waited for a moment, listening for voices, but she heard only a far-off drone—a drone that grew louder as the seconds passed.

Another rocket.

Trinh quickly reached back to the metal rod and began pulling again. Her mouth came free, and then her entire head. Once her left shoulder emerged into the open air, she squirmed to release it from its captivity. When she had, she grabbed the piece of metal with both hands and tried with all of her might to yank the rest of her body clear. With the drone of the rocket increasing, her torso appeared, and then her waist.

The metal rod moved suddenly. Trinh turned her head to look around at it, but then she heard a noise above her. It sounded different from the rocket, an artificial groan like that made by an overburdened piece of metal.

Then Trinh heard something else above her shift. She whipped her head around to look up and saw flickers of ash floating down. She raised her hand to wave them away from her face. That's when she saw a huge mass appear atop the mound beside her, at its edge, maybe seven or eight meters above her. She could make out no details of the object, but its size and smooth surface reminded her of the side of a sarcophagus.

It tottered in place, then began to slide down toward her.

Trinh threw her hands into the ground and pushed, trying to scramble backward. One leg came loose, and she thrust the heel of her boot into the ground for additional leverage. Her trapped foot seemed to snag on something, but then finally came free.

Trinh heard more movement above her, even over the approaching rocket. She had liberated herself, but too late. The massive object slipped down the accumulation of wreckage and then toppled over and into the air. She saw it from the corner of her eye as it fell, and then it slammed her back against the ground.

Trinh stared up into the sky. She felt no pain, but the shock of the impact overwhelmed her. It seemed impossible to make sense of what had just happened.

Somewhere above her, the rocket continued to get closer.

Bending her neck, Trinh peered down the length of her body. The huge object—she saw that it had a vented metal surface and roughly the shape of a rectangular prism—had landed on the middle of her body. She could not see her legs; she could see nothing beyond her navel. Dark patches ran across the bottom of her light-blue uniform shirt, and as she looked on, they spread.

Trinh let her head fall back onto the ground. She had never felt so fatigued. She could no longer deal with all that had happened to her. Sleep seemed like the best of all possible solutions. At that moment, it didn't matter to her if she ever woke up.

Trinh closed her eyes. Somewhere, almost directly above, the rocket roared. She wondered idly whether she would die in the explosion or from the injuries she had just sustained. She had no preference. She would just lie there on the surface of an alien world, in the ruins of a dead city, and wait to see what would happen next.

And then she was gone.

Ten

On the main viewscreen, the image of the second world in the R-836 system grew as *Enterprise* approached it. For Sulu, the seconds seemed to tick away with interminable slowness, so much so that he imagined doing what the aliens had done on their vessels between the moon and the planet: engaging the warp drive for a brief but dangerous jump across local space. But the attack on *Enterprise* had proceeded much as it had in system R-775, without warning or apparent provocation, and with the ship's warp drive as a primary target. Scotty had reported that after the shields had dropped around the starboard nacelle, it had suffered damage from the sustained assault.

"Mister Spock," said Uhura, "we are within communications range."

"Open a channel to every member of the landing party, Lieutenant," Spock said. He had taken a seat in the command chair.

"Channel open," Uhura said.

Sulu heard Spock push a button on the arm of the chair. "*Enterprise* to Captain Kirk," he said, and then,

"*Enterprise* to landing party." When he received no reply, he repeated himself.

"I'm sorry," Uhura said. "The last vessel is still jamming transmissions."

"Keep trying," Spock told her. Then he said, "Ensign Chekov, how soon before we are within transporter range of the surface?"

"One minute, fifty-three seconds," Chekov reported. "We are already within sensor range. I'm reading the upper strata of the planet's atmosphere."

"Scanning for the alien vessel," Sulu said, employing his targeting scanner once more. *If we can't reach the landing party in time,* he thought, *we can still destroy our attackers.* But the notion of revenge held no interest for Sulu. He didn't care at all about causing the deaths of strangers, even murderous ones; he wanted only to save the lives of his crewmates and friends. *And my love.*

"Ship's sensors are directed toward the surface," Chekov said. "I'm scanning for our people."

Sulu heard an intercom channel open, and then Spock said, "Bridge to transporter room."

"*Transporter room,*" responded a voice that sounded slightly tinny. "*Kyle here.*"

"Lieutenant, prepare for an emergency beam-up of all six members of the landing party," Spock said. "We will be within transporter range in one minute, nineteen seconds. We do not presently know if the group is together, so you must be ready to transport from as many as six different locations."

"*Understood, Mister Spock,*" Kyle said. "*I'll multiplex that many of our targeting scanners together to facilitate separate coordinate locks.*"

"Do it quickly, and keep this channel open," Spock said. "Because of Captain Kirk's plan for the landing party, all scans should begin in the center of the city and radiate outward."

At the helm, Sulu saw the alien vessel appear on his scanner. "I've got the last ship," he said. He wanted to hurtle the ship's phasers and photon torpedoes against it, wanted to destroy it as quickly as he could in order to protect *Enterprise*'s crew members on the ground. *To protect Trinh,* he thought, admitting the truth to himself. He hoped to save the entire landing party, of course, but Trinh . . .

Sulu couldn't finish the thought. He knew that firing on the alien vessel would actually endanger the landing party. Any errant phaser beam, any photon torpedo that missed, could end up killing the *Enterprise* crew members on the surface. And even if Sulu managed to cleanly shoot the vessel out of the air, its wreckage would still crash to the planet somewhere.

As the seconds passed, Sulu studied his display, until at last his sensors picked up the city. The readings horrified him. "I'm detecting an explosion on the surface," he said. He felt instantly numb, his voice seeming to originate from somewhere outside his body. "And the alien vessel just launched another missile toward the city."

"Lieutenant Sulu," Spock said, "lower the shields."

"Aye," Sulu said, and worked his panel to comply. "Shields down."

"Mister Chekov, Mister Kyle?" Spock intoned.

"Scanning," Chekov said, and over the intercom, Kyle echoed him. Sulu waited, desperately hoping that the first missile hadn't killed any members of the landing party, and that they'd all be back on the ship before the second one plunged its destructive power onto the surface.

"I'm reading two life signs," Kyle suddenly said. *"And a third. Energizing."*

Sulu could not hear the distinctive hum of the transporter over the intercom, but the sound played inside his head. He visualized Trinh materializing on the platform, healthy and uninjured, as though thinking such a thought might make it so.

"Bridge, we've got them," Kyle said.

"I have another life sign," Chekov said. "Transferring coordinates directly to the—" Chekov stopped in midsentence, and Sulu turned from his scanner to look at him, fearful of what the hesitation might signal. "I've got the last three," Chekov said. "Transferring coordinates directly to the transporter room."

"Coordinates received," Kyle said. *"Energizing."*

Emotion overwhelmed Sulu. A pressure formed behind his eyes, and he realized that tears threatened. He wanted to leap from his chair and race down to the transporter room, but he knew he still had a duty to perform. With an effort, he peered back into his scanner. An instant later, he saw the second missile explode on the surface. He informed Spock.

"Track the alien vessel, Lieutenant," the first officer told him. "We will attempt to capture its crew."

"Aye, sir," Sulu said. He activated a sensor-tracking program.

Several seconds passed, and when no word arrived from the transporter room, Spock said, "Lieutenant Kyle?"

Sulu thought that the intercom channel had been closed, a fact confirmed a moment later when the boatswain's whistle sounded and a voice spoke from the transporter room; it did not belong to Kyle. *"Spock, this is the captain,"* Kirk said. *"What happened? Is the ship all right?"*

"Lieutenant Sulu, raise the shields," Spock said. As Sulu did so, the first officer went on. "Captain, we were attacked by six smaller vessels evidently crewed by the same beings who demolished the city on the planet in system R-Seven-Seven-Five. We have destroyed three of the vessels, incapacitated two others, and are tracking the sixth, which we believe set out to attack your landing party."

"It did," Kirk said. *"And it would likely have killed us all had you not beamed us aboard when you did. Well done."*

"Thank you, sir," Spock said, a reaction Sulu hadn't anticipated. He thought he heard a measure of emotion in the normally stoic Vulcan's voice—not because the ship's captain, James T. Kirk, had appreciated his actions, but because his friend, Jim Kirk, had survived. Sulu understood completely.

"*I'll be up to the bridge shortly,*" the captain said, "*after I stop in sickbay. Kirk out.*"

Sickbay? Sulu thought, and again, he looked away from his scanner. *Did somebody get injured on the planet? Did Trinh?*

Across the bridge, at the main science station, Chekov peered in the direction of the helm. Pavel said nothing, but Sulu could see his own concern reflected in his friend's face.

Kirk waited impatiently in McCoy's office, pacing back and forth. The entire landing party had somehow survived an attack on the city that the captain identified to himself as Dresden. Spock had plucked all six of them from the surface of the planet and deposited them back aboard *Enterprise* after they had survived the first, apparently errant missile strike, and before a second could land. But when they materialized on the platform in the transporter room, it turned out that not all members of the landing party had returned to the ship unscathed.

The captain had been among the last group of three beamed back on board, along with Lieutenant Stack and Ensign Trinh. Doctor McCoy and the other two members of the landing party stood in the middle of the transporter room, looking battered and disheveled, but otherwise all right. Kirk himself had suffered bumps and bruises on his sprint away from the city square, and in his tumble to the ground when the first missile struck. It would turn out that had been true of everybody in the landing party.

But when the golden sparkle of the transporter effect had cleared from the captain's eyes and he'd found himself back aboard *Enterprise,* he witnessed far more serious injuries. Standing on the pad beside him on the platform, Lieutenant Stack held a hand across his left biceps and triceps, where a sizable gash had been opened in his flesh. Blood covered that side of the security officer's uniform, and his arm hung at an awkward angle that left no doubt that it had been broken.

When Kirk had peered around to the back of the transporter platform, though, he'd witnessed a far more gruesome scene. Ensign Trinh lay across two pads, her body mangled and covered in blood, her chest barely rising and falling with her respiration. Kirk saw no burns or other marks that indicated she'd been caught in an explosion, but clearly something terrible had happened to her. A complex mix of emotions roiled within him: pain and sadness for Trinh, anger at the aliens whose actions had caused her injuries, guilt for the role he had played in endangering members of his crew.

McCoy had immediately jumped up on the transporter platform, his hands already working to open his medkit, and while the doctor had spared a glance at Lieutenant Stack, he'd rushed directly to Ensign Trinh. Kirk moved in the other direction, leaping down from the platform and crossing to the transporter console. He heard Spock's voice speaking to Lieutenant Kyle, but the captain ignored his first officer and punched the intercom control with the side of his fist, closing the channel and opening a new one. "Transporter room to sickbay," he said. "This is the captain. We have a medical emergency."

A voice answered at once, and Kirk recognized it as belonging to one of the ship's surgeons, Doctor M'Benga. *"Acknowledged, Captain,"* he said. *"We're on our way."*

That had been nearly thirty minutes earlier. Kirk had waited with McCoy for the emergency medical team, and then had accompanied the group to sickbay. Though anxious to head to the bridge, he first wanted a report on the condition of Ensign Trinh. He'd checked in with Spock from sickbay, providing the first officer with no details on the status of the landing party personnel, but making sure that nothing required his own immediate attention on the bridge.

You just don't want to face Sulu without knowing that Trinh will be all right, Kirk thought cynically, castigating himself for his cowardice. In the first moment he'd seen her on the transporter platform, the captain had believed her dead, such had been the extent of her injuries. He felt relief when he saw her still breathing, but he also knew that small fact afforded no guarantee of her continued survival.

Kirk heard footsteps approaching one of the open doorways on the inner side of McCoy's office, and he turned in that direction. A moment later, the doctor entered. He still wore indicators of their visit to Dresden: a small tear at the bottom of his uniform shirt, a scratch along his left cheek, a smudge of dirt above his right eye. "How is she?" Kirk asked without waiting.

McCoy looked grave. "Not good, Jim," he said. "Doctor M'Benga's having her prepped for surgery." The captain didn't have to wonder why the ship's chief medical officer wouldn't perform the operation, because he knew that McCoy had just spent hours hiking through a dead city before facing his own mortality in a missile attack. "Something large fell on Trinh . . . crushed her body. She's suffered extensive internal injuries, and she very nearly bled out. Doctor M'Benga and I believe that most of her damaged organs can be repaired to some degree, and in one or two instances, replaced, but . . . the base of her spine has been badly compressed and she has several vertebral fractures and significant nerve damage."

Other than finding out that she had died, Kirk didn't think the news could have been any worse. "Will she suffer paralysis?" he asked.

"It's very likely she will," McCoy said. "But there's no guarantee that she'll even survive today's surgery, and the operation today is only the first of many she'll require." The doctor looked away, and in that brief interval, Kirk hoped that the awful prognosis would not get any worse.

But it did.

"Jim," McCoy said, looking back up at the captain, "even if we are successful in repairing the damage and restoring function, it's unlikely that Trinh will survive her injuries for very long."

Kirk felt as though he'd been kicked in the gut. "How long?" he asked quietly.

"It's impossible to say with any certainty right now," McCoy told him, "but I'd say a matter of months, maybe a year. She might even live another three years, but I'm not sure that would be a good thing for her."

Kirk stared at the doctor without saying anything. What *could* he say? What *was* there to say? The two men stood in a laden silence. At last, Kirk simply said, "Bones."

"I know, Jim," McCoy said. "I'm sorry."

"Can Sulu see her?"

"Not for several hours, at least," McCoy said.

Kirk considered how Sulu would feel, and what he'd want to do. "He might want to come down here anyway," he said. "To wait."

"Probably," McCoy agreed. "I'll make sure we take care of him."

"Good," Kirk said. He wanted to say more about

Trinh, to do more, but what could he do? "What about Lieutenant Stack?" he asked.

"Oh, uh, he's fine," McCoy said, as though he'd completely forgotten about the security officer. "He suffered a closed, non-displaced fracture of the humerus, as well as a deep laceration. We knitted him up. I took him off duty for a couple of days and sent him to his cabin."

Kirk nodded. "I'll be on the bridge," he said. "Keep me informed."

"Yes, Captain."

Kirk turned and crossed McCoy's office to the outer door, which opened at his approach. He stepped out into the corridor and headed for the nearest turbolift. As he walked, his mind wandered back to Starbase 25, to his meeting with Admiral Ciana. She'd told him to keep doing what he'd been doing aboard *Enterprise*, that Starfleet Command valued his service.

What service? he asked himself. *Paralyzing members of my crew? Destroying their lives?* What good did all his achievements do if he could not keep safe all the people in his charge?

"No good at all," he said aloud, then glanced around to make sure he was alone in the corridor.

When he reached the turbolift and entered the car, he took hold of the activation wand and stated his destination as the bridge. As the lift began its ascent, Kirk thought about what he would say to Sulu, and then asked himself again what good had come of his captaincy if he had to deliver such news. And again, he answered himself out loud.

"No good at all."

Sulu heard the doors to the turbolift slide open with their familiar squeak. As he'd already done three times since the landing party had been recovered, he turned at the helm to see who had arrived on the bridge. He didn't expect Trinh to appear there, but Sulu wanted to speak with the captain, to make sure that Trinh hadn't been hurt while down on the planet's surface.

At last, the open doors of the turbolift revealed Kirk behind them. Sulu saw at once that the captain still bore the marks of his visit to the planet's surface, and quite probably of the attack on the landing party: dark smudges of grime fouled his gold uniform shirt, a ragged tear left his pants open at the knee, and a slash of red climbing up the side of his face revealed where his flesh had been sliced through and subsequently repaired. He stepped out of the car and peered toward the center of the bridge, to where Spock sat in the command chair. In his peripheral vision, Sulu saw the first officer begin to rise, but then Kirk held up one hand, palm out, clearly signaling to Spock that he should remained seated.

As the captain walked to the portside opening in the railing and descended to the lower level of the bridge, Sulu sought to make eye contact with him, but Kirk did not look his way. Before the helmsman could speak up, the captain addressed Spock. "What's the status of the attacking vessels?" he wanted to know. Sulu turned back to his console, but he would listen for a break in the conversation so that he could talk to Kirk.

"I regret to inform you, Captain, that they have evaded us," Spock said.

"What?" Kirk said. "I thought you disabled two of their vessels, and were tracking the one that attacked us on the planet."

"Both of those details were at one point true," Spock said. "But the vessel that attacked the landing party exited the atmosphere and returned to space at considerable velocity while utilizing effective evasion techniques. As a result, we had no clear opportunity to capture or incapacitate the craft before it engaged its warp drive."

"And *our* warp drive isn't functioning?" Kirk asked.

"The aliens' sustained attacked compromised the shields around the starboard nacelle, which then suffered several direct missile strikes," Spock said. "Mister Scott reports that the damage does not rise to the level of that done to the port nacelle in system R-Seven-Seven-Five. Nevertheless, it will require at least a day to patch, and four more days at a starbase to effect permanent repairs."

"What about the two vessels you disabled?" Kirk asked.

"We have scanned the system, but have been unable to locate them," Spock said. "Readings are inconclusive, but suggest that the attackers might have had sufficient time to mend their craft and depart the system at warp."

"All right," Kirk said. "What about our shields?"

"They have been restored to full strength," Spock said.

"Very good," the captain said. "As long as we're in orbit here, keep them raised. And I want continuous sensor sweeps at maximum range. We need to know at once if the attackers return."

"Understood," Spock said.

Sulu heard a pause between the two men, and when it extended a few seconds, he turned in his chair so that he could ask to speak with the captain. To his surprise, Kirk was already peering down at him. "Mister Sulu," he said, "come with me."

The helmsman knew right away that something had happened to Trinh. All at once, his mind seemed to exist outside his body, which he could no longer feel, as though he had just been stunned with a phaser. He turned back to his station for a moment and secured the helm, then stood up slowly and followed the captain into the turbolift.

Once the doors had glided closed, Kirk took hold of an activation wand and specified their destination. He called out a deck number rather than saying "Sickbay," as Sulu had expected, but they equated to the same thing. The lift began to descend. Without waiting for the captain to speak, Sulu said, "What happened to Trinh?"

"Sulu," Kirk said, "I'm sorry. She's been hurt very badly."

"How badly?"

"She's in surgery right now, and she will be for several more hours," Kirk said. "According to Doctor McCoy, it's likely to be the first of many operations she'll need."

Sulu's vision wavered as tears collected in his eyes. He took a deep breath and fought them back. "Will she live?"

"The doctors don't know," Kirk said. "But even if she does, they don't know for how long. It's likely to be a hard life."

Questions posed themselves in Sulu's mind—he wanted to know what had caused Trinh's injuries, whether or not her mind had been affected, if he could do anything at all to help her, and when he could see her—but they all seemed to hide what he actually felt inside him, and he stopped them before they reached his lips. He looked down at his feet and tried to decide not only what he should do next, but how he should feel. When he peered back up at the captain, he could think of only one thing to say: "Why?"

"I don't know exactly what happened," Kirk said. "We scattered when we were attacked, hoping that multiple targets would increase the odds of our collective escape. While Trinh—"

"No," Sulu said. "I'm not asking how she got hurt." He marveled at the calmness in his voice. "I want to know why you sent her down there." Even with no anger in his tone, he suspected the captain perceived the rage growing within him.

"Sulu," Kirk said. He shook his head while glancing all around the lift, as though he might find an answer somewhere. "I don't know what to say. You were there on the bridge. We found another dead city, and we needed to study it."

"I *was* on the bridge," Sulu agreed. "And I heard a member of your senior staff telling you it would be too dangerous to send anybody down to the planet to explore." Although Sulu hadn't been asked his opinion at the time, he'd concurred with Doctor McCoy's assessment about the hazards involved in transporting down a landing party.

"Sulu," the captain said, "there were differing views. I had to make a choice—"

"You didn't have to make *that* choice," Sulu said. "I was also on the bridge when we found the first dead city, and I was on the planet when the landing parties were attacked." Sulu's voice had begun to rise in volume, but he didn't care. "How could you not see how unsafe it would be to take the same actions when we discovered the second city?"

The turbolift slowed as it reached its destination, but before the doors could open, Sulu reached out and wrapped his hand around an activation wand. "Hold," he said. The lift stopped, and the doors remained closed. He didn't know how many regulations he might be breaking, but he didn't care about that either.

The captain looked at him. "Do you really want an answer?"

"Do you have one?" Sulu said derisively.

Kirk brought his hands together at his waist, then held them apart, palms out, in what seemed like a supplicating gesture. "There's a risk in everything we do," the captain said. "You know that. Right now, we're standing in a tin can in the middle of a vacuum. Outside the hull, it's two hundred and seventy degrees below zero. It's impossible to be completely safe out here."

"That's no answer," Sulu said, almost snarling the words. "I'm not talking about being *completely* safe. I'm talking about you beaming a landing party down to a planet after missiles were launched against other landing parties—and crew members were killed—in almost identical circumstances."

"The circumstances weren't identical," Kirk said, but he did not sound entirely convinced of his assertion. "We scanned for hidden missile installations; there were none."

"Are you going to deny that we were attacked by the same aliens who attacked us the first time?" Sulu said. The captain didn't reply right away, and Sulu didn't wait before continuing. "When Doctor McCoy counseled against sending a landing party down to this planet, do you remember what you said?" Again,

Kirk didn't appear inclined to answer, and the helmsman didn't wait for a response. "You said that you never risk anybody's life unnecessarily."

"I risked my own life," Kirk said very quietly. "I was down there too."

"And that's your choice," Sulu said. "But you also chose to put five other lives in danger, and at least one of them has paid the price for your hubris." The captain's head snapped back, almost as though reacting to a punch. "Tell me," Sulu went on, almost spitting his words out, "what was so *necessary* that Trinh had to be hurt so badly?"

Just tasting Trinh's name on his lips brought Sulu back to reality—to the staggering understanding that the woman he loved might soon die, or if she lived, might never be the same, might never have the life she envisioned for herself. He swayed backward, and his shoulder blades brushed the side of the lift. Tears streamed down his face. "What was so necessary that *I* had to be hurt so badly?"

"Sulu," Kirk said, "nothing I say to you, no answer I give, will seem justification enough for what's happened."

Sulu looked down, defeated. Nothing would ever be the same for him either. But he also knew that he couldn't think about that—not at that moment, and probably not for some time to come. However badly she was hurt, however much help she would need, Sulu had to be there for her.

And I will be.

"I am truly sorry," said Captain Kirk.

Sulu peered up again. "I don't care," he said. "Your sorrow means nothing." He reached for the activation wand and ordered the turbolift to resume its journey. It moved only a short distance, and then its doors parted. "I'll be in sickbay, Captain," he said. He strode forward and out of the lift, leaving Kirk behind.

Sulu did not look back.

Eleven

Trinh awoke slowly, drifting upward from what must have been a dream. She could still see herself walking across the University of Alpha Centauri campus, beneath the canopies of the ancient trees that towered over the main quad. The school library stood in front of her, a glass-fronted, four-story building in which she'd spent many days and not a few nights.

In a backpack she'd slung across one shoulder, Trinh toted something heavy, so she guessed that she hadn't actually been headed for the library, but probably past it, to the complex of buildings known familiarly around campus as the Age Factory. The university's galaxy-class archaeology program resided there, with faculty offices, classrooms, labs, a specialty library, and two massive structures that allowed for amazing simulations of digs from around the Federation.

In her dream, Trinh hadn't been able to recall what she carried with her, and so she'd stopped at a bench in the quad and pulled her backpack from her shoulder. She unsnapped the opening of the main compartment, reached in, and pulled out a miniature, but still heavy, sarcophagus. She held it up with both hands and studied it, trying to read the ideograms marching along its black surfaces. Nothing looked recognizable.

As she'd turned over the relic—or the model of a relic—in her hands, examining it, it started to feel heavier to her. At first, Trinh thought she must be imagining it, but the object's weight continued to increase. She struggled to hold it aloft, and realized that if she didn't put it down soon, it would crash to the ground—and if it did so with her hands still around it, she'd be apt to lose a finger.

An odd dream, Trinh thought as she opened her eyes, but already the details of her nighttime apparitions had begun to fade. In the dimly lighted room, she wondered about the time. She gazed upward and saw a ceiling she didn't recognize, though perhaps she would once she turned on a light.

Except the ceiling's so big. As she followed the lines of lighting panels—all dark, but she could make them out—she knew she couldn't be in her small room in the dormitory, or even in the smaller place she'd stayed off campus.

No, she told herself. *School was a long time ago.*

But even after that, when she'd been away on digs or on research projects, she'd never stayed in such a large space. Not even after she'd met Luke and they'd begun living and traveling together.

Where then? she asked herself. *Maybe the* Enterprise—

Like a thunderbolt, it all flashed back into existence for her: the dead cities, the rockets, being buried alive, and escaping that terrible fate, only to exchange it for one even worse. Her lips quivered as her tears began. In the days and nights since suffering her injuries, she had wept a lot, usually stopping only when she slept, or when the medications pushed her mind past the point of experiencing reality.

Trinh looked up at the ceiling—at the *overhead*—and remembered that even the *Enterprise* now lay in her past. How long ago had her injuries occurred? Ten days? Two weeks? She didn't remember. She could recall only snatches of the first few days back aboard the ship, though she'd collected some other details along the way. It had taken at least a day after the attacks for Lieutenant Commander Scott and his engineering staff to repair the warp drive, and then a week or more to reach Starbase 25. The ship had arrived there four days earlier, at which time Trinh had been off-loaded to the station's infirmary.

Off-loaded, she thought. *Like a piece of meat.*

But that's all she was now, wasn't it? And not even fresh meat. *Spoiled* meat.

Slowly—not out of any sense of caution, but because she could move no faster—Trinh reached up with one hand—the hand at the end of an arm not attached to an uncountable number of machines. She pulled aside the bedclothes. Lifting her head from the pillow, she squinted through the dim light at what remained of her body. She had done so many times already, but she felt powerless to stop herself from examining her wounded form again, foolishly hoping each time she looked that she would find that she had sustained her injuries in a cruel dream, rather than in an even crueler reality.

Covered by a medical gown, Trinh mercifully could not see her flesh above her feet, which stuck out near the end of the bed—feet that actually appeared healthy, but that she would never be able to use again. She had seen what lay beneath the thin fabric covering her from shoulders to ankles, though: from the base of her ribs, down to her waist, and on to her thighs, her skin had become a deep, unhealthy purple color, the shade of rotting apples. It had the texture of paper, and felt as thin. Because of the severity and magnitude of her injuries, the surgeons had been unable to utilize an autosuture to seal her wounds and incisions, and so fine black strands had been used to tie the outer shell of her body back together. She looked like the image she envisioned of the creature Doctor Frankenstein had cobbled together from separate body parts in Mary Shelley's novel.

Worse than that, though, and something she could make out even covered by her medical gown, her body had withered. Through her terrible injuries, through four surgeries and facing still more, her internal organs had been ruined, her thigh bones splintered, her pelvis crushed. Doctor M'Benga and Doctor McCoy had repaired some of her viscera, had replaced what they could, but her overall physical system had suffered tremendously.

Yeah, my physical *system suffered,* she thought. *But my mental and emotional sides are doing just fine.* Her tears continued even through her bitter sarcasm. When she could stand the pain—the physical pain—and the medications didn't addle her, she could maintain an inner monologue. Speaking remained a terrible chore, though, one that caused her extreme fatigue in just moments.

Hikaru had stayed with her as much as possible. Since her injuries, almost every time she'd awoken—or regained consciousness—he'd been by her bedside. At first, when she couldn't speak at all, when she could barely move, he just sat with her, sometimes talking to her, sometimes just looking at her with his love still burning in his eyes. He smiled a lot, and never cried in front of her, but she saw the redness in his eyes, the puffiness of his face, and she knew that, alone in his quarters, he shed many, many tears.

Trinh hated him for that. Loved him, and hated him. Loved him, because she would have expected nothing less of this wonderful man than for him to stand by her, for him to do everything he could to make this time as positive as it could possibly be, for him to continue to love her. Hated him, because it was all a lie. Not his love, not his steadfastness, not the beauty of his spirit, but the promise, unspoken at first, that times would one day be better for them, that her health would improve and they would resume joyously spending their lives together.

She knew none of that could ever happen. In the first few days after her injuries, in those few moments here and there when she would float up to consciousness, and when only members of the *Enterprise* medical staff had been present, she'd asked—in tortured fragments of speech—and later she'd begged for them to give her a diagnosis and detail her chances for a full recovery. For some reason, the doctors and nurses experienced little difficulty in listing and explaining the state of her massively wounded body. Yet when she questioned them about her condition not in that moment, but in a year hence, or two years, or ten, they hemmed and hawed, hid behind "uncertainties" and "possibilities." But Trinh had wanted probabilities, and nobody wanted to provide her with those.

Maybe because they know me, Trinh speculated. She dismissed that idea, though, both because Leonard McCoy and Jabilo M'Benga didn't know her all that well, and because she thought it unlikely that two such accomplished physicians and surgeons would choose even pretty lies over their ethical responsibilities. She suspected, though, that her exceedingly weakened condition, especially in those first days, had prevented the two men from telling her anything that would deprive her of hope and therefore potentially complicate her convalescence.

Despite her depleted state, though, Trinh had apparently improved, since Doctor Rellan had not hesitated to discuss her prognosis with her. *Or maybe it's because she's Vulcan,* Trinh thought, though she doubted that the stoicism of Starbase 25's chief medical officer had anything to do with it. When Trinh had been transferred from the *Enterprise* sickbay to the starbase's infirmary, Trinh had asked Doctor Rellan about what she could expect, medically, in the future, and the doctor had promised to review her records and examine her readings to make a determination.

Trinh learned that she had no future. Or not much of one. She would never walk again, though it seemed at least possible that she could be fitted into an automated wheelchair at some point. She would always require significant doses of numerous medicines, including those to combat chronic pain, which would only work completely when they robbed her of full consciousness. No longer could she easily perform the most basic of bodily functions, but would need the use of various devices. Doctors and nurses and medications and machines would occupy her entire existence.

Existence, Trinh thought. *Not life. I'll exist, but I won't live.*

And she wouldn't even *exist* for long. Doctor Rellan estimated her maximum life expectancy at three years, although she believed one year a more likely scenario. For Trinh's physical condition would likely

244 DAVID R. GEORGE III

not improve much more than it already had, but even maintaining that level of severely compromised health would require intensive means that simply could not be sustained. Medical science could only delay for a short time the deterioration of her mangled body.

Trinh wanted none of that. All she wanted was to die.

When Sulu walked into the infirmary on Starbase 25, he saw both Doctor Rellan and Nurse Garcia on duty, the former seated at a workstation in the main compartment to the left, the latter studying a remote diagnostic panel and making some notes on a data slate in the ward to the right. The lieutenant headed into the ward and over to the nurse, pleased to be able to consult with him rather than the doctor about Trinh. Sulu trusted Rellan's medical abilities completely, but he thought he could more readily get what he wanted from Garcia.

"Good morning, Sean," Sulu said, working to keep his tone upbeat and conversational.

"Hikaru," the nurse said, offering him a welcoming smile. "How are you?"

"I'm all right," Sulu said, forcing a smile onto his face even though he hadn't felt all right in days. Ensign Garcia surely must have understood that, but the two always exchanged pleasantries anyway. *Enterprise* had been at the starbase for four days, and as much time as Sulu had spent in its infirmary, he couldn't have helped but become friendly with the medical staff. "How are you doing?"

"I'm fine, thank you," Garcia said. He nodded toward a door panel at the end of the ward that stood halfway open. "Ensign Trinh is awake."

"Good," Sulu said, and then he dropped his voice to a more serious tone. "How is she today?" This was the question he'd wanted to ask the nurse, rather than the doctor. Rellan would have provided him with perfectly accurate information about Trinh's condition, of course, but she would not have given him the answer he needed.

"Physically, about the same," Garcia said. "Mentally and emotionally, though, I think this may be her best day here, at least so far." Sulu smiled again, his expression actually genuine. "She was crying earlier," Garcia said cautiously, as though it pained him to say so, "but not as much as the past few days, and she's been more talkative too."

"That's great," Sulu said.

"She asked about you, of course," the nurse said.

Sulu shook his head. "I meant to be here before she woke up, but I was . . . checking on some things I needed to do for Starfleet," he said. He didn't want to reveal to Garcia or anybody else the decision he'd made before he spoke to Trinh. "Is she awake now?" Since suffering her injuries, Trinh spent a majority of her days either asleep or unconscious, depending on the timing of her surgeries. Sulu knew that rest would play a major role in her recuperation, and so he never wanted to rouse her.

"She was awake just a couple of minutes ago," Garcia said. "Let me check." The nurse set his data slate down on a nearby shelf, then crossed the ward to the half-open door. He peered inside, then turned back toward Sulu and nodded.

As Sulu walked over to the room Trinh occupied—he did not wish to think of a compartment in a sickbay or in an infirmary as "Trinh's room"—the nurse reached up and touched a control mounted on the bulkhead. The door quietly slid open the rest of the way, and Garcia entered.

"Hi there, Ensign Trinh," he said. "You've got a visitor."

Sulu reached the doorway and looked in at the woman he loved. He watched her turn her head toward him, her movements slow and careful. She didn't smile when she saw him, but she nodded almost imperceptibly. Sulu didn't even know if she could smile, at least without discomfort, considering the length of pale tubing that reached from the corner of her mouth and disappeared into a glut of devices crowded around the head of her bed.

When Sulu stepped inside the room, Nurse Garcia moved away from the bed to let him pass, then started back toward the door. "I'll be right outside," he said. "Call me if you need anything."

"Thank you, Sean," Sulu said.

Once the nurse had left, Sulu moved in close to the bed and peered down at Trinh. Her face still had no color, her eyes no depth, and the form of her body beneath the bedclothes appeared unnaturally gaunt, as though even the mildest current of air could carry her away. *Of course she looks* unnaturally *gaunt,* Sulu thought. *All of this—all of her pain and suffering— didn't happen* naturally, *and needn't have happened at all.* The vitriol he felt for Captain Kirk burned like a fire within him.

Sulu showed none of that hard emotion to Trinh, though. Instead, he fit another smile onto his face. "Good morning," he said. "I hope you slept well." He did not *ask* whether she had, because if she hadn't, he didn't want her to have to wallow in anything negative, no matter how minor. He reached over and smoothed her dark hair, then leaned in and gently touched his lips to her cheek. "I love you."

As Sulu pulled back, Trinh's eyes followed him. She blinked at him, slowly and deliberately, and he understood the meaning she intended her gesture to carry: *I love you too.* She could speak, he knew, but she still found it painful and exhausting to do so.

"So," he said, actually excited about the news he'd brought with him that morning, "the doctors tell me that it will be a few more weeks before they'll allow you to travel. Well, I just found out that, by that time, a Starfleet vessel, the *Algonquin,* will be here, and when it departs, it's headed back to Earth."

Trinh stared at him for a moment, and then the slightest crease drew down between her eyebrows. Sulu recognized her look of confusion.

"Yes, Earth," he said. "I received a message from your mother overnight."

Trinh shifted her head on her pillow, and Sulu saw her brow knit once more.

"When all this happened," Sulu said, rushing through even the brief reference to her injuries, "Starfleet of course contacted her. I decided to do so too, and I found her reply when I woke up this morning." Sulu had considered loading Nguyen Thi Yeh's message onto a data slate and bringing it with him, but he didn't know what sort of impact seeing her mother's anguish would have on Trinh. "She's upset about what happened, but she sends you her love and says she's looking forward to seeing you again."

Trinh's eyes went wide. "What?" she croaked in her weak, dry voice.

"You don't have to speak, Trinh," Sulu said. "It's all right." The simple declaration stuck in his throat, because of course *nothing* was all right. He reconsidered, then recast his sentiment from the grueling present to the improved future: "Everything will be all right."

Trinh rolled her head gradually to the left on her pillow, then back over to the right, her eyes darting about. "Are you looking for something?" Sulu asked. "Do you want your data slate?"

Trinh laboriously moved her head back to the

center of the pillow, then, instead of nodding, closed and opened her eyelids: *Yes.*

Sulu looked over at the rolling cart that had been set up beside the bed. He saw a number of personal objects he'd brought her: a few brightly colored slabs that contained some recent vids Trinh had wanted to see, a copy of an ancient medallion she'd found at an archaeological dig on Berengaria VII, a photograph of the two of them at the top of the climbing wall at the starbase, and a number of other small items. Among them sat Trinh's data slate. Though she found it hard to speak, and even harder to move almost any part of her body, she could use her left hand enough to write. He picked the slate up, activated it, and confirmed its current function. He started to remove the stylus from its place, but then recalled that Trinh preferred simply to use her finger.

Sulu adjusted the bedclothes, then set the slate down. He then lifted Trinh's hand and place it atop the screen. "It that okay?" he asked.

Trinh's index finger moved. *"Yes."* Since she had used her data slate before her injuries to record messages, Sulu had been able to program the device to speak in her normal voice. When Trinh had begun using the slate for the purposes of communication a few days ago, she'd asked him to do that. He'd done so cheerfully, but he actually found the experience mildly unnerving.

Trinh wrote more with her finger. *"Earth? My mother seeing me?"*

"I want to take you back to Mars," Sulu told her. Trinh had lived for most of her teenage years in Bradbury Township on the red planet. Her father had since passed away, but her mother still lived there. "Your mother and I want to work together to help you get better."

"You? On Mars?" said the data slate, and then Trinh added more. *"Your career?"*

Sulu leaned back in over the bed and looked into Trinh's dark brown eyes. He wanted her to see his sincerity, and more than that, the depth of his love for her. "I'm going to resign my commission," he said, trying to keep his tone both light—*This really doesn't matter*—and committed—*I want to do this.* "There will—"

"No."

"Yes," Sulu insisted. "This is not something—"

"No." Trinh tapped successively on the slate's screen, on the single word she'd drawn virtually, with her fingertip: *"No. No. No. No. No."*

Sulu waited. He hadn't expected such resistance from Trinh. He knew that she had a good relationship with her mother—something Nguyen Thi Yeh's moving message to him had confirmed—and she couldn't possibly want to stay in Starbase 25's infirmary indefinitely. What better place could there be than her mother's home to spend her recovery, and who better to be there for her than two of the people who loved her most?

When he saw that Trinh would not command the slate to keep repeating *No,* he said, "Your mother wants to take care of you, wants to help you, and so do I."

"Career."

"It's not important," Sulu said, and meant it. He'd worked hard to enter Starfleet, and to succeed once he'd made it there, and yes, he'd hoped one day to rise to the position of starship captain, but none of that was more important to him than Trinh. "There will be plenty of things for me to do on Mars," he went on. "With your mother there—and she says that your sister's also planning to come out from Luna for some extended visits—I'll have time enough when you start to improve to maybe pick up a freighter or transport run now and again."

Trinh peered up at him, but her hand didn't move.

"I promise you, it'll be fine," Sulu said, suddenly uncomfortable with the silence. When Trinh still did not raise her finger to the slate, he said, "I want to do this. I love you."

Finally, Trinh touched the slate again: *"No."*

"Yes," Sulu said.

Trinh wrote more. *"I don't love you."*

Sulu knew differently, knew it as surely as he knew anything at all, trusted it more than all the proofs he'd worked through as a mathematician. Still, it hurt to hear the words spoken in Trinh's voice. "You do love me," he told her. Then, trying to be funny, he said, "Is this your medication talking?"

"It's me," Trinh made the slate say. *"Go."*

"I know it's not you," Sulu said. "I know what we've shared, what we have between us." He pressed the flat of his hand against the left side of his chest, over his heart, even before he knew he meant to do so.

"We have THIS between us." After the slate had spoke her words for her, Trinh moved her head in a sluggish circle, as though to take in everything in the room, defining for him what she meant by *THIS*.

"This," Sulu said, spreading his arms wide, "is not you. *You*—" He pointed at her. "—are still you."

"Not anymore." Then: *"Never will be."*

Sulu leaned back in and gently caressed Trinh's cheek. "You are still you in here," he said, and he brushed his hand lightly atop her head. "All of this—" He waved his other hand above her diminished body. "—just carried you around."

Trinh tried to pull her head from beneath Sulu's touch. He stood back up and withdrew his hand, giving Trinh the space she apparently wanted. She reached to her data slate again.

"Not funny."

The comment wounded Sulu. "I wasn't trying to be funny," he said. "I know who you are, Trinh, and all of that is still here."

"Not all of me . . . Part is gone . . . The rest will be soon."

"Trinh, I don't want to do this because I like you," Sulu said. "I'm not doing it out of guilt or obligation.

I'm not doing it because of anything I've said to you, any promises I made. I'm doing it because I love you, not just yesterday, but today and tomorrow." He leaned in toward her again. "I *love* you."

"*You won't.*"

"I will."

"*Luke.*"

The name startled Sulu. He knew about Trinh's first husband; she'd spoken of him early in her relationship with Sulu. They'd met at graduate school on Alpha Centauri—he'd also been an archaeologist— and had wed soon after earning their doctorates. Because of their shared vocation, they spent a lot of time together, mostly staying at home on Alpha Centauri, but also traveling farther afield on various digs.

It had been on one such expedition, to Ophiucus III, that Luke had fallen. In a dig on the fringes of New Dakar, an ancient and previously unknown burial chamber had given way beneath him. He plummeted ten meters and survived, but he also struck his head and suffered a traumatic brain injury. He lived for six months in a hospital before slipping into a coma; he died three months after that.

Sulu understood the parallel Trinh wanted to draw. He also knew she was wrong. "Yes, I remember what you told me about Luke," he said. "It's not the same thing. You lost him as soon as he endured his head injury. You lost who he was."

"*Doesn't matter. Loved him, so I stayed.*" Sulu

wanted to say more, but Trinh kept writing. *"At end, I hated him . . . Hated living in hospital . . . Hated putting my life on hold . . . Hated him leaving me . . . Hated myself not being a better person."*

"It's not the same thing," Sulu repeated.

"Mostly hated myself because I knew Luke . . . I knew he wouldn't want me to stop living life to care for his carcass."

"You are *not* a carcass," Sulu said, finally unable to prevent his voice from rising with his frustration. He paused to calm himself before he said more, but then Trinh used her slate again.

"I am."

"You are injured," Sulu said. "And you're the woman I love."

"I was."

"You *are*."

Trinh pulled her hand away from the slate and held it up, fingers splayed in a halting motion. He waited while she wrote. It took several minutes. *"You love me. And I want it to stay that way. When I remember Luke now, I remember him after his fall. I remember interminable days, watching him deteriorate, and being able to do nothing about it.*

"Do you think you can make me more comfortable physically? So what? Caregivers can do that. My mother can do that. But if you do that, it will end up hurting me. I don't want the man I love to live like that. And I don't want you to remember me like that . . . like THIS!

"We've had seven months together. The best seven months of my life. We both know that nothing you do can ever change that; nothing between us will ever be better. Let's end it there."

A thousand thoughts seemed to vie for supremacy in Sulu's mind. Trinh had said so many things and he wanted to refute them all. "You'll hate me if I take care of you," he said, picking up one thread of Trinh's argument, "but you won't hate your mother?"

Trinh wrote again. *"Mother's known me thirty-seven years . . . It's different . . . She'll remember me as baby, as girl, as teenager . . . But if it's not different, I'll go somewhere else . . . Hospice . . . I don't have much time . . . Have they told you that?"*

Although he had promised himself that he would not cry in front of Trinh, that he would always smile and be a source of strength for her, he had not expected to hear her acknowledging her own mortality. He could not stop his tears. "I'm sorry," he said. "I don't want to lose you."

"Already have . . . Who I was is not just dying . . . Who I was is already dead."

Trinh looked up from her data slate at him, and for just a moment, he thought he saw an intensity in her eyes. But she was right: it wasn't there. She wrote one more thing.

"Please, Hikaru . . . let me stay dead."

She pulled her hand away from her data slate and closed her eyes. For a few minutes, Sulu watched her.

Trinh's chest rose and fell with her raspy breath, but its rate didn't change, so he didn't think she'd fallen asleep.

"Do you really want me to go?" he asked her, but he might as well have asked the empty room.

He watched Trinh for another few minutes, trying to memorize her features, the position of her body beneath the bedclothes, the sound of her labored breathing. He didn't care what she'd said; he wanted to remember *everything*. He wiped away the tracks of his tears from his face and watched her some more.

Finally, he turned and walked from the room. He stopped just outside the doorway. Nurse Garcia saw him from across the ward and came over to him. "How's she doing?" he asked, his tone one of genuine concern.

"She's . . . it's already been a difficult day," Sulu said. "You should keep checking on her."

"Sure, of course," the nurse said. "I'll go in right now. It's good to see you, Lieutenant."

Garcia headed through the doorway into Trinh's room, leaving Sulu alone in the compartment. He considered going back inside, trying to convince Trinh, or even just simply ignoring whatever she had to say. But then he heard the data slate speak in her voice one last time.

"Nurse, Lieutenant Sulu is no longer permitted to see me."

Sulu walked quickly through the ward and out

into the corridor. He couldn't stay in the infirmary. He turned left without thinking about it. He kept walking, but he knew that he didn't want to stay on Starbase 25.

Up ahead, a series of large, round ports lined the outer bulkhead, looking out into space. As Sulu passed them, he glanced in that direction. Through them, he spied an arc of Dengella II, the planet about which the starbase orbited, and where he and Trinh had once flown a kite together.

Sulu also saw a pair of starships floating in space, and he stopped to gaze out at them. Several umbilical lines tied the *U.S.S. Courageous* to the starbase, and a hectic cloud of activity surrounded the *Miranda*-class vessel. Nearby, free of any encumbrances and freshly repaired, *Enterprise* kept station. Its crew, Sulu knew, prepared to leave the starbase behind and return to their mission before the day ended.

Earlier, Sulu had made the decision that he would not be aboard *Enterprise* when it departed Starbase 25. He'd intended to resign from Starfleet and begin planning to relocate Trinh to Mars. *That can't happen now,* he thought. *The woman I love won't let me care for her.*

Sulu supposed that he could force the issue, that he could refuse to stay away from the infirmary, that he could continue to make plans. But he knew Trinh, and he understood that she would not make it easy. If he had to endure such circumstances on his own, Sulu wouldn't have hesitated, but he feared that compelling Trinh to fight that battle against him would hurt her, and make her recovery all the more difficult. He couldn't do that to her.

Sulu peered back out into space. He looked at the ship on which he'd served for nearly five years, and where his Starfleet career had begun to flourish. His anger toward Captain Kirk flared, but he tamped it back down, knowing that he should not make his next decision based on emotion.

Except that emotion's all I have left, Sulu thought. He had love, but no one with whom to share it. Love, but no lover.

Sulu regarded *Enterprise*. He did not want to go back there. And yet he knew he must.

Sulu turned from the port and headed for the nearest turbolift. He would ride the car to one of Starbase 25's transporter rooms. Then he would beam over to *Enterprise* one last time.

Twelve

Kirk sat at the desk in his quarters, staring across the cabin to where his alpha-shift helmsman stood. Sulu had arrived unannounced a few moments earlier and asked to speak with the captain. It marked the first time that Kirk had seen him since the lieutenant's outburst in the turbolift—an incident the captain had been content to leave in the past, unreported and un-addressed.

Since appearing at the door to Kirk's cabin, Sulu had conducted himself courteously, if formally. He respectfully declined to take a seat, stating his prefer-ence to stand. He indicated that what he wished to discuss would not require much time.

On the day after Trinh had suffered her injuries, Sulu had appealed for emergency leave, submitting his request through Spock. The captain normally would have spoken with an officer asking for time away from his duties, but it seemed eminently clear that the lieutenant wished to avoid interacting with his com-manding officer as much as possible. Kirk approved the request, choosing to ignore the obvious fact that Sulu still blamed him for what had happened to Trinh.

The captain understood his anger, even felt it justified, although he also knew that there would have to be at least a professional rapprochement when the lieutenant returned to his position.

Kirk presumed that Sulu's visit related to his emergency leave, and perhaps to a proposed timetable for him to resume his duties, though it also seemed possible that he might instead ask to extend his time away from the ship. The captain had received regular medical reports from Doctor McCoy during the time Trinh had spent in sickbay, and then from Doctor Rellan aboard Starbase 25 once the A-and-A officer had been transferred to the station's infirmary. According to both McCoy and Rellan, Sulu had devoted virtually all of his waking hours to visiting Trinh, even at those times when she had not been conscious and awake. The doctors unanimously agreed that no hope existed for Trinh to ever fully recover, and so Kirk had no notion of precisely when Sulu would want to come back to *Enterprise*.

"What can I do for you, Mister Sulu?" the captain said. He took care with his words and tone, wanting neither to antagonize the lieutenant by being forceful with him, nor to encourage further insubordination by treading too lightly. And truly, Kirk empathized with Sulu. He did not blame the man for the antipathy he'd expressed toward him, but the captain had to maintain discipline aboard ship, specifically in the overall service of safeguarding the crew.

"Captain, I'm here because . . ." Sulu's words, barely started, trailed off. The helmsman looked away, apparently unsure of what he wanted to say—or perhaps *how* he wanted to say it. Kirk waited. Finally, Sulu peered back over at him and said, "I'm here because I can no longer function effectively as a Starfleet officer aboard this ship."

"What?" Kirk said, surprised by the declaration. He leaned forward in his chair, his arms poised against the edge of the desk. "I'm afraid I can't agree with that assessment, Lieutenant."

"It's not a question of assessing the matter, Captain," Sulu said. "It is a statement of fact."

Kirk shook his head. "I don't see it, Mister Sulu. You're a fine officer. You've served this ship with distinction. I see no reason to believe that will change."

Sulu paused and took a deep breath. "I beg your pardon, Captain," he said, though he did not sound apologetic. "I didn't say that I wasn't an effective officer; I said that I could no longer be one aboard *this* ship."

"I see," Kirk said, realizing that the lieutenant's anger toward him had not abated at all. Sulu seemed to be challenging him, a situation the captain needed to defuse. He pushed back from his desk and stood up, wanting to face the helmsman on an equal footing. "That's not really the case either, is it?" Kirk said. "It's not that you believe you can't serve well aboard the *Enterprise*; it's that you've decided that you no longer wish to serve under my command."

"This is not a matter of making a decision," Sulu said. "It simply is what it is."

"Because of what happened down on the planet?" Kirk said, injecting a sympathetic note into his voice. "Because of what happened to Ensign Trinh?"

Sulu hesitated, then said, "I have no desire to discuss this on the record."

Kirk believed the lieutenant's assertion, but he also thought it demonstrated confusion in Sulu's emotional state. "Why not?" the captain asked. He circled out from behind his desk and stepped in front of Sulu. "If you truly believe I acted irresponsibly, that I *unnecessarily* endangered members of the *Enterprise* crew, then why not make a formal report? Why not go to Starfleet Command with it?" Kirk thought he knew the answers to those questions: Sulu would not raise the issue of the captain's recklessness because he did not genuinely believe the captain had acted that way.

The lieutenant stared at Kirk, but said nothing.

"You don't have an answer?" the captain said. Then, wanting Sulu to consider his own feelings, and sincerely hoping to learn the truth himself, he asked, "Could it possibly be that I'm just a convenient target for your anger right now?"

"There's nothing 'convenient' about this situation," Sulu said, his voice dropped to a very low tone. "But I have other matters to concern me besides how Starfleet Command allows you to captain this starship."

The response disappointed Kirk. He took a few paces away before turning back to the lieutenant. "So why are you here, then?" he asked. "To resign your commission?"

"No," Sulu said at once. "I want to transfer to another ship."

"And what reason will you give?" Kirk wanted to know.

"I don't wish to make my personal reasoning a formal part of my request," Sulu said. "I believe that there is no requirement that I do so."

"No, there isn't," Kirk agreed, "but without a compelling justification, your request might be denied."

"It might be," Sulu said. "I guess that will mostly be up to you."

"That's right," Kirk said. "And I don't want to lose a good officer, and a good man."

Sulu nodded, but the movement seemed absent of meaning. "Transfer is my first choice," he said, "but resignation is also an option."

"Sulu . . ." Kirk said, searching for the right way to speak with him.

"In the meantime," Sulu went on, "I've already completed a request for transfer. Once I leave here, I intend to submit it, both to you and to Starfleet Command."

Feeling that he'd botched the entire conversation and wanting to make it right—wanting to bring it to a different conclusion—the captain crossed the cabin again to face Sulu at close range. Emotion roiled within Kirk, and he opted to let it show. He reached up and put his hands on the outsides of Sulu's upper arms, a gesture he meant to express the esteem and friendship he felt for him. "Sulu," he said, and then reconsidered. "Hikaru," he began again, "I understand the seriousness of this situation, of everything that's transpired." Kirk thought of the woman he had loved more than any other, the woman he'd wanted to spend the rest of his life with, and how he'd had no choice but to allow her to die. The light had left her eyes right in front of him, and so he really did understand so much of what Sulu felt. "There's no need to do this. We've served together on the *Enterprise* for almost five years. You know me as the captain of this ship, and I think you know me as more than that. What happened to Ensign Trinh . . . what happened to Ensign Trinh was a terrible thing, but nothing can change that. What you're feeling right now, though, that *will* change."

Sulu looked at Kirk for a long time. The captain waited, hoping that he'd gotten through to him. It seemed as though he had, and—

"No, Captain," Sulu said. "I'm going to do this."

Kirk dropped his hands from Sulu's arms. "I'm sorry to hear that," he said. He paced back across the cabin and sat behind his desk. "You're dismissed, Lieutenant."

Sulu left without another word. Kirk watched him

go, and continued staring at the door of his cabin even after it had closed behind the lieutenant. The captain could deny Sulu's transfer request, or if he wanted to push the responsibility off onto somebody else, he could approve it, but ask Starfleet Command to deny it. He felt sure he could contact Admiral Ciana to make sure that the transfer didn't go through.

But he wouldn't do that. Even with all the pain Sulu clearly felt clouding his judgment, even with his mistakenly blaming Kirk for Trinh's injuries, the lieutenant deserved the respect he had earned. The captain would approve his transfer, and he would make sure that Command did so as well.

The only thing Kirk wondered was whether or not he would ever see Hikaru Sulu again.

Pillagra

III

Thirteen

Sulu glanced at the chronometer on the top right of the engineering console he manned. It pleased him to see that only ten minutes remained in alpha shift. As had become his habit of late, he looked forward to leaving the bridge.

Before he could do that, though, he needed to complete his calibrations on the helm of *Courageous*. During the observation and investigation of a proto-nebula a week earlier, the ship had been buffeted by plasma surges. *Courageous* appeared to weather the storm with no ill effects, but when Sulu took the helm several days later—a task he rarely performed since his transfer—he noticed a sluggishness in its response. He brought it to the attention of the alpha-shift helm officer, a Tellarite woman named Teglas, but the lieu-tenant had initially been unable even to measure any variance. Over the course of the next few days, Sulu had worked with her, first to precisely define the prob-lem, and then to resolve it.

Earlier that shift, with helm operations routed to a peripheral station, Teglas had installed the fix, which had included replacing two duotronic components in the main console, as well as upgrading its firmware. After that, the only remaining task had been to recalibrate the updated panel. Sulu had taken on that job, which he'd nearly completed.

"Captain, long-range sensors are detecting a warp signature," said Ensign Trenna from the primary science console. Sulu peered over at the Vulcan to see her operating her controls with elegant precision.

As the captain, Michael Caulder, looked over from the command chair at Trenna, the first officer, Jordan Costley, walked from his station over to the primary science console. Leaning in over Trenna's shoulder to look at her monitors, Costley said, "It's a big one. Or maybe several little ones."

"Track it back to see if you can find out where it might have come from," Caulder ordered.

"Yes, sir," Trenna said.

Costley stood back up and moved over to the vacant secondary science station. "I'll take a look the other way," he said. "Maybe we can see where they're headed."

As Trenna and Costley worked the ship's sensors, Sulu returned to his calibrations. He'd already executed a pair of diagnostic tests on the updated helm, and then made necessary adjustments. He hoped that his third diagnostic, which had only a few more minutes left to run, would confirm fully restored helm function. Until then, Sulu watched intermediate results reveal themselves on his readouts, and he hunted among them for any potential inconsistencies.

"Captain," said Trenna, "the warp vessel's path has taken it through some of the R-Seven-Hundred sectors." Sulu turned in his seat at the mention of that particular region of space. It had been on a planet there that he had almost been killed by a missile. "We're too distant to know whether or not the vessel originated in one of those sectors or only passed through them."

"I don't have the same difficulty on the other end," announced Costley. "We're too far to pick up detail on the vessel itself, but I can see that it's passing through the R-Eight-Hundred sectors."

R-Eight-Hundred! Sulu thought, the designation screaming through his head. And before he could avoid thinking about it: *R-Eight-Three-Six!* On the second planet in that system, Trinh—

But he couldn't think about that. Except that, in truth, he still thought about little else. During the two months he'd served aboard *Courageous*, he'd kept in touch with Trinh's mother, Nguyen Thi Yeh. She sent him sporadic subspace messages about Trinh, whose condition had not improved since her return to Mars. Yeh did not provide much detail in her communications, but she always mentioned her gratitude to him for filling her daughter's life with joy, and for then letting her go. Sulu still had trouble reconciling his actions with something positive; he still felt that he'd abandoned the woman he loved when she'd needed him most.

"Log it," Captain Caulder said. "Bundle the sensor readings and transmit them to Starfleet Command and Starfleet Operations."

"Captain," Sulu said, and it surprised him to see not just Caulder, but every crew member on the bridge turn toward him.

"Lieutenant?" Caulder asked.

Sulu stood up and padded to the center of the bridge. "Captain, the *Enterprise* crew had some adversarial encounters with several vessels out in those sectors, but failed to establish communication with the alien crews. Perhaps it would be a good idea for us to find out where they come from and where they're headed."

The captain—a tall man with a barrel chest and shoulder-length blond hair, along with a full beard and mustache—looked at him for a moment without saying a word. "I'm sorry, Lieutenant," he finally said. "I must've misheard you. You couldn't possibly have suggested that we pursue an unknown alien vessel across sectors of space."

"I . . . I know it'd be an unusual mission for us," Sulu admitted, "but there could be considerable value in being able to identify—"

"Lieutenant," the captain said, cutting him off. "It wouldn't be an 'unusual' mission for us; it would be an inappropriate one."

"Sir, I know—"

"Lieutenant," the captain said again, his deep

voice growing firmer. "I know you were accustomed to serving on the *Enterprise,* but this isn't a *Constitution*-class starship. We're a small ship on a scientific research mission. We're not heavily armed, we're not all that fast, and we have a crew comprising mostly scientists."

Sulu wanted to respond. He wanted to explain his thinking to the captain, and to try to impress upon him the importance of learning whatever they could about what had already proven a threat to the Federation. He knew, though, that Captain Caulder would not listen.

"Am I understood?" the captain asked him.

"Yes, sir," Sulu said.

"Good." Caulder stood up to his impressive height—he easily stood two full meters tall—and looked over at Costley. "Commander," he said, "we're almost at the change of shift. You'll make the handover to Pearson for me?"

"Yes, sir," Costley said.

"Very good," Caulder said. He offered Sulu a final, reproachful glance, then marched into the turbolift.

Once the captain had gone, Sulu returned to the engineering station. There, he resumed monitoring the intermediate results of his latest diagnostic. Behind him, he heard the beta-shift personnel arrive and relieve their alpha-shift counterparts. Because of Sulu's position on *Courageous*—relief helmsman, mathematician, and second officer—no supernumerary needed to take over for him.

What was I doing? the lieutenant asked himself. He'd transferred to *Courageous* from *Enterprise* because he could not tolerate Captain Kirk unnecessarily risking the lives of his crew, and yet Sulu had just suggested to Captain Caulder that he order their science vessel to trail a ship potentially crewed by dangerous aliens. *Aliens who already damaged a* Constitution-*class starship and caused the deaths of several crew members,* he thought. *Aliens who stole Trinh from me.*

Sulu had initially been surprised by Caulder's reaction to him, but upon reflection, it seemed justified. *Is that the type of starship captain I'd be?* he thought. *Racing my vessel and crew into harm's way without a second thought?* The idea disgusted him.

A tone on the engineering panel chirped, and Sulu saw that the diagnostic had at last finished running, confirming the accuracy of his calibrations to the helm. Thankful that he wouldn't have to remain on the bridge, he secured the station and started for the turbolift. In the center of the bridge, Costley handed a data slate to Ensign Pearson, then apparently finished speaking with him. Sulu stepped into the turbolift, and the first officer followed him inside.

When the doors had slipped closed behind them, Costley reached for the activation wand, then looked over at Sulu. "Where are you headed, Lieutenant?" he asked. "Anything on your agenda for tonight?"

"Just to my cabin," Sulu said. "I'll have some dinner, maybe catch up on some correspondence."

Costley nodded slowly, almost as though he didn't believe what Sulu had told him. Though taller than the lieutenant, the first officer did not reach anywhere near the height of the captain, nor did he fill out his uniform as broadly. Sulu thought of him as lanky.

In the odd silence of the turbolift—the cars always hummed while in operation, but Costley hadn't yet specified any destination—Sulu realized his own poor manners. The first officer had asked him about his evening, but Sulu hadn't reciprocated. "What about you, Commander?" he said, trying to sound as though he hadn't felt forced to pose the question.

"I thought I'd head down to the gym, maybe spar a little," Costley said. He raised both his fists and playfully punched at the air. "You wouldn't care to join me, would you?" The first officer sounded as though he already knew the answer to the question before he'd even asked it.

"No, thank you," Sulu said. "Sparring's not really one of my interests."

"No?" Costley said. "So what are you interested in?"

"Oh, well . . ." Sulu didn't want to say anything that would then get him invited to some other activity. "I guess I really don't have any."

Costley nodded. "Okay," he said. "Just thought I'd ask." He reached again for the activation wand and turned it. "Deck Three, then Deck Ten."

The car began to hum as it descended, but the atmosphere seemed awkward to Sulu. Trying to normalize it, he motioned toward the turbolift doors, and by extension, to the bridge. "He doesn't really like me very much, does he?"

Costley didn't pretend not to know what Sulu meant, but addressed the issue directly. "No, I don't think it's that the captain doesn't like you," he said.

Sulu snorted in disbelief. "No?" he said. "Then what is it?"

The first officer appeared to consider whether or not to say anything. "Look," he finally said, "this has to stay between you and me, but—"

The turbolift doors parted. Costley looked out into the corridor, then said, "We can talk about this another time."

Sulu took hold of the activation wand and ordered the turbolift to resume. The doors closed again, and the car continued down. "I'd prefer to talk about it now, if that's all right."

"Sure," Costley said. "What I was going to say is that it's not that the captain dislikes you; it's that I don't think he trusts you."

"What?" Sulu asked, shocked. He could far more easily understand somebody not liking him on sight, just based on a visceral first impression, but he knew of nothing he'd done that could have earned Caulder's distrust.

"Lieutenant, you've been aboard the *Courageous* for . . . what? Two months?" Sulu nodded. "Well, your shift just ended, and you're heading to your cabin to have dinner by yourself."

"I didn't say I'd be alone," Sulu bristled.

Costley's eyebrows rose on his narrow face. "*Are* you having company?" he asked.

"No," Sulu admitted sheepishly. He wondered why he'd feigned indignation when the first officer had said nothing untrue.

Costley shrugged. "You're not even eating in the mess. I have to say, Lieutenant, it even seems . . . note-worthy . . . to me that you're not making any friends here. You don't even seem to be trying."

"I wasn't aware that was a requirement of service," Sulu said.

"It's not a requirement, of course," Costley said, "but . . . it *is* natural. Hell, even Trenna and Teglas are friends—a Vulcan and a Tellarite—and that's not usually the way to get a party started."

"I guess I didn't come here to make friends," Sulu said.

"Why *did* you come here?" Costley asked. Before Sulu could reply, the turbolift once more slowed to a stop and the doors opened. Costley stepped out of the car onto Deck 10, but then he reached back and held an arm out to prevent the lift doors from closing. "I'm not being facetious or rhetorical; I really want to know."

Sulu debated with himself for a moment—*Do I really want to have this conversation?*—then exited the turbolift. As the doors shut behind him, he peered down the corridor. He saw several of the crew, but nobody within earshot. Looking back at Costley, he said, "Before I transferred here, I was a helmsman and a third officer. Now I'm a second officer. I've moved up in the food chain."

"Yeah, but you dropped down in weight class," Costley said, which Sulu took as a boxing metaphor. "I mean, I love the *Courageous,* but you served on the *Enterprise.* And under Captain Kirk." At the mention of the captain's name, Sulu felt his jaw tense. He forced himself to relax, but apparently too late to avoid the first officer's notice.

"Oh," Costley said. "You know, Lieutenant, the only things in the universe that travel faster than light in normal space are rumors."

Sulu's stomach clenched. "You heard something?" he asked. "About me? About Captain Kirk?"

"The talk is that you threw him out an airlock," Costley said.

Sulu understood the idiom: people believed he'd sacrificed Captain Kirk's good name out of self-interest. "What exactly did you hear?" he asked.

"I heard that you reported him to Starfleet Command and demanded a transfer," Costley said.

"That's not what happened," Sulu said. "And what did I supposedly report him for?" Then he realized that it didn't matter, because he had taken no such action. *I mean, I did essentially force Captain Kirk to transfer me, but—* He wondered if Kirk himself had started the rumor, but he couldn't imagine that being the case.

"I never heard what you supposedly reported him for," Costley said, "and I don't think that Captain Caulder did either, but I think that's another reason he might be having trouble trusting you."

Sulu raised a hand to the back of his neck and rubbed it for a moment. "Do I need to have a talk with the captain?" he asked.

"No, I don't think that would help," Costley said. "But I'll say something to him. Nothing on the record, just conversationally."

"I'd appreciate it," Sulu said.

Costley shrugged. "I'm the ship's first officer," he said. "It's part of my job to boost morale. Can I give you some advice, though?"

"Sure," Sulu said. He didn't actually want to hear any of the first officer's suggestions—or anybody's suggestions, for that matter—but he thought it would be blatantly rude to say so.

"Don't spend all your off-duty hours in your cabin," Costley urged him. "We're a relatively small crew, we're out here studying astronomical objects and phenomena, but believe it or not, we're a fun group.

You might find that you'll like some of us. Maybe even many of us."

Sulu thought about that. He certainly hadn't been looking for fun in his life when he'd transferred to *Courageous,* but he thought that the first officer made a larger point. Sulu had officially joined the *Courageous* crew, but he hadn't actually become a part of that crew. He really didn't want to become a part of a crew. *Or a part of anything,* he thought. But that didn't mean that he shouldn't.

"Did you say that you were going to the gym to spar?" Sulu asked.

"Yeah," Costley said. "And you're still invited to tag along."

"Thanks," Sulu said. "I'd like that."

Fourteen

Jim Kirk perused the hardcover volumes that ran along the shelf above his bed. The day before, he'd finished Derivon Sanger's *Declaration Red*, a compelling tale of a man's struggles to survive the War of Martian Independence. The captain had been forced to read the novel on his data slate, though, rather than in hard copy; since the book had been published only recently, physical editions hadn't made their way out to the edges of the Federation—and certainly not *beyond* UFP space. Kirk preferred the feel of a book in his hands, the sound of a page turning, the smell of the paper—all prejudices he'd learned from his mother, who had so loved to read. With the critical notices *Declaration Red* had received, though, and considering his interest in the subject matter and the pedigree of its seventh-generation Martian author, the captain hadn't wanted to wait.

Just back in his cabin after dinner with Bones and two frustrating games of three-dimensional chess with Spock—Kirk's intuitional gambits didn't always win the day—he decided to start not only another novel but an actual *book*. Although he had several yet to read, editions he'd picked up a couple of months ago on Starbase 25, he gravitated instead to a volume he'd already made his way through a number of times: *David Copperfield*. He slid the handsome volume from the shelf—it had been a gift from his aunt on his fourteenth birthday—settled himself onto his bed, and cracked open Charles Dickens's masterpiece. He had read only the brilliant first line—*Whether I shall turn out to be the hero of my own life, or whether that station will be held by anybody else, these pages must show*—when the boatswain's whistle interrupted.

"Bridge to Captain Kirk," followed the voice of Lieutenant Palmer, the beta-shift communications officer.

The captain tapped the intercom button by his bed. "Kirk here. Go ahead, Lieutenant."

"Captain, we're receiving a transmission from the Procyon, *an* Antares-*class transport,"* Palmer said. *"It's from Admiral Ciana."*

Admiral Ciana? Kirk thought. He flipped *David Copperfield* closed, swung his legs off the bed, and bounded to his feet. While he didn't always relish hearing from Starfleet Command—and he supposed that they didn't always relish hearing from him—he had to admit a sense of anticipation in speaking with Lori Ciana again. During their brief meeting when *Enterprise* had been moored at Starbase 25, she had charmed him.

"Pipe it down to my quarters, Lieutenant," he said. "*Aye, sir.*"

"Kirk out." He closed the intercom channel.

The captain set his book down on the bed, then made his way around the half wall separating the two sections of his quarters and over to his desk. He sat down there, then reached forward and activated the monitor on the desktop. The skewed chevron of the *Enterprise*'s emblem appeared on the screen, then blinked off, replaced by the image of the commander in chief's aide.

"Admiral Ciana," Kirk said, "it's good to see you again." He noticed the slightly wild look of her silver-blond hair and wondered if she'd just been awakened for some reason.

"*It's good to see you, Captain Kirk,*" she said. She spoke easily, in a manner that did not suggest she had contacted him out of exigency. "*I hope you've been well.*" She paused very briefly, then added, "*You certainly look well.*"

Despite his perception that Ciana had flirted with him during their first meeting, the compliment surprised him—though he did not object to it. "Thank you," he said. "I can clearly say the same for you."

"*Can you now?*" Ciana said. "*I bet you say that to all the admirals.*"

"No, not to all of them," Kirk said through a grin he couldn't entirely control. "Only to you and Admiral

Walkowski." Considered something of an institution within Starfleet, Louis Walkowski had recently celebrated his seventh decade in the service. Though still vital, he had lived a quarter of the way into his second century and looked twice his age.

Ciana laughed, a warm sound with a musical lilt to it. *"Flatterer."*

Kirk's grin grew broader. "So tell me, Admiral, to what do I owe this pleasure?" he said. "Am I being reassigned already?" He asked the question lightly, but he valued anything at all he could learn about the future course of his Starfleet career. After all, a mere three months remained of *Enterprise*'s five-year mission.

"No, not yet," Ciana said, her tone becoming serious.

"I had hoped Starfleet Command might inform me in advance of my next posting," Kirk said. "Or my continuation at *this* posting."

"That's reasonable to expect," Ciana said. *"Especially for somebody with your service record. But you know how . . . bureaucratic . . . Starfleet Command can be. I know how Admiral Nogura feels about the work you've done aboard the* Enterprise*—and I think you do too—but I'm not as sure about some of the other admirals."*

Kirk accepted Ciana's comments at face value. He didn't want to contradict her, but he actually didn't feel that he knew Nogura's mind about his situation, no matter what Admiral Ciana had told him. The commander in chief had a deserved reputation as a hard, often inscrutable leader, though most also considered him fair.

"*I will keep my eyes and ears open, though,*" Ciana continued. "*I'll try to find out something credible for you, Captain, if not definitive. I know you want to stay out there exploring the depths of space, and even to the casual observer, that's clearly where you belong.*"

"Thank you, Admiral."

"*Although,*" Ciana said, tilting her head down slightly, "*I have to believe that you would enjoy being stationed at Starfleet Headquarters.*"

The comment seemed almost coquettish to Kirk, though perhaps he'd misinterpreted the admiral. Still, he felt his cheeks coloring. "San Francisco is a beautiful city," he said. Unsure what more to say, though, he decided to turn his attention to other matters. "But I'm sure you're not contacting me to talk about the City by the Bay."

"*No, unfortunately not,*" Ciana said. "*A science vessel conducting astrophysical research near the Federation border has reported the detection of a considerable warp signature belonging to a ship, or possibly several ships, traversing some of the R-Seven-Hundred and into the R-Eight-Hundred sectors.*"

"Did any of the ships match the configuration of

those that attacked the *Enterprise* at R-Eight-Three-Six?" Kirk asked.

"The science vessel, the Courageous, *was too distant to determine such details,"* Ciana said. *"But Starfleet Tactical analyzed their sensor readings, and while they couldn't positively ascertain the configuration of the ships, they were able to conclude that the magnitude of the warp signature resulted from an aggregate reading of six to eight separate vessels."*

"But you can't identify whether they're friend, foe, or stranger," Kirk said.

"No," Ciana said, *"but the warp signature comprises the drive output of enough ships that they would have to be relatively small."*

"Smaller than those that attacked the *Enterprise*?"

"Yes," Ciana said. *"In fact, Starfleet Tactical believes that the size of the ships might match the size of the warp ships that you and your crew found outside the cities in the R-Seven-Seven-Five and R-Eight-Three-Six systems."*

Kirk nodded, seeing the conclusion that Tactical had obviously reached. "Starfleet thinks that these vessels might be part of another colonization effort?" he said.

"We think it's a strong possibility," Ciana said. *"Command has therefore decided that they want it investigated. The* Enterprise *is the closest ship."*

"What's our mission?" Kirk wanted to know.

"*First, investigate,*" Ciana said. "*Determine whether or not the ships belong to whoever attacked the Enterprise. If they do, then do not engage, and immediately report back to Starfleet.*"

"And if they're not the attackers?" Kirk asked. "If they are colonists?"

"*Make contact,*" Ciana said. "*And if they're the same people who built the two destroyed cities you discovered, then warn them about what happened, if they don't already know. If you perceive that the destruction of the two cities was an internal matter, then tread lightly and bring that information back to Starfleet Command.*"

"Understood," Kirk said.

"*Because of the obvious dangers in those sectors, Command wanted to send you backup, but there aren't many Starfleet vessels near your position.*" Continuing on its mission of exploration, *Enterprise* had traveled outside of Federation space. "*I'm able to communicate with you because I'm traveling between starbases, on the* Procyon, *in the region of the Federation that your ship is closest to. But she's a transport that's unable to provide you any cover or support. We're sending the* Courageous *and the* Lexington *your way, but the latter won't arrive for at least two weeks.*"

"Do you want the *Enterprise* to wait?" Kirk asked.

"*No,*" Ciana said. "*Because the cities you found were built and destroyed so recently, we believe that time may be a factor here. If these are colonists settling on an*

*empty world, we want to help them avoid the fate of the
other two cities. You'll rendezvous with the* Courageous
*in seventy-two hours, at coordinates I've packaged with
this transmission."*

"Understood, Admiral," Kirk said. "Is there anything else?"

"No," Ciana said. *"Except . . . be careful, Jim."*

Again, the admiral surprised Kirk—she had called
him by his given name—and again, he did not object.
"Thank you, Lori."

She offered him a smile, then said, *"Ciana out."*
She reached forward and the screen went dark. Kirk
thumbed the monitor off, then activated the intercom.

"Kirk to bridge."

"Bridge here, Captain," replied Lieutenant Palmer.

"Lieutenant, have you received a set of coordinates
from Admiral Ciana?" Kirk asked.

"Aye, sir," Palmer said. *"The admiral appended them
to her communication."*

"Very good," Kirk said, and then, "Lieutenant
Arex."

"Yes, sir," replied one of the ship's relief navigators.
Kirk knew that the month's duty roster positioned
Arex as the beta-shift bridge officer.

"Set course for those coordinates," Kirk ordered.
"Adjust speed so that the *Enterprise* will arrive there in
seventy-two hours."

"Yes, sir," said Arex.

"Kirk out." The captain closed the channel, then sat

back in his chair. He thought for just a moment about what would happen to his career in three months, and then for another moment about Admiral Ciana. *Lori.* But then he put all of that out of his mind and started thinking about the R-800 sectors and what his crew would find there.

He did not pick up *David Copperfield* again that night.

Fifteen

Sulu sat at the helm of *Courageous* and cursed his luck, not for the first time. Directly in front of him, the main viewscreen displayed the image of Captain Kirk standing in the center of the *Enterprise* bridge. Sulu had transferred out from under Kirk's command specifically so that he would no longer have to take orders from the man responsible for—

Stop it! Sulu told himself. It didn't matter that he found himself on a mission with Captain Kirk again. It didn't even matter that Starfleet Command had placed Kirk in charge of the mission. Sulu would perform his duties as required, and soon enough, *Courageous* and *Enterprise* would go their separate ways.

The two ships had arrived a day earlier at the edge of the R-800 sectors. Together, the crews of *Courageous* and *Enterprise* conducted methodical sensor sweeps, seeking out any indications of warp activity in the region. It didn't take long. Within twelve hours, the crews tracked half a dozen drive signatures, all leading to an unexplored star system that Starfleet called R-855.

The two crews had traveled to the system and then

entered it cautiously, using its gas giants to conceal their approach. Once there, scans revealed a squadron of ships—nearly two dozen—orbiting the third planet, an M-class world. The configuration of the vessels did not match those that had attacked *Enterprise*, and for that, Sulu felt grateful. The anger he felt toward Captain Kirk could not match the absolute rage he harbored for those who had assaulted an *Enterprise* landing party with missiles.

"Our sensors show that they're all warp-capable vessels, despite their relatively small size," Captain Caulder said from where he sat in the command chair.

Kirk nodded. *"They also appear similar to the vessels we discovered disabled or destroyed outside the two dead cities,"* he said.

"Most of them are carrying either agricultural, construction, or electronic supplies," Caulder said, "in addition to some heavy machinery we haven't yet been able to positively identify, but that we think may relate to power generation."

On the viewscreen, Captain Kirk peered up at his first officer, who stood beside him. *"All infrastructural elements for a society,"* Spock said.

"But not nearly enough for a city the size you found on the two planets," Caulder noted. "I've reviewed your reports, Captain Kirk, and they suggest likely populations of between one hundred and two hundred thousand inhabitants."

"They may just be starting," Kirk suggested.

"Or just finishing," offered Commander Costley, standing up from where he'd been sitting at one of the bridge's science stations.

"If those vessels are indeed supporting the construction of a new city," Spock said, *"the builders may be anywhere along the construction cycle. It may be the case that the number of ships employed in their efforts does not reflect the ultimate extent of the city, but simply the number of ships the builders have available to them."*

Although he'd had no intention of speaking, another thought occurred to Sulu. "Based on the observations of the *Enterprise* crew in the two lost cities," he said, "we know that those warp ships land. It may be that there are additional ships on the surface."

"Perhaps," Kirk said. He reached up and wrapped a hand around the front of his jaw and absently rubbed his chin, a gesture Sulu had seen him make numerous times. He looked pensive for a few seconds, then seemed to arrive at either a conclusion or a decision. *"Captain Caulder,"* he said, *"from the evidence we have, I believe that these aliens are the same ones who constructed the other cities the* Enterprise *crew found, and I'm willing to bet that they're in the midst of building another one on the third planet in this system. I'd like to approach the planet and try to establish contact with them."*

"Do you want the *Courageous* to accompany the *Enterprise,*" Caulder asked, "or to hang back?"

As Kirk appeared to the consider the question, he stepped over to the *Enterprise*'s command chair and sat down. *"Let's approach together,"* he said. *"We're going to be making first contact, so I don't want to take any actions that could be construed as duplicitous. There are a lot of ships in this system, and more may be coming. If the* Courageous *is discovered hiding, it could give the wrong impression of our intentions."*

"I understand, Captain," Caulder said.

"We'll travel at full impulse," Kirk said. *"Captain Caulder, keep the* Courageous *on our starboard flank. Lieutenant Uhura will open hailing frequencies and attempt to make contact. Monitor our communications."*

"Yes, Captain," Caulder said.

"Kirk out."

Sulu felt relieved as the image of Captain Kirk vanished from the viewscreen, replaced by a head-on view of *Enterprise*. As he watched, the *Constitution*-class starship rolled to starboard and started toward the planet. Captain Caulder ordered Ensign Riordan to monitor communications on all frequencies, then called out Sulu's name. "Put us fifteen hundred meters off the *Enterprise*'s starboard flank and match its speed," he said.

"Aye, aye, sir," Sulu said. He operated his controls, working to properly position *Courageous* and accelerate to the correct velocity. The day had not been comfortable for Sulu to that point, but as he moved *Courageous* through the R-855 system, he noticed the responsiveness of the helm and felt a moment's pride for a measurable contribution he'd made to his new ship.

Kirk rose from the command chair as *Enterprise* approached the third planet in the system. He watched the blue-and-white marble grow to fill the screen, and he tried to pick out the forms of the vessels in orbit. Before he could, Spock spoke up from his science station.

"Captain, our presence within the system has been detected," he said. "The ships above the planet are breaking orbit and heading in our direction."

"Thank you, Mister Spock," Kirk said. "Lieutenant Uhura, open hailing frequencies."

The captain heard the snap of buttons being pressed behind him. "Hailing frequencies open."

"This is Captain James T. Kirk of the *U.S.S. Enterprise*," he said. "We represent the United Federation of Planets and come in peace." He waited for a response, but received none. He repeated his greeting, and when no reply came, he said, "Uhura?"

"Nothing, sir," said the lieutenant. "They are receiving us; they're simply not responding."

"Captain," Lieutenant Rahda said at the helm, "I'm detecting five more vessels lifting off from the planet's surface."

"Sensors can now confirm the presence of a city there," Spock said. "It is roughly the same dimensions as the other two we have investigated in this region . . . but it is intact." He paused, and Kirk glanced across the bridge to see his first officer bent over his hooded viewer. "The city appears to be largely complete, but for a section on its northern end, which is evidently still under construction. I'm reading a population of approximately thirty-seven thousand."

"Captain," Lieutenant Rahda said, "the vessels are converging on the *Enterprise* and the *Courageous*."

"Magnify," Kirk said. The image on the main viewer jumped, and a section of the planet expanded to fill the entire screen. Visible against that backdrop, numerous ships advanced on *Enterprise*. Though not all of the same design, they seemed mostly similar: wedge-shaped craft that narrowed from stern to bow, with a blunt nose and a pair of nacelles depending from the main body.

"The vessels appear to be powering their weapons, though they're not yet in range to be able to use them," Rahda reported. "Should I raise the shields?"

"Weapons?" Kirk said. "Spock, I thought the one ship we were able to examine in the first city didn't have weapons."

"It possessed only a relatively low-yield laser cannon," Spock said, "which we counted more as a tool than as a weapon, since it would prove ineffective against the *Enterprise* if employed as an armament."

"Those are the types of weapons I'm reading," Rahda said as she peered into her scanner. "Laser-based."

"How ineffective, Spock?" Kirk said.

"Without shields, the *Enterprise* could suffer some minor external damage from the lasers," the first officer said, "but it would take a prolonged attack from numerous ships to pose a serious risk. The *Courageous* does have some sensitive scientific equipment on its hull, though, which the lasers could harm or even destroy."

"Lieutenant Rahda, let's leave our shields down for the moment, and our own weapons off line," Kirk said. "The *Enterprise* doesn't appear to be in any danger, and I don't want to appear provocative." He turned to face the communications station. "Uhura, contact Captain Caulder," he said. "Have him raise his shields, but for right now, make sure he keeps his weapons powered down."

"Aye, sir," Uhura said.

Kirk waited as *Enterprise* and *Courageous* approached the planet and the squadron of alien vessels. He heard Uhura speaking with Captain Caulder, but kept his attention focused on the main viewscreen. Suddenly, a vivid blue beam streaked out from one of the ships. *Enterprise* trembled momentarily.

"Direct hit," Rahda said. "No damage."

"Let's try this again," Kirk said. "Uhura, hailing frequencies."

"Hailing frequencies open," the lieutenant said.

"This is Captain James T. Kirk, commanding the *U.S.S. Enterprise* and representing the United Federation of Planets," he said. "We mean you no harm and seek only to open a dialogue."

Kirk waited. "Still nothing," Uhura said.

All at once, lasers shot from every vessel on the viewscreen. *Enterprise* rocked far more dramatically than it had with the first strike. "Multiple direct hits on both the *Enterprise* and the *Courageous*," Rahda said. "I'm reading minor buckling on some of our outer plates. The shields of the *Courageous* are holding and the ship is unharmed."

Kirk sighed. "Raise shields," he said.

"Shields up," said Rahda. "They're firing again."

Kirk continued to watch the futile display of primitive firepower. With *Enterprise*'s shields raised, it became almost impossible to even perceive that the ship had been struck by weapons. The vessels fired again, and again. He waited, hoping that the aliens would recognize the clear advantage of *Enterprise*'s defenses and accept his invitation to talk.

"Sir, I have Captain Caulder for you," Uhura said.

"Put him on audio, Lieutenant," Kirk said, wanting to keep an eye on the alien vessels.

"Caulder to Enterprise."

"We read you, *Courageous*," Kirk said. "Go ahead."

"Captain, perhaps we need to demonstrate a show of force," Caulder said. *"Nothing to do any damage, more like*

a shot across their bow. Maybe a well-placed photon tor-
pedo detonating in front of them would get their attention."

Kirk glanced over at Spock, who arched an eyebrow in obvious disapproval. Kirk agreed. "Captain, I
think that, for now, the relative imperviousness of our
defensive screens to their weapons amply establishes
our military superiority. Resisting the temptation to
display our own weaponry may go a long way in suggesting our moral standards and the benignity of our
intentions."

"*I understand what you're saying, Captain,*" Caulder
said, "*but those crews have opened fire on us unpro-*
voked."

"I don't know, Captain," Kirk said. "Circumstances
suggest that these people have recently had two of
their cities destroyed, and now two unknown starships have entered the planetary system where they're
building a third. Perhaps that's provocation enough."

Caulder did not respond for a few seconds, but
then said, "*Acknowledged, Captain. Courageous will*
stand by for your orders."

"Thank you, Captain. Kirk out."

On the viewscreen, the alien vessels continued to
fire their laser cannons. Kirk crossed the bridge to
starboard and mounted the steps to the outer deck,
where he approached the main science station. "What
do you think, Spock? Does it seem reasonable that
they're attacking us on sight because of the recent destruction of at least two of their cities?"

"Fear can be a strong motivator to action," Spock said.

Kirk folded his arms across his chest and looked back at the viewscreen. The alien vessels continued to fire on the *Enterprise* and the *Courageous*. "At the moment, they seem quite single-minded. How do we get them to talk to us?"

"I believe that your decisions to keep the *Enterprise*'s shields down until we were fired upon, and to keep our weapons off line, make a compelling argument about our intentions," Spock said. "However, since the aliens have refused our attempts at communication, perhaps an additional, diplomatic act would be in order."

Kirk turned back to his first officer, pleased that Spock's thoughts echoed his own. "Exactly what I was thinking," he said. "How well would one of our shuttlecraft withstand the aliens' laser cannons?"

"The defensive screens of the shuttles are obviously smaller than those of the *Enterprise,* both in terms of size and strength, but they should withstand several such attacks," Spock asserted. "Having said that, I would not necessarily recommend sending a shuttlecraft into the field of fire. There are simply too many unknowns to be assured of complete safety."

"We have to do something, Spock," the captain said. "If I get into trouble out there, I can always return to the ship."

"Captain," Spock said, "it would not be appropriate

for you to pilot a shuttlecraft in these circumstances. The risk is too great."

"You just said that the risk is *unknown*," Kirk reminded his first officer. "And you said that a shuttle could stand up to these attacks."

"To a point," Spock said. "But what if the aliens attempt to take you hostage?"

"I won't let them get that close," Kirk said.

"And if the shuttlecraft's drive should become incapacitated?" the first officer persisted.

"You can always haul me back here with the tractor beam," Kirk said.

"I must point out that we have only just encountered these aliens and know virtually nothing about them," Spock said. "We do not know what they are capable of, either technologically or morally."

"Technologically, Spock?" the captain said. He pointed toward the viewscreen. "They're firing on us with laser cannons. It's not as though they're more advanced than the Federation."

"The aliens who attacked us in the R-Seven-Seven-Five and R-Eight-Three-Six systems attacked us with missiles, but also possessed warp-powered vessels more agile than the *Enterprise*. Technology can advance asymmetrically within a civilization."

"Duly noted," Kirk said. "But Spock, I've been charged by Starfleet Command to make a first contact. It is therefore appropriate that I be on that shuttle."

"And if something unforeseen happens and you are captured or killed?" Spock asked.

"In that case, I will have failed," Kirk said. "Take the *Enterprise* and the *Courageous* back to Starbase Twenty-Five and make a full report to Starfleet Command."

"Yes, sir," Spock said.

"You have the bridge," Kirk said. He followed the curve of the outer deck around to the turbolift. As the doors parted, Spock called after him.

"Captain," he said. When Kirk stopped and looked back, Spock said, "Be careful, Jim."

Kirk entered the lift, and the doors closed behind him. He noted with mild amusement that Spock had used the same words that Admiral Ciana had when she'd ordered him on the current mission. Kirk thought that he would need to exercise more caution when it came to dealing with Starfleet Command about his career than would be necessary with the aliens firing on *Enterprise*.

The captain took hold of the lift's activation wand and stated his destination: "Hangar deck."

Zeden Pego felt the icy touch of terror stealing up his spine. When he peered down at the external-sensor readout, that feeling intensified. The panel, one of many set into the surface of the trapezoidal instrument table in the middle of the similarly shaped control center, showed activity he didn't quite understand.

But then, I don't understand much these days, do I?

When they'd recently received word that the second colony had been lost—apparently destroyed by the same unknown faction that had destroyed the first—morale had plummeted, both on the support ships and down on the planet's surface. Governor Velura and the other leaders debated whether or not to abandon their new city—Pillagra—and return home. Emotions ran both ways, with some wanting to choose discretion over their pioneering dreams.

For Zeden, the choice had been based on practical concerns, and had therefore been simple. The three fleets of ships hauling the equipment and other materials to establish the various colonies had all left home around the same time. They each traveled significantly different distances to their colony sites, and thus for significantly different spans of time. Zeden's convoy arrived at their site last, hundreds of days after the first convoy reached theirs.

The building of Pillagra had begun immediately, with a focus on making provisions for basic needs. Once that had been accomplished, the fleet of personnel transports—already done with their work at the first two colonies—began to appear in orbit, delivering thousands of colonists at a time. Those colonists in turn joined in the continuing construction of the new city. Overall, the relocation of so many citizens would require multiple trips, and though many more colonists were on their way, the effort to that point had already taken half a year; evacuating them from Pillagra would take just as much time, and also demand the turning back of the next transports already en route. Zeden agreed with the community's decision to remain.

Or at least I did, he thought, not without a note of bitterness. As he looked at the three other crew members in the control center, and as they all faced the possible ends of their lives, he reconsidered. It suddenly seemed foolhardy to have allowed practicality to drive a decision about life and death.

More than the logistics of vacating Pillagra and going back to their homeworld, though, the idea of abandoning the colony offended many. People did not wish to leave a place that they had made together, that so many had struggled to build. When they had chosen to be colonists and to construct something new, they had brought their hearts with them.

Zeden studied the confusing readings on the sensor panel and tried to tamp down his fear. He did not worry about himself—although he had no wish to perish just yet—but about all of the people in his charge. The support vessels that had come to the new planet did not carry soldiers; for the most part, other than their crews, they transported artisans and craftspeople, builders of the physical, guardians of the societal, and supporters of the spiritual. They did not deserve to die simply because they sought to forge a fresh life for themselves.

"What is that?" Zeden asked. His second in command, Viran Stovol, stepped up beside him and looked at the sensor panel.

"I'm not sure," Viran said, and he turned and paced toward the narrow, front end of the control center, where two wide ports peered out into space ahead of their vessel. Zeden joined him, and together they gazed out at a confused panorama. All about, the thin blue bands of the construction lasers flashed through space, pounding into the two alien ships.

Except pounding *might not be the best way to describe it,* Zeden thought. Neither ship seemed in the least affected by the impacts of the lasers against their defensive screens.

"There," Viran said, pointing through one of the ports and out at the larger of the alien vessels. Zeden tried to follow the direction of Viran's gesture, but at first saw nothing. Then movement beside the lower section of the larger ship caught his attention.

"Is that another ship?" Zeden said.

"It does look like a small craft of some kind," Viran said. "I think it launched from the aft end of the larger ship."

"It could be a weapon," Zeden said. He headed back toward the external-sensor panel and worked its controls to scan the newcomer on the field of battle. Viran walked up beside him.

"Anything?" the second in command asked.

"No," Zeden said. "Just defensive screens. I'm not detecting any weapons systems."

The two men watched as the small craft flew slowly into the middle of the battlefield. There, it decelerated and then stopped. Zeden waited, but nothing more happened. He thought about directing the lasers to fire on it, but it occurred to him that perhaps that's what the aliens wanted him to do, that such an act would trigger some terrible destructive force.

"Are there any life signs?" Viran asked, and Zeden checked.

"There's one," he said.

"Just one?" Viran asked.

"Yes," Zeden said.

On the other side of the instrument table, Gan Delan looked up from the communications panel. "That one life sign on the small vessel is hailing us," she said. "It seems to be the same person who tried to contact us before."

Zeden looked at Viran, at a loss for what to do. He hadn't trained for combat, or to protect thousands of ground-based citizens from a threat in space. "What should we do?" he asked Viran.

"Maybe we should talk to them," Viran said.

The idea frightened Zeden. He'd trained in diplomacy and alien relations no more than he had in warfare. He worried that anything but a show of strength would invite the destruction of the colony.

What show of strength? he asked himself. He

turned and looked out again through the forward ports and saw the most powerful force they could muster essentially bouncing off the screens of the other ships.

"All right," he said, more to himself than to the others. He looked to Gan. "Tell everybody to stop firing their lasers," he said. "Then open communications to the aliens."

Kirk piloted *Columbus* away from *Enterprise,* taking the shuttlecraft into position directly ahead of the alien ships. He flew on instruments, using sensor navigation to ensure that he didn't steer the shuttle into the path of any of the lasers. Spock had told him that the shields would hold, and he believed his first officer, but Kirk had no particular desire to see his defenses weakened.

Halfway between *Enterprise* and the closest alien vessel, the captain brought the shuttle to a stop. Touching a control on the main console, he then lowered the panels covering the three ports that lined the bow of *Columbus.* Peering out into space, he saw the irregular line of alien vessels facing in his direction. The bright blue rays of their lasers shot through the darkness, speeding past the shuttlecraft toward *Enterprise* and *Courageous.* Peering out at the scene, Kirk thought it looked as though *Columbus* had been trapped within a lattice of energy, much like the Tholians employed.

Reaching across the main console to the communications panel, the captain opened a channel. "Kirk to *Enterprise*," he said, his voice sounding isolated in the empty cabin.

"Enterprise, *Spock here*," came the immediate reply.

"Well, Mister Spock," the captain said, "as I'm sure you can see, I've thrown myself into the middle of the battlefield. So far, I'm being ignored."

"That is not necessarily a bad thing, Captain," Spock said.

"Perhaps not," Kirk said, "but I'm going to try to get the attention of the aliens again. I'll keep you informed. Kirk out."

The captain closed the channel, then opened hailing frequencies. "This is James T. Kirk, captain of the *U.S.S. Enterprise*, from the United Federation of Planets," he said. "We are on a mission of peace. Please respond." He thought about mentioning the *Enterprise* crew's discoveries of the two lost cities, but concluded that revealing such knowledge could implicate the Federation, in the estimation of the aliens, as having had something to do with those attacks.

Kirk waited a few moments, then decided to try again. "This is Captain James Kirk of the *U.S.S. Enterprise*. Our mission is one of peace." He waited again, and while he did, he saw the alien vessels all at once cease firing their laser cannons. A moment later, he actually received a response to his hails.

"This is Zeden Pego," said a male voice. *"You are*

trespassing in our space and you are requested to leave at once."

"We do not mean to trespass," Kirk said. "We do so only because we believed it the only way to attract your attention so that we could speak with you."

"We do not know your people," Pego said. *"Why would you wish to speak with us? And why should we wish to speak with you?"*

"For two reasons," Kirk said, happy to finally be able to state his case. "First, the mission our people have set ourselves is one of exploration, of seeking out new life and new civilizations in our galaxy. Second—" The captain hesitated, still concerned that if he spoke of the destroyed cities, the aliens might believe him and his crew somehow responsible. "Second," he finally went on, "we have come into the possession of some information that we believe may be of great import to your people."

Pego then asked the question that Kirk hoped he wouldn't. *"What is this information?"*

Again, the captain hesitated, worried about how Pego would react to news of the lost cities. With other species, Kirk sometimes found it difficult to judge inflection and tone, never more so than when communications involved translators. Still, Pego sounded scared to him, and of more import, he did not sound like a leader. The captain chose to use that judgment to see if he could proceed past him.

"Zeden Pego," Kirk said, "are you the head of your government?"

"*I am not,*" the alien said. "*I run this ship, though, and the others with it.*"

"I understand," Kirk said. "But I would like to meet with your leader. I am prepared to travel to the surface of your world in order to do so. I will come alone and unarmed. If you have scanned this vessel, then you know that I speak the truth."

Silence followed. Worried that Pego had opted not to relay his request, Kirk checked the communications panel to ensure the channel remained open. It did.

At last, Pego said, "*I do not have the authority to make such a decision.*"

"I urge you to seek the counsel of those who do," Kirk said.

"*How do I know that you have the information you claim?*" Pego asked.

"You don't," Kirk said. "But you can make a determination about the character of my people. Your sensors must show that your weapons had virtually no effect on either of our two ships. And despite the fact that you fired upon us, we have not retaliated. If we wished, we readily could have destroyed one or more of your vessels to demonstrate our strength. Even now, we could use the might of our ships to land on your world and seek its leaders. We have not done that, nor would we ever consider doing so. Our people believe that true strength does not reveal itself in violence, particularly when used by the strong against the weak."

Again, Pego did not reply at once. Even if Kirk hadn't been told that Pego did not lead the government, even if he hadn't heard fear in his voice, he could have guessed as much, merely from his hesitancy.

"*I will pass your request on to our governor,*" Pego said.

"I will wait here for an answer," Kirk said. "I would also tell you that time may play a critical factor in the information we have to pass on."

Pego closed the channel without another word.

Sixteen

Kirk studied the navigation console of *Columbus* carefully, reassuring himself that the sensor lock maintained the specified distance from the four alien vessels that escorted the shuttlecraft down to the surface of the planet. It had taken two hours for Pego to relay a response from the colony's governor, and the captain suspected that most of that time had been taken up with debate about the situation. When the aliens finally agreed to allow the captain to meet with their leader, they provided strict conditions under which that meeting would occur. The seriousness of their concerns, combined with their reaction to the appearance of *Enterprise* and *Courageous* in the star system, convinced Kirk that they must already know about the two lost colonies.

Spock, of course, had been concerned about the captain traveling unaccompanied to the planet surface, and Captain Caulder had shared those apprehensions. Kirk reminded both men that *Enterprise* and *Courageous* boasted enough firepower to lay waste to every alien vessel in orbit and their entire city, a compelling enough reason for the aliens to treat the

captain with civility and guarantee his safety while
in their company. In addition, Kirk secured permission for both Starfleet ships to enter orbit about the
planet—a good distance from the colony support
ships, but still in orbit—which would allow Spock to
immediately beam his commanding officer back to
Enterprise should the need arise. The first officer intended to keep a sensor lock on the captain during his
visit on the planet.

As the shuttlecraft neared the surface, Kirk took
a moment to stand and glance through the forward
ports. The city that spread out before him had clearly
not been completed; as Spock had noted, the north-
ernmost section appeared under construction. The
majority that had been finished, though, enchanted
Kirk. He could not honestly say that the collections of
buildings and green spaces, of neighborhoods and pedestrian thoroughfares, of statuary and public squares
matched the images he'd envisioned when walking
through the destroyed cities, but even viewing those
features from above, he saw them filled with vibrant
life. Subdued but pervasive colors adorned many
structures, and the natural landscape surrounding
the colony had been embraced and brought inside,
with grass and flowers and trees running throughout
it. Kirk also saw at least one narrow river snaking
its way in and out of the city, and in other locations,
elaborate fountains added movement and artistry to
the scenery.

As *Columbus* continued to descend, the edge of the city passed beneath it. Kirk could discern the figures of people walking along the avenues below, and as he peered through the ports, he spotted many heads turning up toward the shuttlecraft, and several arms thrusting skyward. From his vantage, the aliens appeared humanoid, a deduction he and his crew had already made after finding the broken statue in the first ruined city.

Gazing ahead, Kirk saw where it seemed *Columbus* would alight, and he felt a flutter of anticipation. He sat back down at the main console, then monitored the shuttlecraft as its four chaperones guided it to a landing. When he felt *Columbus* touch down, the captain stood, walked over to the hatch, and as he'd been instructed, waited.

Moments later, he heard a rapping on the outside of the hatch. Kirk reached up and worked the control pad set into the bulkhead. The two upper portions of the hatch parted, and the bottom section folded outward across the port nacelle. Just outside waited a party of three people, a man and two women. The man and one of the women—both appeared young, quite tall, and fit—hung back in what the captain recognized as the characteristic positioning of security officers. Kirk saw no weapons, but assumed that they carried them. The second woman did not appear as physically imposing as the others; possessed of a rich, dark complexion, she wore an almost regal bearing. All three looked nearly indistinguishable from humans, with the exception of—

"You are James Kirk?" asked the second woman from her forward position.

"I am," he said.

"Welcome to Pillagra."

Kirk stepped out onto the step formed by the bottom of the hatch and looked around. *Columbus* had set down in the center of the city, in a cobbled square of roughly the same dimensions as those he and his crew had observed—that they had walked through—in the lost colonies. But where those had been bordered by the ruins of wrecked buildings, the one before the captain nestled within the entrancing confines of stately architecture. Kirk felt as though he stood in fallen land somehow reclaimed.

"Is Pillagra the name of your city or of this world?" he asked the regal woman.

"It was the name we chose for our colony," she said, "but now we let it stand for the planet as well."

"I am very pleased to be here," Kirk said.

"And we are pleased to have you here," the woman replied. "My name is Alitess Lan. The governor has asked me to escort you to your appointment with her."

"Thank you."

Kirk stepped down onto the cobblestoned surface of the square, then closed and secured the shuttlecraft's hatch. He then followed Lan as she led him away from *Columbus*, between the two alien vessels that had landed in front of the shuttle. The air felt cool and slightly damp, and from the position of the sun not that far above the horizon, Kirk estimated the time as midmorning. He noticed only a handful of people about, all of whom remained stationary, leaving him to believe that the square had been locked down by Pillagra's security.

Lan led Kirk toward the tallest building in sight; it reached to three stories, while most of the buildings that fronted on the square rose only two. In front of their apparent destination stood a fountain. In the center of a round reservoir, a graceful pedestal supported what looked like a large chest that had been hinged open, and which revealed a heavily textured, ornately carved hourglass figure within it. Water poured from the opening in the chest and cascaded down into the basin with a rush of white spray. Kirk found it beautiful.

Inside the building, Lan and Kirk entered a mid-sized atrium, into which spilled the morning light. Large plants lined the columned space, interspersed with several sitting areas. The room clearly functioned as a place for guests to wait. Again, Kirk saw only a small number of people about, and once again he assumed them all security officers.

Lan directed Kirk to a tall wooden door set into the left-hand wall. She opened it before him, allowing him to enter first. After telling him that the governor would be in shortly to see him, Lan withdrew and closed the door behind her.

Though not as tall as the atrium, the room still rose to a considerable height. Framed artwork adorned the walls; large paintings of various styles and subject matter seemed designed to appeal to eclectic tastes. Nicely but sparingly appointed with a pair of sofas and a number of chairs and small tables, the room appeared to Kirk to serve as a reception area, a place to meet guests before moving on to other rooms in the building.

The captain walked around the room, looking at—and in some cases admiring—the artwork. Only a short time passed before a second door opened. A woman entered, scanned the room until she saw Kirk, and then headed toward him. Short, with a bit of a round shape, she had wavy black hair and a smile that, even from a distance, seemed extraordinarily genuine.

"I am Velura Sant," the woman said as she approached. "I am the governor of Pillagra."

"James Kirk, captain of the Federation vessel *Enterprise*," he said. "It is a pleasure to meet you, ma'am. Thank you for seeing me."

Sant motioned toward the nearest sofa and said, "Shall we sit?" Once they had settled themselves, the governor said, "I am told, Captain, that you put quite a scare into the crews of our support vessels in orbit."

"I can assure you that was not my intention," Kirk said, "and I apologize."

"I am also told that you claim to have important information for me and my people," Sant said. "I hope you will not be offended when I tell you how unlikely that seems to me."

"I understand how it must sound, Governor Sant, but—"

"Excuse me, Captain, but I am addressed as Governor Velura." She seemed to offer the correction as a statement of fact, with no trace of having been insulted.

"Pardon me, Governor Velura," Kirk said. "I truly do have information to impart to you, and which I believe you will find of great import, but I am reluctant to speak of it without first learning how much of this information you already know."

Velura lifted both of her eyebrows. "Again, I mean no offense, Captain," she said, "but that sounds deliberately obfuscatory. I'm afraid I don't understand."

"Governor, this colony, Pillagra, is not the only one of its kind, is it?" A shadow seemed to pass over Velura's features. "I ask because the information I have concerns two other colonies that we believe your people might have settled."

"Then I can imagine what that information might be," the governor said. "And yes, I can tell you about those other colonies.

"When we set out from our homeworld to reach this planet and build Pillagra, we did so as part of a movement. We were one of three sets of ships that went out. The first colonists reached a planet they called Gelladorn and began constructing a city there.

As they did, transports began ferrying more settlers there, ultimately delivering nearly a hundred thousand people."

Although that number fell within Starfleet estimates of the city's capacity, the figure nevertheless staggered Kirk. He could only hope that all of the inhabitants had not perished with Gelladorn.

"The second colony was built in the same manner," Velura continued. "It was called Velat Nol, and it was farther from our homeworld. Farther still is the third colony, which is Pillagra."

"But something happened to Gelladorn and Velat Nol," Kirk said gently.

The governor's jaw clenched. "Both were annihilated, Captain," she said. "Utterly destroyed, from what we understand, without a single survivor." She paused and breathed in deeply, as though trying to fight back deep emotion. "When communication was lost with Gelladorn, it was assumed to be a technological problem, and so a ship was sent with experts to conduct any needed repairs.

"The ship was never heard from again.

"Another expedition was sent to investigate," Velura went on. "Proceeding with extreme caution, they examined the ruins of the colony, and while doing so, were attacked by missiles launched from elsewhere on the planet. They managed to escape, but it was suggested that the Gelladorn colonists might have built their city on the site of an existing, automated military post."

"Belonging to whom?" Kirk asked.

"We don't know," the governor said. "But the colonists of Velat Nol immediately set out to explore their seemingly pristine world to make sure that a similar fate would not befall them. They found no missile installations, but a short time later, communication was lost with Velat Nol as well. A subsequent expedition found only wreckage where once the colony had been."

"And Pillagra?" Kirk asked.

"By the time we learned that Velat Nol had fallen," Velura said, "we had already settled Pillagra. We discussed the possibility of leaving, but we chose not to. As you can imagine, though—as you've witnessed— the appearance of strangers, particularly those in powerful starships, can set our people on edge."

"Of course," Kirk said, understanding completely.

"And now, Captain, what have you to tell me?" the governor asked.

"The starship I command, the *Enterprise,* is on a mission of exploration," Kirk said. "My crew seek to learn about our universe, and to meet the others with whom we share it."

"That sounds . . . noble," Velura said.

"I think there is an aspect of nobility to it," Kirk agreed. "And when it's done for the right reasons—for curiosity, for the enrichment of us all—there also has to be an element of humility. I also find it romantic.

"Sometimes, though, it can be hard," the captain

continued. "My crew discovered the remains of both the Gelladorn and Velat Nol colonies." Kirk described in detail the events surrounding the *Enterprise* crew's visits to the two lost cities. He included his decision to obliterate the missile installations, and the ambush of *Enterprise* by six other vessels. When he finished, he asked the governor whether her people had any idea who had destroyed their cities and killed their citizens, and why they had done so.

"No," Velura said. "We talked about some sort of territorial issue, but the regions of space where the colonies were established seem to be largely unoccupied."

"That has been our experience as well," Kirk said.

The governor seemed to consider this, then asked, "So is that the information you wished to provide me and my people, Captain?"

"For the most part, yes," Kirk said. "When our people observed what might have been a colonization effort, we chose to see for ourselves. When we confirmed the similarities of Pillagra to the lost cities we encountered, we wanted to warn you."

For the first time since they'd begun talking about the lost colonies, a smile crept onto Velura's face. "On behalf of my people, I thank you," she said. "Particularly after all that's happened, it's nice to learn that there are other kind beings in the galaxy. This confederation of yours . . ."

"The United Federation of Planets," Kirk said.

"We are an amalgam of more than a hundred different worlds and species, people who share many ideals and goals, while at the same time retaining our distinctiveness."

"That sounds impressive," Velura said.

"And your people, Governor?" Kirk asked.

"My people?" Velura said. "We are the Bajorans, from the planet Bajor."

Seventeen

Sulu walked along the avenues of Pillagra in a state of numbness.

After Captain Kirk had conducted a successful first contact with the Bajoran colonists, Captain Caulder had announced to the crew of *Courageous* that the two Starfleet vessels would remain in orbit about the planet for several more days. The additional time would allow *Enterprise*'s first-contact specialists to better acquaint themselves with the Bajorans, as well as to lay the foundation for a potential relationship between Bajor and the Federation. Governor Velura and her ministers also agreed to permit a small number of *Courageous* and *Enterprise* personnel—no more than two dozen at a time—to take shore leave in their city.

Sulu had not even considered requesting any off-duty time. He had joined the *Courageous* only a few months earlier, and as second officer, it seemed to him an abuse of power to take leave prior to the rest of the crew. But on the fourth day at Pillagra, just before the start of alpha shift, Commander Costley informed him that the two of them had been included on the list of crew members beaming down to the planet.

"The first and second officers get shore leave when it's limited to only twelve of our complement at a time?" Sulu had protested to Costley. "The rest of the crew are going to transport us into open space."

"I agree," Costley had said. "But I think it's the captain's way of ensuring that I help you integrate with the crew."

Knowing that it would only hurt his already tenuous standing with the captain to protest, Sulu had accepted the situation and transported down to Pillagra. He, Costley, and four other crew members—the second group of six to beam down from *Courageous* that morning—materialized in the square at the center of the colony. Back on R-775-I—or, as the Bajorans called it, Gelladorn—Sulu hadn't seen that part of the wrecked city, nor had he visited the surface of R-836-II—Velat Nol. Trinh had been a member of landing parties to both worlds and both cities, though, and she had seen the squares there. She had described the first one in detail to Sulu.

Trinh's words had returned to him as soon as he'd arrived in Pillagra. Although she had walked through obliterated cities, seeing nothing but ruins that marked the deaths of tens of thousands, she'd looked beyond the fallen present and into the living past. As an archaeologist, she possessed a talent for doing so. And so when Trinh had spoken to him about her experiences visiting those lost colonies, she'd also peeled away the layers of destruction, the layers of time, and illustrated for Sulu what once had been, despite the fact that she had never been there to see it.

The group of six in which he'd beamed down had initially stayed together as they explored Pillagra. They walked through the square, enjoying the art and architecture, the old-fashioned look and feel of the cobblestones, the fountain in front of what one Bajoran described to them as the governor's residence and offices. They met and spoke with some of the colonists. Sulu said little, instead listening to his memories of Trinh.

As the six crew members had spread out from the square onto the pedestrian thoroughfares that ran through the city, the first officer had noticed his reserve. At first, Costley attempted to joke with him about it, tried to draw him out, just as he'd taken to doing aboard ship. As the day wore on, though, Sulu perceived the first officer's mounting frustration. As various crew members peeled away from the group to go off on their own, Costley stayed with him, but grew increasingly exasperated with his continued reticence. Sulu tried once to explain what occupied his mind, but he found it difficult enough to think about Trinh without also having to voice those thoughts.

Eventually, Costley had left Sulu to his own

devices. The first officer didn't seem angry or upset when he did so, but genuinely concerned. Despite the short time that the two men had known each other, Costley seemed to understand that something troubled Sulu deeply, and he might have even suspected that it had in some way driven him from *Enterprise*. To that point, the first officer hadn't asked about it, but Sulu worried that he might suddenly find himself ordered by Starfleet to consult a counselor.

Maybe that wouldn't be such a bad thing, Sulu thought as he paced through Pillagra by himself. *Maybe it could even help.* He knew that one of the doctors aboard *Courageous* carried a specialty in psychiatry, and so he could avail himself of the opportunity to speak with her.

Walking along without seeing much, mired in his remembrances of Trinh and in the guilt he still felt for not staying with her despite her protestations, Sulu saw little of Pillagra. Numerous Bajorans noted the presence of a visitor to their city and smiled in his direction when he passed, and he tried to be mindful of their graciousness and return it with a smile of his own. Although Sulu found smiling back at the Bajorans a relatively easy and natural act—they looked very much like humans, but for a series of small ridges at the tops of their noses—he had difficulty concentrating on the world around him, as opposed to the one within.

When he rounded one corner, though, he noticed a spacious meadow bounded by occasional stands of trees. The park drew him in, and as he strolled across the grass, the landscape brought him back to the day on Dengella II when he and Trinh had flown the Vietnamese kite that they'd made together. The memory tasted both bitter and sweet, and Sulu wondered how—*if*—he would ever get past that portion of his life.

I don't want to get past it, he thought. *I never wanted it to end.*

Several concrete benches dotted the park, and Sulu found one beneath a leafy tree. He sat down and leaned forward, placed his elbows on his knees, and tried to see a clear way forward. He had continued to send messages to Trinh, but since last seeing her in the infirmary on Starbase 25, he had not heard back from her. He had to satisfy his hunger for information about Trinh with the few, often sketchy replies he sometimes received from her mother.

I should resign my commission and just go to Mars, he thought. He could show up there, at the home of Nguyen Thi Yeh and demand to see the woman he still loved. Sulu knew Trinh, though, and he understood her strength of will. She would resist him, and for his own good.

Alone on the bench in the park, Sulu shook his head. Had their roles been reversed, had he been the one permanently incapacitated, had he been the one given only months or years to live, how would he have reacted? Sulu told himself that he would have wanted Trinh by his side, but could he trust that, since that's how he wanted her to feel? Would he really have accepted her staying with him as he descended inexorably to his death? Could he have done that to the woman he loved? He didn't know.

Maybe if I just go for a visit, Sulu thought. *Would Trinh accept that? Would she—*

The twin tones of Sulu's communicator sounded. He reached for the device and flipped open its cover. "Sulu here," he said.

"Lieutenant, this is Ensign Riordan." Even in the communications officer's few words, Sulu heard the urgency in his voice. *"Captain Caulder is conducting an emergency recall of all personnel."*

"What is it?" Sulu asked, rising to his feet. "What's happened?"

"We've detected a group of ships entering the system," Riordan said. *"Stand by for transport."*

Sulu took a few steps forward, away from the bench on which he'd been sitting. "Standing by," he said.

He heard a familiar hum, and then a golden haze clouded his vision. The transporter effect swept him up in Pillagra, then set him down on *Courageous.* By the time he materialized, the ship had already gone to red alert.

Sulu leaped from the platform and raced for the bridge.

• • •

"Five vessels closing fast," said Lieutenant Rahda from the helm, where she peered into her targeting scanner. "Estimating arrival in five minutes, forty seconds."

In the command chair, Kirk fought the urge to ask about the identity of the vessels. His people knew their jobs, and they would tell him what he needed to know as soon as they found out themselves. *But I already know, don't I?* Kirk thought. He feared that he did, given the destruction of the first two Bajoran colonies, and the presence of a third on the world below. He eyed the main viewscreen, which displayed the curve of the planet's horizon. *Courageous* hung in orbit nearby, as did a number of Bajoran ships.

"The vessels are of the same configuration as those we encountered in system R-Eight-Three-Six," Spock said from his science station.

"Red alert," ordered Kirk, disturbed but not surprised by the report. The ship-wide klaxon immediately blared out its pulsing call to battle stations, and the rectangular signal lights around the bridge began flashing brightly. "Spock, are any of those ships the same ones that attacked us?"

"Difficult to know with certainty," said the first officer, "but two of the vessels show hull damage consistent with the *Enterprise*'s weapons."

"Uhura, hailing frequencies," Kirk said, rising from the command chair.

"Hailing frequencies open, sir," Uhura replied at

once. At the same time, the alert klaxon cut off, and Kirk knew she'd silenced it on the bridge.

"This is Captain James T. Kirk of the *U.S.S. Enterprise*," he said. "You are approaching a civilian population. You are warned to withdraw immediately, or we will open fire on you." He glanced over his shoulder at Uhura, who had a hand raised to the silver earpiece she monitored. She gave a brisk shake of her head. He looked back at the viewscreen, mindful of the thousands of people living peacefully on the planet's surface. "This is Captain James Kirk of the *Enterprise*," he said again. "We have no desire to fight, but if you do not withdraw, we will fire on your vessels. Please respond."

"No reply, Captain," Uhura said.

"And no change in course or speed," Rahda added.

The captain turned and walked past the command chair, stepping up to the communications console. "Raise the *Courageous*," Kirk ordered.

Uhura operated her console with practiced skill. "You're on, sir," she said.

"*Enterprise* to *Courageous*," Kirk said.

"*Caulder here.*"

"Captain, our repeated attempts to hail the approaching vessels and warn them off are being ignored," Kirk said. "The vessels are of the same configuration as those that attacked the *Enterprise* in system R-Eight-Three-Six." Kirk knew that when Starfleet Command ordered *Courageous* on their mission,

Caulder had been provided full reports on the *Enterprise* crew's discoveries of the lost cities, as well as on their encounter with vessels like those headed in their direction.

"What are your orders?" Caulder asked.

"Captain, I know that the *Courageous* has a scientific mission profile," Kirk said, "but we need all hands on deck. I have no doubt that those vessels out there intend to attack, with the ultimate goal of destroying Pillagra. We can't let that happen."

"Understood," Caulder said without hesitation.

"Good luck, Captain," Kirk said.

"And you."

"Kirk out." Then, looking to Uhura, he said, "Notify the Bajoran governor."

"Aye, sir," Uhura said.

Kirk moved quickly over to the science station. "Recommendations, Spock?"

"From our experience, we know that the alien vessels are extremely maneuverable," said the first officer, "but their armaments are rudimentary, and their defenses do not measure up to ours."

"Hit them fast, then, and hard," Kirk said.

"Yes, sir," Spock said. "I would also point out that the Bajoran support ships in orbit have virtually no weaponry of their own, and minimal defenses. They will make easy targets."

"We can't send them out of the system unprotected," Kirk said.

"No, sir," Spock agreed.

Kirk nodded, understanding that he had few ways to protect the Bajoran ships. He turned back toward Uhura, whose skillful hands continued their dance across the communications panel, doubtless transmitting a report of the situation to Velura Sant. "Lieutenant," Kirk said. Uhura looked up, but the captain noted that her fingers did not stop working her controls. "Broadcast a signal to all Bajoran ships in orbit. Have them descend to the planet's surface at once." He thought a moment, then added, "They should not land anywhere near Pillagra." If the aliens intended to obliterate the Bajorans, Kirk would not make it easy for them.

"Aye, sir," Uhura said.

"Contact in one minute," Rahda said.

"Break orbit," Kirk said. He headed to the starboard steps and down to the center portion of the bridge, where he sat in the command chair. "Move to intercept. Full impulse, ready phasers and photon torpedoes."

"Bringing the ship about," Rahda said, the thrum of the impulse engines rising. "Readying all weapons."

On the main screen, the planet fell away to port. Kirk caught a brief glimpse of *Courageous* also in motion, and then the view centered on a patch of stars. "Full magnification," Kirk ordered. The image blinked, and the barest outlines of the black, blade-shaped vessels became visible, lined up horizontally on the screen. As the captain watched, four of them broke their formation, each moving off in different directions: up, down, port, and starboard. The fifth vessel continued forward on its linear course.

Kirk leaped from the command chair and leaned in over the helm. "Rahda, target the closest vessel. The instant we're in weapons range, open fire, phasers and photon torpedoes. Fire in a wide spray to counter evasive maneuvers."

"Aye, sir."

"All five vessels have launched missiles," Spock said. "They are targeting the *Enterprise* and the *Courageous*."

"Main phasers," Kirk said. "Fire on the missiles until the vessels are in range."

"Firing phasers," Rahda said. The feedback pulses of the ship's weapons keened through the bridge, once, twice, half a dozen times, and more. On the viewscreen, red beams streaked from *Enterprise*. Though Kirk could not clearly see the black missiles against the backdrop of space, the silent explosions of their destruction made for a welcome sight.

"The vessels are launching missiles continually," Spock said, explaining Rahda's incessant firing. "Our phasers are obliterating them."

Even as Rahda operated her weapons subpanel, she looked into her targeting scanner. "First vessel entering range," she said. The squawk of the ship's phasers calmed for a moment, then resumed in force, joined by the beat of photon torpedoes being propelled into space. "Firing on the first vessel," Rahda said, her voice steady.

Kirk saw the image on the viewer swing around to follow a cone of phasers and photon torpedoes tracking one of the alien vessels. A torpedo found its mark and detonated, and the vessel veered quickly to one side, directly into a line of phaser fire. A burst of white light bloomed, then faded to nothingness.

"Direct hit," Rahda said. "The vessel has been destroyed."

The bridge suddenly shook. "Missile strike on the primary hull," Spock said. "Minimal damage to the shields."

"Captain, two more vessels are in range," Rahda said.

"Ignore the missiles if necessary," Kirk said, knowing that they posed little threat to the ship in the short term. "Concentrate on those vessels."

"Targeting," Rahda said, even as *Enterprise* bucked under additional missile strikes.

Both alien vessels appeared on the main viewscreen, missiles firing out ahead of them. Suddenly, a salvo of *Enterprise*'s photon torpedoes spread across the screen. Great bursts of light and flame blazed momentarily into existence as missiles exploded in the line of fire. The vessels jockeyed in all directions, evading the torpedoes, but then multiple lines of phased red energy sprang from *Enterprise*. A phaser blast caught one of the ships, sending it twisting away, seemingly out of control. The other ship pursued a serpentine course, dodging the weapons fire. It dived down, and Rahda followed it with *Enterprise*'s phasers, but then it suddenly darted up and leaped forward, heading directly for the ship.

Before he could bark an order, *Enterprise* rolled hard to port. Kirk was pitched in that direction, barely keeping his feet as the inertial dampers faltered for a fraction of a second. He looked back up in time to see the black ship filling the viewscreen. He braced himself for impact.

It never came.

"Firing phasers and photon torpedoes," Rahda said, but already the sounds of *Enterprise*'s weapons filled the bridge.

"Direct hit," Spock said. "A second vessel has been destroyed." He paused, then announced that *Courageous* had vanquished a third vessel.

Kirk stepped back over to the helm and laid a hand on Rahda's shoulder. "Excellent evasion, Lieutenant, and good shooting," he said. Rahda glanced up briefly, then returned her attention to her controls. "Find the last two vessels," Kirk told her. He turned and headed toward the main science console, though he remained on the lower, inner section of the bridge. "Spock," he said, "they tried to ram us."

"I am at a loss to explain it," Spock said. "They

appear to be bent on destroying the *Enterprise*, no matter the cost to themselves."

"That doesn't sound right, Spock," the captain said. "We don't even know who it is we're battling."

"Captain," Rahda called from the helm, and Kirk turned toward her. "The *Courageous* is engaging one ship, and I've tracked the other by a radiation leak it must have suffered when it took our phaser strike. Its engines appear to be off line, and it's drifting."

"Take us to the *Courageous*," Kirk said.

"Aye, sir."

The captain looked back up at Spock, then mounted the steps to join him at his console. "Any hypotheses?" Kirk asked.

"I have none," Spock said. "Whoever is piloting those vessels seems obsessed with destroying us. From what we witnessed in the R-Seven-Seven-Five and R-Eight-Three-Six star systems, they seem focused on the Bajorans in the same way."

"But until a few days ago," Kirk noted, "the Federation had never even had any contact with the Bajorans. It seems unlikely that there's a connection."

"Perhaps *we* are the connection," Spock said.

"Explain."

"It is our belief that these aliens, whoever they are, destroyed the Bajoran colony called Gelladorn," Spock said. "They then apparently constructed automated missile emplacements to further protect the planet, which they did when they detected our presence. We then destroyed those installations.

"The aliens then apparently destroyed the Bajoran colony called Velat Nol," Spock continued. "But they did not then build missile facilities."

"Perhaps because they didn't have the time?" Kirk ventured, trying to follow his first officer's reasoning.

"Perhaps," Spock said. "Or perhaps they lacked the materials, or the support, or some other vital component. But they did not lose interest in the planet, which they attempted to protect against our presence. Now, here again at Pillagra, we have appeared, this time in defense of the Bajorans."

"We've made ourselves the enemy," Kirk said.

"By effectively allying ourselves with Bajoran colonists," Spock said.

Kirk wondered briefly if he had chosen the wrong side. *Who knows what the Bajorans have done to incur the wrath of the aliens.* That might be true, but the *Enterprise* crew had scanned Pillagra and detected no weapons, and though it could have been a deception, the Bajorans had seemed friendly and open during their days of meetings.

"Captain," Rahda said from the helm, "we are approaching the *Courageous.*"

Kirk peered up at the viewscreen to see bright-red phaser beams streaking from the *Miranda*-class vessel and slicing through space toward one of the alien vessels, which darted to and fro. "Add our fire to theirs as soon as we're in range," Kirk said.

But as Rahda acknowledged his order, Kirk saw the alien vessel streak up suddenly, then reverse direction and dive. The captain knew what would happen next, but was powerless to stop it. He watched in horror as the alien vessel crashed into *Courageous*.

"Fire phasers!" Captain Caulder ordered.

At a peripheral engineering station, Sulu watched as one of the alien vessels bore down on *Courageous*. The red rays of the ship's phasers shot out into space, seeking a target. The alien vessel flashed its impressive maneuverability, eluding the lethal streaks of energy.

Suddenly, the alien vessel rushed upward. Intuition sent Sulu leaping to his feet. On the viewer, the alien vessel swung back down, avoiding the phaser blasts meant to stop it. Sulu turned toward the helm and opened his mouth to scream the words in his head: *Hard over!*

But before he could utter a sound, the bridge of *Courageous* jolted violently. An unimaginable thunder ripped through the compartment, accompanied by the terrible plaints of rending metal. The lights darkened and control panels went black. The red alert klaxon shrieked one final call, and then even that stopped.

The front end of the alien vessel plowed through the upper decks on the starboard side of *Courageous*. Kirk saw sections of hull plating, loosed from the ship, turning end over end in space, blinking with the reflected light of the system's star as it did so. He felt sick to his stomach.

"Uhura," he said from where he stood beside Spock, and the communications officer looked over at him, an expression of complete dismay on her face. "Hail the *Courageous*."

"Aye, sir," she said, though Kirk could barely hear her. She reached up to work her console.

Kirk turned to his first officer. "Spock?" he asked quietly, though the Vulcan had already bent to peer into his hooded viewer.

"Scanning," Spock said, and even he seemed affected by the awful spectacle, his voice lowered to a somber level. "I'm reading more than a hundred fifty life signs, most of them strong."

Kirk knew that the complement of a *Miranda*-class vessel ranged as high as two hundred twenty, so the toll could have been much worse, though that provided cold comfort. He gazed back at the viewscreen and saw that the momentum of the alien vessel had caused it to pinwheel across the hull of *Courageous* and float off into space. "Ship's status?"

"Collating," Spock said. "Structural integrity fields are struggling to contain the sections of the ship opened to space, but life support is operating. Engines appear unaffected, while starboard-side weapons systems and shields are down."

"What about the alien vessel?" Kirk asked, but then the *Enterprise* bridge brightened. On the viewer, the captain saw the source of that light fading where the alien vessel had been.

"Captain," Uhura said, "I'm having trouble raising anybody on the *Courageous*."

"Keep trying, Lieutenant," Kirk said. "They'll answer when they can." Then to Spock, he said, "With their starboard shields down, we can beam medical and repair teams to the *Courageous,* and their survivors over here. I'll contact McCoy and Scotty—"

"Captain," called Lieutenant Rahda. "Sensors are detecting two more vessels heading this way."

Kirk looked at Spock, then headed back down to the inner section of the bridge. "More of the alien vessels?" he asked Rahda.

"No, sir," she said, peering into her scanner. "There is a physical resemblance, but these are much larger, roughly the same size as the *Enterprise*."

As Kirk hoisted himself back into the command chair, he started to call for a red alert, but saw that the signal for general quarters still flashed on and off. *One battle barely ended before the next begins,* he thought, and then realized that the first wave of smaller ships had been a ruse, meant to soften the defense of Pillagra provided by *Enterprise* and *Courageous.*

And it worked, Kirk thought.

"Uhura, hailing frequencies," the captain said, but

he held out little hope that the aliens would suddenly want to talk.

Sulu regained consciousness in complete darkness. He had no idea how long he'd been out, and at first, he couldn't even be sure of his location. He pushed himself up and recognized the feel of the deck beneath him. An odd sort of silence surrounded him, one he'd rarely if ever heard aboard a starship. Through his hands, though, he felt a vibration, and he knew that at least some function had not been lost.

Slowly reaching about him, Sulu found the bottom portion of the nearest console, confirming his place at the periphery of the bridge. He rolled up onto his hands and knees and began to crawl, following the line of stations. Somewhere, he thought he heard movement, and he called out into the darkness, his voice sounding lifeless to his own ears.

When no one responded, Sulu moved his hand forward and pushed up against a body. He quickly fumbled to find an arm, then worked his way down to the wrist. He felt a pulse and, satisfied, he set the arm down and continued crawling forward.

When he reached the alcove that led to the turbolift, he noted that the doors did not part. He felt around the lower section of the bulkhead beside them. He found the recessed latch there, inserted his fingers, and pulled it open. A small light within activated. Sulu had to look away for a few moments until his eyes adjusted from having dilated in the pitch blackness.

When he could finally tolerate the light, Sulu peered into the emergency cache. He picked out a communicator and then a handheld beacon, which he activated and snapped onto his wrist. He shined the beacon across the bridge. He saw bodies everywhere.

Opening the communicator, he said, "Bridge to sickbay." He waited only a moment before trying again. On his third attempt, a voice finally responded.

"Sickbay, this is Tejada," said the ship's chief medical officer.

"This is Lieutenant Sulu," he said. "We need an emergency medical team on the bridge immediately."

"We need emergency medical teams everywhere," Tejada said. Sulu believed her. She sounded harried.

"Doctor, the captain and first officer are down," Sulu told her. "I think the turbolift to the bridge may be off line, so you'll need to either transport in or climb up the turboshaft."

"Are the transporters working?" Tejada asked.

"I don't know," Sulu said. "I'm blind up here. You'll have to find out."

"I will," the doctor said, and she seemed to calm down as her medical responsibilities asserted themselves. *"I'll get somebody up there to do triage, and if we can, we'll transport the wounded to sickbay."*

"Good. Sulu out." He flipped the communicator closed, affixed it to the back of his belt, then used the beacon to light his way over to the captain, who lay in a heap halfway across the bridge from the command chair. Again, Sulu felt for a pulse. He didn't find one.

Looking around, he finally spotted the first officer. Costley's body had folded over and wedged beneath the navigator's station. Sulu went to him and checked once more for signs of life. Costley's heart beat, though weakly.

Sulu glanced around. He wanted to check on the rest of the crew and do more for all of them than simply check for their pulses, but *Courageous* had been in a firefight. If Sulu didn't find out what was going on out in space around the ship, they could all be blasted out of existence at any moment.

Standing, Sulu reached again for the communicator. "Bridge to transporter room."

"Berenson here," answered the transporter chief, the swiftness of the reply a surprise.

"Ensign, this is Lieutenant Sulu. Are the transporters on line?"

"They are, sir, yes," he said.

Sulu removed the beacon from his wrist and set it down atop the navigation console. Though emergency teams would doubtless bring their own lighting, he wanted to leave the bridge partially illuminated in case any of the officers regained consciousness before help arrived. Once he'd done that, he said, "Beam me there at once." He knew that auxiliary control stood next to the ship's main transporter room. With the bridge out of commission, Sulu could find out the situation and run the ship from there.

"*Energizing*," Berenson said.

When Sulu materialized on the transporter platform, he saw Doctor Tejada and two of her nurses rushing in from the corridor. He jumped down to the deck and started past them, toward the door, when the doctor stopped and reached up toward his head.

"Are you all right, Lieutenant?" Tejada asked.

Sulu raised a hand to his forehead. His fingertips came away tacky with his own blood. "Don't worry about me," he said, knowing that, at that moment, he needed to take command of the ship. "Worry about the captain and the rest of the bridge crew."

Without waiting for a response, Sulu raced out of the transporter room.

By the time he activated the small viewscreen in auxiliary control, Sulu had received relatively positive reports from engineering, particularly for a ship that had just experienced a collision in space. Though starboard shields and weapons no longer functioned, both the impulse drive and the warp engines remained operational. The ship's chief engineer, Mieke Wass, had rerouted power from the damaged systems to life support, making the internal environment of *Courageous* sustainable, at least in the short term.

Once he'd learned the ship's status from Lieutenant Commander Wass, Sulu had quickly run down a list of ship's officers, trying to contact each. He stopped when he'd found a navigator, an engineer, and a science officer to join him in auxiliary control. He redirected all command functions, then activated the small viewscreen while he awaited his new bridge crew.

The monitor winked to life, showing an empty starfield. Sulu quickly touched a control to focus the visual display on the objects nearest in space to *Courageous*. The screen flickered, then showed an image of *Enterprise*.

The ship was not alone.

Sulu spied two vessels of a configuration he had never before seen, but they shared enough characteristics in common with the other alien ships that he did not doubt their origin. Black, they comprised two bladelike hulls, connected lengthwise along the center of each, so that they possessed a plus-shaped cross section. They appeared roughly the size of *Enterprise* itself.

As Sulu looked on, phaser blasts, photon torpedoes, and missiles raced through the space between the Starfleet vessel and enemy ships.

Behind Sulu, the doors parted, and two of the three officers he'd called to auxiliary control entered on the run. "Come on," he yelled. "We need to get *Courageous* moving."

"Aft shields down to thirty-five percent," Spock reported.

From the command chair, Kirk said, "Rahda, drop our stern. Protect the aft shielding."

The bridge continued to rattle under the relentless onslaught of the two alien vessels. Although they had shown no weaponry more advanced than their smaller counterparts, they evidently carried a great deal more ammunition, and the ability to fire it in salvos. One missile by itself did not tax *Enterprise*'s shields, but both vessels fired five or more at once, and they kept coming. The alien vessels also targeted individual shields, obviously working to overload them. Kirk knew that once the first shield collapsed, the rest would fall like dominoes.

But the aliens won't need to wait for all the dominoes to fall, Kirk thought. With even one of the shields down, the right weapons strike could destroy the entire ship.

"Captain, the alien vessels are moving farther apart and beginning to circle," Rahda said.

Like sharks, Kirk thought, and he suddenly had a clear vision of the deadly Earth creatures swimming through the corridors of the alien vessels, relentless, cold-blooded predators expanding their killing fields.

"Keep the stern out of the line of fire," Kirk said again, but he knew that Rahda could only do so much. Alone against two vessels, with them maneuvering about *Enterprise*, it would only be a matter of time before one of their missiles brought down the aft shields.

And we can't fall back, Kirk thought, *because that would leave the Bajoran city vulnerable.*

"Captain," Spock said, "the *Courageous* is moving . . . heading toward us."

"Yes," Kirk said. "Spock, which of the two alien vessels is most vulnerable? We need to knock out their ability to launch their missiles."

"The one presently located off our starboard side," Spock said.

"Rahda, concentrate all phasers and photon torpedoes on that ship, targeting their missile tubes," Kirk ordered.

"Aye," Rahda said as she worked her controls.

Kirk turned toward the communications station. "Uhura, can you raise the *Courageous*?"

"Still trying, sir," Uhura said. "The alien ships may be jamming transmissions."

Of course, Kirk thought. When the *Enterprise* had faced the aliens in the R-836 system, they'd done the same thing. He hoped he wouldn't need to communicate with Captain Caulder, though; if the *Courageous* captain saw *Enterprise* concentrating its weapons on one target and ignoring the other, Kirk trusted that he would understand, and join in that effort.

The captain peered at the viewscreen, which showed only one of the alien vessels. Lines of missiles ran out toward *Enterprise,* shaking the ship and further weakening the shields. Phasers and photon torpedoes rushed in the other direction, some landing, some not; despite their greater dimensions, the alien vessels possessed a maneuverability similar to their smaller counterparts.

In the distance, beyond the alien vessel, Kirk saw *Courageous* pass the field of battle. *What's he doing?* Kirk thought, but then he remembered that the starboard shields on *Courageous* had failed. Caulder needed to protect that side of his ship.

Phasers suddenly shot from the port side of *Courageous* and slammed into the same vessel that *Enterprise* was attacking. But then the second alien vessel appeared on the screen, headed for *Courageous*. Kirk tried to will Captain Caulder not to break off his attack, but just as he thought that, the second vessel fired. A barrage of missiles assaulted *Courageous*. Some found its starboard side, and Kirk saw more pieces of the ship's hull blasted away into space. *Courageous* ceased fire and veered away.

On the screen, the second alien vessel disappeared from view as it attempted to flank *Enterprise*. Kirk debated whether to break off their attack on the first ship in order to protect the aft shields, or to continue in the hope of victory. Just then, the multitude of missiles launching from the first ship ceased.

"Captain, I believe we have crippled their launching system," Spock said. "But our starboard shields have now fallen below twenty-five percent and are on the verge of collapse."

"Rahda, now, target the second ship, come at him on our port side," Kirk said. "Spock, keep an eye on the first. Make sure it doesn't try to ram us."

Kirk watched the viewer as the image swung around to the second alien vessel, its missiles continuing to fly at *Enterprise*. Once more, Lieutenant Rahda sent rails of phaser fire and runs of photon torpedoes back in response.

"Captain," Spock said, "the first ship is moving off."

"We'll let them go for now," Kirk said, "until we can defang the second vessel."

The bridge continued to shudder with every missile strike.

"Captain," Spock said, "the first ship is headed for the planet."

"What about their missiles?" Kirk asked. "Did they decoy us?"

"Negative," Spock said. "Their launchers remain down."

"Then what—?" But then Kirk understood. If the aliens could not fire on the city, then they would use the only weapon remaining to them, the one they had used against *Courageous*. They intended to ram their starship into the Bajoran colony.

On the small viewscreen in the auxiliary control room, Sulu saw the orb of the planet loom into view as *Courageous* tracked the alien vessel. Because its weapons had been incapacitated, the lieutenant and acting captain knew what the aliens intended. Sulu didn't think twice about what to do.

"Ramsey," he said, addressing the relief navigator

who sat at the console beside his. "Plot a pursuit course."

"Into the atmosphere?" Ramsey asked. "But we've lost our starboard shields, and the structural integrity field is barely holding. We can't—"

Sulu turned to the young man. "Ensign, we can, and we will."

"Lieutenant," Ramsey said, "traveling at speed within an atmosphere will probably collapse the integrity field." Sulu looked the young officer in the eyes and saw no fear; he did see an abundance of caution, and a desire to save the remainder of a crew who had already been hit hard.

"Ensign, if we don't try," Sulu said, "the thirty-seven thousand people who live in the city on that planet are going to die. Now, am I going to have to repeat any more orders, because I can get another navigator in here."

Ramsey worked his controls. "Laying in a pursuit course," he said.

"Plot an intercept," Sulu said. "We need to destroy that ship before it gets anywhere near the city."

"Yes, sir," Ramsey said.

Sulu waited for the course to come up on his panel, then pushed *Courageous* forward. On the viewer, the planet quickly grew to fill the screen as the ship hurtled toward it. Sulu searched for the alien vessel ahead of them, but couldn't see it. The helm console in auxiliary control did not control weapons, and so had no targeting scanner. "Science officer," he called back over his shoulder, not remembering the name of the woman who had reported to auxiliary control. "I need sensors. Where's our target?"

"Scanning," the science officer called back.

Sulu boosted *Courageous* to higher speed. He felt the ship shimmy as it entered the upper reaches of the planet's atmosphere. Turning to his left, he pointed over at the engineer, who had rerouted weapons to auxiliary control. "Jackson, when we have him on sensors, lock photon torpedoes, all available tubes. We need to vaporize him."

"Yes, sir," Jackson called back. Sulu saw him studying his panel, doubtless waiting for the results of the science officer's sensor sweep.

Moments passed, and Sulu worried not only that they had lost the alien vessel, but that by the time they located it, it would be too late. He saw that the cloud cover still lay well below them, and so he hoped that there might still be time.

"Sir," Ramsey said, his voice low, "structural integrity field is fluctuating."

"Let it fluctuate," Sulu boomed back at him.

"Lieutenant, I have the alien vessel," the science officer called. "Transferring coordinates to navigation and weapons control." Both Ramsey and Jackson called out that they'd received the data.

"Get me a new course," Sulu said, but an instant later, it appeared on his panel. He worked his controls to bring *Courageous* onto its new heading. When he looked back at the viewer, he saw the alien vessel. "Hold your fire," he said. "I don't want to shoot toward the ground." From their height and the angle at which they approached the surface, a photon torpedo miss would likely not hit the city, but Sulu could not take that chance. Instead, he drove *Courageous* faster.

A huge bang resounded in the auxiliary control room. "What was that?" asked the science officer, but Sulu already knew.

"We just lost structural integrity," Ramsey said.

In his mind, Sulu saw pieces of the hull peeling away from *Courageous* as it flung itself toward the planet. On the viewer, he saw the gap with the alien vessel closing. "Be ready," he told Jackson. "As soon as we overtake it." Out in space, the alien vessels had utilized their impressive maneuverability to evade weapons strikes. Sulu didn't think that would work inside an atmosphere.

He increased speed. On the viewscreen, he saw *Courageous* pull even with the alien vessel. "Now," he cried, and a volley of photon torpedoes lashed out into its hull. "Keep firing," Sulu said. "Every last photon we have."

But one of the torpedoes Jackson had fired had been the last one they would need. The alien vessel exploded.

"Captain, the *Courageous* has destroyed the alien vessel," Spock said.

"Now we just need to complete our business up here," Kirk said, buoyed by Captain Caulder's success. *If more alien vessels don't suddenly show up.*

"Our aft shields just collapsed," Spock said.

"Noted," Rahda said. With only one adversary, protecting one side of the ship would be far easier than with two. But if the starboard shields also collapsed—

Sulu righted *Courageous* relative to the planet's gravity and slowed the ship's downward velocity. To Ramsey, he said, "Get me a flat piece of ground to set down on and give me a trajectory. Ten kilometers from the city." With the failure of the structural integrity field and the ship sliced open, *Courageous* could not safely return to space.

"Yes, sir," said the navigator.

While Sulu waited, he looked around at the young officers who had worked with him. "Good job, everybody," he said. They all thanked him. They all looked exhausted.

Once Ramsey had provided a place to land and a course by which to reach it, Sulu worked the helm to bring *Courageous* onto the new heading. Once he had, he pulled the communicator from the back of his waist. He knew that the alien vessels had jammed transmissions out in space, but he hoped that wouldn't be true down on the planet.

Flipping the communicator open, he said, "*Courageous* to Governor Velura."

• • •

The bridge continued to rumble beneath the alien attacks. The deck quaked. The battle in space had raged for nearly two hours, with *Enterprise* and the alien vessel trading blows like weary heavyweights in the final round of a bout.

Except that we're not landing nearly as many punches, Kirk thought, beset by his own fatigue. The incredible agility of the alien vessel had allowed it to avoid many of *Enterprise*'s weapons strikes. At the same time, the aliens' missiles lacked the destructive power of phasers and photon torpedoes, allowing *Enterprise* to withstand massive numbers of direct hits. But like drops of water eroding solid rock, so many missiles landing on its shields had taken their toll. *Enterprise*'s aft shields had failed, as had the starboard shields, forcing Rahda to conduct her continued assault with one hand tied behind her back, as best she could keeping the ship's port side facing their attacker. They had tried every feint, every maneuver, everything they knew to administer a killing blow— or, short of that, a crippling one—but nothing had worked.

And then suddenly, the bridge stilled. The sound of the ship's phasers firing continued, but the crash of missile strikes and the trembling of the deck ceased. Kirk stared at the viewscreen, where the alien ship had gone still. The climax of a book he had once read, H. G. Wells's *The War of the Worlds,* occurred to him:

after invading Earth and conquering humanity, an alien race falls victim to terrestrial bacteria. Wells wrote of the stillness that descended when the Martians fell. The present circumstances reminded Kirk of that, though the captain knew that the aliens the *Enterprise* crew battled had not suddenly perished.

"Spock?" he said.

"Our sensors cannot penetrate their hull," Spock told the captain, "but I believe they have exhausted their supply of missiles."

Kirk stood up, astonished that such a simple thing could end the battle. *Enterprise* had used the last of its photon torpedoes an hour earlier. "Rahda," Kirk said. "Cease fire."

An unnatural quiet seemed to fall over the bridge like a veil. "Let's see if they'll talk to us now," Kirk said. "Uhura, open hailing frequencies."

"Hailing frequencies open, sir."

"Alien vessel, this is Captain James Kirk of the *U.S.S.*—" On the main screen, the alien ship streaked away, racing quickly from view.

"Spock?"

"They are headed to the planet," Spock said. "Toward the city."

Enterprise rushed down through the atmosphere, just as *Courageous* had done. But the second alien vessel flew vertically, headed for the city from directly above it. As a consequence, Kirk could not employ

Enterprise's phasers to attempt to destroy the attacker, for fear that a miss would strike the city. And while the alien ship had avoided destruction out in space by evading many of *Enterprise*'s weapons, Kirk wondered if it could do so within the atmosphere. He had one more punch to throw.

"Rahda, deploy the tractor beam," Kirk said.

On the viewer, a white beam lanced from *Enterprise* and struck the alien vessel. "Slow us down, Lieutenant," Kirk said. The labored sounds of the overburdened hull groaned through the bridge as *Enterprise* tried to restrain the alien vessel.

"They are attempting to shear away," Spock said.

Kirk hit the intercom button. "Bridge to engineering."

"Scott here, Captain," came the reply.

"I need all available power to the tractor beam," Kirk said.

"Aye, sir," Scotty said.

"Kirk out."

The sounds of strain increased.

"They are pushing their engines to the limit," Spock said.

"Then push ours," Kirk said.

"Uhura, can you get through to the Bajorans?" Kirk asked.

"Trying, sir," Uhura said, and then, "Negative. The aliens are continuing to jam transmissions."

"Spock, if we can contact the Bajorans, have them evacuate the city . . ."

"I am not sure how long we can maintain this position," Spock said.

"However long it is, Spock, the Bajorans might
be able to move at least some of their people out of
danger," Kirk said. The captain activated the intercom
once more. "Bridge to Hadley," he said, contacting one
of the ship's helmsmen.

"Hadley here, sir," he replied.

"Lieutenant, report to the hangar deck."

Fifteen minutes after Hadley had departed *Enterprise*
in a shuttlecraft, a heavy whine rose, interrupted by
the sound of the boatswain's whistle.

"Scott to bridge."

Kirk activated the intercom. "Kirk here," he said.
"Go ahead, Scotty."

*"Captain, the engines canna take much more of
this,"* said the chief engineer. *"If we burn them out,
then either that ship or gravity is gonna drag us
down."*

"Scotty, stand by," Kirk said, then to Spock, "Do
you see any movement down there?"

Spock examined his sensors. "No, sir."

By that point, the captain had hoped to see the
Bajoran support ships moving in to begin evacuating
the city.

"Spock, how many people in the city right now?"

"Scanning," Spock said, leaning over his hooded
viewer. When the first officer stood back up, Kirk saw

something he'd only rarely seen on the Vulcan's face: a look of surprise. "Captain, the city is empty."

"What? How can that be?" Kirk asked, incredulous himself. "Are the aliens interfering with your sensors?"

Spock bent over his viewer once more. "Negative," he said. "Scanning the area, I am reading clusters of people . . . all at a considerable distance from the city."

"They already evacuated," Kirk said, and then realized that the inhabitants must have begun doing so after *Courageous* prevented the first ship from crashing into the city.

"Lieutenant Rahda," Kirk said. "Release the tractor beam." On the viewer, the shimmering white rays connecting *Enterprise* to its attacker vanished. The alien ship immediately hurtled forward and was quickly lost to sight.

Seconds later, a massive explosion erupted in Pillagra.

Eighteen

"Captain, I have it on sensors," Spock reported from the science station.

"Well done," Kirk said. "Transfer the coordinates to navigation."

Spock worked his controls, and then Chekov said, "I've got them, sir. Laying in a course."

"Ensign Walking Bear, take us there," Kirk told the relief helmsman. "Full impulse." After the tremendous effort Lieutenant Rahda had put in during the battle with the alien vessels, the captain had sent her to her quarters for a well-deserved rest.

"Full impulse, yes, sir," Walking Bear said. The drone of the impulse engines rose.

The stars on the viewscreen veered to one side as *Enterprise* started on its new course. It took only ten minutes to find their quarry. The small alien vessel that *Enterprise* had damaged during the battle floated uncontrolled in space.

"Are you still unable to penetrate their ship with sensors?" Kirk asked.

"Affirmative," Spock said.

"Ensign Walking Bear, prepare to deploy the

tractor beam," Kirk said. The captain remained determined to find out who had perpetrated such violence against the Bajorans, as well as against the crews of *Enterprise* and *Courageous,* and he wanted to know why. Since his crew could not scan the aliens aboard the vessel, they could not transport them from their ship. Though he knew he would have to exercise caution, Kirk intended to haul the vessel back to the planet, then physically take its crew into custody.

"Before we take them in tow," Kirk said, "let's try this one more time. Uhura, open hailing frequencies."

"Hailing frequencies, aye," Uhura said.

"This is James Kirk of the *U.S.S. Enterprise,*" the captain said for what felt like the hundredth time in his attempts to speak with the aliens. "Please respond."

"Nothing, Captain," Uhura said.

"No, of course not," Kirk said. "Alien vessel, we intend to take your ship with us in tow. You will be remanded to Starfleet security and Federation custody, where you will no doubt be charged with crimes—"

Unexpectedly, the main screen blinked, the view of the alien vessel tumbling through space replaced by the visage of an unfamiliar being. It wore what seemed to be a formfitting silver shell that looked like metallic armor, though the covering possessed a fluid-like appearance. The color of the being's face closely matched that of its armor. It had large, golden eyes, fluted around the edges. When it spoke, several seconds passed before the ship's translator succeeded in deciphering the alien language, and in the interim, Kirk heard a high, melodic voice. The translator picked up the being's words in midsentence.

"—*permit you to do so. We do not know if you falsely worship the True, the Unnamable, but you have picked over the bones of those who do, and then protected them.*" Kirk did not recognize the references to the True or to the Unnamable, but he understood that the alien spoke of the *Enterprise* crew visiting the dead Bajoran cities, and then protecting them at Pillagra. "*You have raised weapons against the Ascendants. You will pay for your transgressions.*"

"I do not know who you speak of as the True," Kirk said, "but our beliefs need not intrude on your—"

"*Your beliefs are immaterial. You would not have drawn the wrath of the Ascendants if you did not abide and abet those who worship falsely.*"

"We meant no disrespect," Kirk said, attempting a different approach. "We would seek peace and understanding with your people. If we can accept—"

"*You are fortunate that the Ascendants are not here.*"

"I thought you said that *you* were an Ascendant," Kirk said, confused.

"*I am an Ascendant, lost through a burning Eye, perhaps a view onto the Fortress itself. We would have returned to our people if we could have but found the burning Eye again. But while we have not, we have carried on the Quest, even so far removed from where we started. But here, in this space, we are the last.*"

Kirk did not understand the meaning behind all the words, and he wondered if something had been lost in translation. He didn't know, but he would leave that to the experts. "As I said, we are going to tow your vessel—"

"*No, you are not,*" the Ascendant said, and it reached forward, out of view on the screen. A loud noise erupted before the transmission ceased. The image on the screen disappeared, replaced by a view of space directly ahead of *Enterprise,* where a brilliant, white flash briefly lighted the night. Then the explosion that had consumed the alien vessel—the *Ascendants'* vessel—faded away, leaving nothing behind.

Kirk stared at the viewscreen for several moments. Had all of this—the destruction of two Bajoran cities, the murder of hundreds of thousands of people, and the attempted murder of tens of thousands more—had all of this been done in the name of some religious orthodoxy? Kirk reeled at the possibility. As tired as he already felt, the thought drained him even more.

"All right," Kirk told his bridge crew. "Let's return to Pillagra, retrieve the crew of the *Courageous,* and make our farewells to the Bajorans. Ensign Walking Bear, take us back to the planet."

Nineteen

Kirk sat at the desk in his quarters, his hand holding a stylus poised over a data slate. He gazed at the screen of the device, which as yet held only a salutation, a formal greeting to the parents of an *Enterprise* crewman who had been killed during the Ascendants' attack at Pillagra. The captain closed his eyes as he waited for the words to come, a process that seemed to take more and more time with each year that passed and each letter he wrote. Although he had learned to work past the deaths of those in his charge, he had never become inured to those losses, or to the pain he knew it caused the loved ones left behind.

With his eyelids still shut, Kirk allowed the thrum of *Enterprise*'s warp engines to wash over him. As the crew headed back toward Federation space—to deliver the complement of *Courageous* survivors to the nearest starbase, to allow *Enterprise* to undergo needed repairs, and finally to conduct the last few months of the five-year mission—the days aboard ship had settled into a lull. Kirk had returned to his quarters an hour earlier, after manning his post on the bridge through a mercifully uneventful alpha shift.

Once off duty and back in his cabin, the captain had stripped off his uniform and headed into the 'fresher, where he'd eschewed a modern shower for the old-fashioned kind. While he appreciated sonic cleansing technology and understood its hygienic benefits, it never quite reinvigorated him the way a powerful spray of hot water did. Afterward, he grabbed a towel and dabbed his body dry, then donned a new uniform. Even with his day's shift on the bridge complete, he still had duties to perform.

At his desk, he struggled with what to write to the families of *Enterprise* crew members who had fallen on his watch. He abhorred contacting survivors, but even though regulations did not require that he do so—Starfleet maintained a dedicated Casualty Notification Department—he felt a tremendous responsibility to follow up with loved ones impacted by his command decisions. But the words never came easily, and sometimes they threatened not to come at all.

The door buzzer sounded. Kirk opened his eyes and checked the chronometer on his desktop monitor; it surprised him that another half hour had passed, bringing him to the time that a Starfleet officer had asked to see him. The captain switched off his data slate and pushed it to the side of this desk, setting the stylus down atop it.

Kirk stood up and said, "Come." The door panel glided open, revealing Hikaru Sulu standing beyond it. "Lieutenant," he said. "Please come in."

Sulu stepped inside, and the door whisked shut behind him. "Thank you for agreeing to see me, Captain," he said. "I appreciate it."

"After your performance at Pillagra?" Kirk said, his tone light but his words earnest. "I'm ready to pin a medal on your chest."

Sulu smiled, though the expression did not seem to reach his eyes. Kirk motioned to the chair on the other side of his desk and invited the lieutenant to sit. When he'd done so, the captain took a seat as well.

"I'm serious, Sulu," Kirk said. "You showed great foresight in compelling Governor Velura to evacuate the city when you did. You saved tens of thousands of lives."

"I didn't, not really," Sulu said. "It was the governor and her people, using all of their ships to carry their citizens out of the city and into the countryside. They managed to do it efficiently and without instigating a panic. There were a few injuries during the evacuation, but nothing serious."

"I understand that you contributed the *Courageous*' shuttlecraft to the evacuation effort," Kirk said, "along with the ship's transporters."

Sulu nodded mutely. Kirk could see that something troubled the lieutenant, but he didn't know what. "Sulu, if you're upset about our last meeting—"

"I am," Sulu said. "I am upset about that meeting . . . about what I said to you . . . about what I thought and felt at the time." He stood up, as though if he sat still, his emotions would overwhelm him. He paced the short distance across the cabin, and when finally he turned back toward the captain, he peered down toward the deck, as though unable to face what he had come to Kirk's quarters to say. Still looking down, and with his voice dropped to a barely audible whisper, he at last said, "People died on the *Courageous*."

"I know, Sulu," Kirk said. "The ship was attacked. There was nothing more that Captain Caulder or you could have done."

Sulu peered up at Kirk. "I'm not talking about the results of Captain Caulder's orders or actions, or even yours, sir," the lieutenant said. "I'm talking about members of the *Courageous* crew dying after *I* assumed command."

"In a battle you didn't start," Kirk insisted.

"When I took the *Courageous* into the atmosphere with the structural integrity field failing . . ." Sulu said, but then he stopped and shook his head. "I should have known better. The integrity field was bound to give way, and with the ship's hull already compromised, it was inevitable that . . ." He couldn't seem to finish his thought.

"It was inevitable that the crew would be at greater risk," Kirk said gently.

Sulu nodded.

"You made a command decision," Kirk said. "From my vantage, Lieutenant, it was the right decision."

"I don't think I can see it that way," Sulu said. "People died following *my* orders. People died, leaving their families and friends to mourn them. I'm not sure how I can live with that. If I'd done something different, maybe more of the crew would have survived . . ."

Kirk stood up and walked out from behind the desk to face Sulu. "Maybe," Kirk said. "Maybe you could have made different decisions and saved the lives of more *Courageous* personnel. But then you could have given different orders and more of your crew might have been lost. And maybe thirty-seven thousand Bajorans would have died."

Sulu expelled a breath. "Is that how we're supposed to evaluate command decisions?" he asked. "By measuring the number of lives lost against the number saved? Ten died, but twenty lived, so it's a good day?"

"No, I didn't mean to suggest that it works like that," Kirk said. "You do what you feel is right, and then you take responsibility for those actions."

"It's a terrible burden," Sulu said.

"It can be," Kirk agreed. "But somebody's going to be out here making decisions—sometimes life-and-death decisions. I'd rather those choices get made by somebody for whom it *is* a burden. I don't want the commander of a starship issuing orders without knowing the gravity of a situation . . . without understanding the possible repercussions of their orders."

Sulu looked down without saying anything, then

stepped forward and reached out his right hand. "Thank you, Captain," he said.

Kirk took the offered hand. "Let me tell you something, Hikaru," he said. "Someday not that far into the future, you're going to make a fine starship captain."

Sulu smiled again, this time with genuine emotion. "I'm not sure I see that for myself," he said. "I did once, but I'm not so sure anymore."

Kirk shrugged, then tried to lighten the mood by saying, "Well, I understand that you're no longer the second officer aboard *Courageous*."

"No," Sulu said. "At the moment, she's not spaceworthy, and I'm not sure how long it's going to take to get her back to the Federation and repaired."

"There's always room here for you," Kirk said. "We already have a second officer in Scotty, but we haven't added any new helmsman in the time you've been gone."

"Thank you, sir," Sulu said. He appeared relieved and genuinely grateful. "I may take you up on that."

"I hope you do," Kirk told him.

Exit
The Rendering of Allegiant Thanks

Just weeks before the scheduled end of *Enterprise*'s five-year mission, a subspace message arrived. It pleased Sulu to see that Trinh's mother had sent it, but when he listened to her message, she told him that Trinh had been able to hold on no longer. Once more, Nguyen Thi Yeh thanked Sulu for being such an important part of her daughter's life, no matter how short the course of their days together. She also invited him to visit her on Mars if he ever made it back to Earth.

As it happened, Sulu would be there in less than a month. And he decided that he would indeed make the trip to Mars.

Kirk sat on the edge of his bed and closed his eyes. As *Enterprise* headed toward Earth, he listened to the sounds of the ship he had commanded for nearly five years, recognizing every one of them. The captain listened, and he remembered, and he thought about the future.

Except that the future can be tiring, Kirk thought.

More than anything, that's what he felt those days. A year earlier, he had begun hearing rumors about what would happen after the end of the mission, and in the time since, he'd heard others. It had worn him out. He'd thought he knew what he wanted, but, in recent days, that certainty had abandoned him. Yes, he wanted to captain a starship, but he also wanted . . . a beach to walk on, with no braid on his shoulders. Sulu had experienced firsthand the burdens of command, and he'd been right about them. And maybe Kirk had borne enough of them.

Sulu had been right about something else too: all the deaths. It didn't matter how good Kirk's reasoning, how sound his choices, it still tore a piece of him away every time somebody died on his watch. And people had died . . . people who, like everybody else, left behind mothers and fathers, sisters and brothers, lovers and friends. He'd lived with that for a long time. Maybe too long.

He didn't know anymore, didn't feel he could know. He would take *Enterprise* back to Earth and then see what happened. And if he ended up an admiral at Starfleet Headquarters . . . well, at least he knew a particular admiral he might like to take out to dinner.

Acknowledgments

Writing a novel seems, by its very nature, a solitary affair. I sit at the desk in my home office, my fingers capering across a keyboard as I read on a computer screen the images and ideas I have conjured in my mind and translated into words. Nobody watches me. Nobody answers my questions. Nobody helps me.

Except, of course, that picture does not capture the full experience of penning a novel. There are editors—Ed Schlesinger and Margaret Clark—who approach me for the project in the first place, who tender me a contract, who start me off in the right direction. And even though they live and work on the other side of the continent, those editors—by way of the postal service, e-mail, and telephone—*do* watch what I'm doing, *do* answer my questions, *do* help me. The process of getting a book into print (and, in this modern age, into pixels and electrophoretic ink) is highly collaborative. My words, my story, my characters, my dialogue, my themes are all examined and either approved or flagged for discussion. The subsequent conversations between writer and editors often enough result in changes to my outline or to my actual manuscript, and those changes are *always* for the better. My editors are my allies. To them, and to their able assistant—I'm looking at you, Julia Fincher—I offer my grateful appreciation.

And while I'm talking about writing and editing, I'd also like to take a moment to express my gratitude to all the readers out there. Clearly, I could not do what I do if you did not do what you do. Reading and writing are two sides of the same coin, and it's a currency that can enrich the world. Thank you.

Beyond the professional, I am also sustained on a personal level. Writing a novel, even with editorial assistance, can be a daunting task. I always feel a mixture of ambivalence, fear, and excitement when I face that first blank page, knowing that I have tens of thousands of words to produce before I even come close to reaching the end of that initial draft. I could not start, endure, or complete the process without all the wonderful people just on the other side of my door.

This time around, I want to start with the "L.A. Family." My life has been made all the better by a cornucopia of bright, creative, loving people: Louis Herthum, Pascale Gigon and Van Boudreaux (five vowels and only four consonants, but who's counting?), Roger Garcia and Sean Stack, Phil McKeown, Kat' Ferson, and Bruce Ravid. I adore you all.

Walter Ragan is another person who provides me with tremendous support. He is also a role model, a man easy to admire. I'm fortunate to have him in my life.

Colleen Ragan, Anita Smith, and Jennifer George are my sisters—one of them by blood, all of them by choice. There can be nothing more life-affirming than being surrounded by such loving, strong, and happy women. I am a better man simply for knowing them.

Patricia Walenista has many passions—reading, Civil War history, hockey (especially the Pittsburgh Penguins), football (especially the Pittsburgh Steelers and my Clemson Tigers), and international travel, just to name a few. Fortunately for me, she continually shares her zest for living, offering a daily example of what it means to be a whole and happy human being. I am grateful for the many joys she has contributed to my life.

Finally, as always, I want to thank Karen Ragan-George. Karen is my earthbound star, whose continuous love and support make everything possible. As she begins on a fresh artistic journey, I look forward to watching her blaze a new trail through her life. Karen's passion, determination, and courage are exemplars of a life well and fully lived. My respect and admiration for her are surpassed only by my love . . . for now and ever.

About the Author

With *Allegiance in Exile*, DAVID R. GEORGE III has penned an even dozen *Star Trek* novels. David returns to the original series after writing the *Crucible* trilogy to help celebrate the fortieth anniversary of the show's premiere. Those three novels center on the events of the episode "The City on the Edge of Forever," using Doctor McCoy's accident, Commander Spock's bitter knowledge, and Captain Kirk's tragic love affair to explore each of those characters. *Provenance of Shadows* chronicles the dual lives of Leonard McCoy, unspooling in two different timelines. *The Fire and the Rose* examines Spock's struggle to reconcile his human and alien selves. And *The Star to Every Wandering* visits the impact that the death of Edith Keeler has on James T. Kirk.

David has also contributed frequently to the saga of *Deep Space Nine*. Most recently, he wrote a loose trilogy of novels featuring DS9 and its once and future crew members, all set against the backdrop of the Typhon Pact, the six-member alien alliance designed to challenge the United Federation of Planets. *Rough Beasts of Empire* follows the renewed Starfleet career of Captain Benjamin Sisko, beginning with the Borg invasion and moving into the Romulan schism; the story also involves an older Spock, and introduces the previously unseen Tzenkethi. *Plagues of Night* and *Raise the Dawn* round out the three-book set, tracking the Typhon Pact's continuing efforts to tip the balance of power in their favor, and detailing explosive events on Deep Space 9 itself.

Prior to that, David visited the continuing post-television *Deep Space Nine* saga in two other novels. *Twilight (Mission: Gamma, Book One)* features Commander Elias Vaughn leading an exploratory mission into the Gamma Quadrant, and Captain Kira Nerys dealing with the possibility of Bajor finally joining the Federation. *Olympus Descending* (in *Worlds of Deep Space Nine, Volume Three*) delves into the Great Link, examining the nature of the Founders, their culture, and their collective mind-set.

Coauthored with Quark actor Armin Shimerman, *The 34th Rule* marked David's first journey into the *DSN* universe. Set during the series' fourth season, it is a tale that peers not only into the avarice promoted by Ferengi culture, but into their cunning manipulation of others in their ongoing quest for treasure. Played not for comedy, but for drama, *The 34th Rule* features Quark and Rom, Benjamin Sisko and Kira Nerys, and Grand Nagus Zek.

David also wrote a *Lost Era* novel, set in the interregnum between the time of Captain Kirk's command of *Enterprise* and that of Captain Picard's. *Serpents Among the Ruins* takes readers aboard *Enterprise*-B, commanded by Captain John Harriman and First Officer Demora Sulu, and it discloses the tale of the Tomed incident, referenced in the *Next Generation* television series. David followed up *Serpents* with another Demora Sulu story, a novella called *Iron and Sacrifice*, which appears in the anthology *Tales from the Captain's Table*.

David also composed an alternate-history *TNG* novel, *The Embrace of Cold Architects*, which appears in the anthology *Myriad Universes: Shattered Light*. He also cowrote the television story for a first-season *Voyager* episode, "Prime Factors." Additionally, David has written nearly twenty articles for *Star Trek Magazine*. His work has appeared on both the *New York Times* and *USA Today* bestseller lists, and his television episode was nominated for a *Sci-Fi Universe* award.

You can chat with David about his writing at facebook.com/DRGIII.